PRAISE FOR *WHAT THE LIVING DO*

"Between a day job dealing with the dead, an unresolved traumatic past, and a cancer diagnosis, Brett Catlin must push her way from self-protection towards learning how to love. Told with elegant, sometimes breathtaking prose, *What the Living Do* is a satisfying, beautifully written story of one woman's journey to wholeness."

— Lauren Carter, author of *Places Like These*, *Swarm*, and *This Has Nothing to Do With You*

"Masterfully, Susan Wadds entices readers with her stunning prose across a rich, complex emotional topography. *What the Living Do* is a brilliantly crafted portrait of a woman grappling with her demons and the challenges she must overcome to find hope, healing, and redemption. An incredible debut, this novel is moving and unforgettable and will resonate in your soul long after the final page."

— Jennifer Manuel, author of *The Heaviness of Things That Float* and *The Morning Bell Brings the Broken-Hearted*

"Susan Wadds has written a fierce and fearless novel about a woman drawn to self-destruction yet desperate to live—and maybe even love. A deeply moving and memorable debut."

— Alissa York, author of *Fauna* and *Far Cry*

"Susan E. Wadds' debut novel, *What the Living Do*, tells a heartfelt and gripping story that speaks of survival and hope, of how one woman rises above challenges in life and uncovers stories—sometimes falsely remembered and retold—that upend her life. Readers will come to love Brett Catlin for her tenacity and spirit. Even as her world seems to crumble around Brett, she puts one foot in front of the other and strives to find contentment in her life, endearing herself to readers through her struggles."

— Kimberly R Fahner author of *Emptying the Ocean, These Wings,* and *Some Other Sky*

"Susan Wadds writes from a place of deep compassion. She understands her characters' hearts and minds and because of that she is able to paint their landscape and allow them to pass through their rights of passage in an utterly convincing way. *What the Living Do* unveils a poignant mirror, carefully formed to reassure its readers that the shadow-corners of their lives are both seen and understood."

— Nick Bantock, author of *Griffin and Sabine, The Trickster's Hat,* and *Dubious Documents*

"Could you deal with survivor guilt and having been molested as a child? Brett Catlin has struggled for twenty-four years. How this strong woman copes and tries to make sense of her world and her relationships with people in it will take the reader on an emotional roller-coaster ride so finely are the plot and the central character and her supporting cast drawn. Effortlessly weaving real-time and backstory the author lets Brett show us how events in her past have shaped her today. And it is today's Brett who must face a life-and-death decision. You will ache for her. Not only is the story compelling in its emotional complexity, it is told in scintillating prose which on occasion, verges on the poetic. A must read."

— Patrick Taylor, author of the *Irish Country* series

"Compassionate, courageous and lyrical, *What The Living Do* is the passionate and powerful debut novel from Susan E. Wadds. Wadds has the courage to go where few other authors venture, into the deep recesses of a psyche damaged by tragedy and misplaced love. In exploring the deep wounds of the past we slowly begin to discover the possibilities of the healing Wadds' protagonist Brett Catlin has denied herself for so many years. It is a story laden with hurt, but ultimately a story of redemption and reclaimed hope. Of healing in the face of terrible odds. And of the power of compassion and understanding. It's a remarkable achievement."

— Phil Dwyer, author of *Conversations on Dying*

"'I can't go,' says Brett, the life-sized protagonist of this absorbing debut novel, 'and I can't stay.' With trenchant insight and agile prose, Susan Wadds conjures a woman snagged on the horns of the most fundamental of human dilemmas. If neither life nor death will have you, what then? Stick around."

— John Gould, author of *The End of Me* and *Kilter*

WHAT THE LIVING DO

Susan Wadds

Regal House Publishing

For Ben, my ma'iingan, the light of my life,
and for Sue

1

When Michelangelo peeled the skins of cadavers, he was searching to uncover a mystery beyond how muscle attaches to bone. In the dead, I search for something beyond a tag to identify a dog's owner.

I clamp on my hard hat as Mel eases the truck to a stop. The dog at the roadside is a mixed breed with a delicate snout and brindled coat. A turkey vulture drops a rope of its intestine and lifts away into a hard blue sky. Overhead, the big bird carves a dark circle while Mel drags the shovel out of the truck bed. Even though I know the dog is dead I squat to touch it just in case. Its jaw gapes, its legs are stiff as branches, its milky eyes open. There's no tag. I touch a rib bone that pokes through the skin like a tire spoke. Was he abandoned or did he simply leave, the scent of wild things pulling him from the safety of home?

Mel drives a boot onto the shovel's edge and begins to dig the hard-packed summer dirt, releasing the scents of metal and stone. The only sounds are the steady rasp of Mel's breathing and the crunch of the shovel.

We didn't bury my sister, Goldie, or my father. After the fire, they brought two clay urns to the edge of the Kootenay River. The wind picked up the ash and bits of bone, casting them in a wide arc over the cold river. Before it settled, a gust of wind caught a handful and flung it into my mouth.

When we slide the dog into the hole, its skull shows white through the split in its fur. This doesn't cause me to gag the way it used to. I still smell smoke, though, whenever the dull moon of an eye lies exposed like this.

Mel labors onto one knee and opens his fist, letting a confetti of tobacco drift over the small corpse. I keep my eyes on the still form while Mel lifts his head to intone a prayer. I hear *nimoosh* and *miigwech*, the Ojibwe words for *dog* and *thank you*.

The first roadkill I buried was a fox. Nothing about it seemed dead that cool spring morning. It was as if the fox had simply lain to rest in the middle of the Second Line, the white tip of its tail curled over the sun flare of its body. I sensed Mel's focus on me even though he faced straight ahead. I removed my gloves to search for a pulse and found a hardness that made me rock back on my heels.

"*Waagosh,*" Mel said.

The fox smelled of juniper and cedar. Turning my head so Mel couldn't see my face, I heard the metal-on-metal of the shovel across the truck's side.

It was the prayer that undid me, the soft syllables like a lullaby.

Once we were back in the truck, Mel touched a finger to the box of tissues tucked into the console and started the engine. I yanked one, turned away, and made as if to check traffic through the passenger window.

Mel is the only one I ever want to ride with, the only one who's never made lame lunges to grab my ass on the pretense of helping me into the cab, and the only one who doesn't bitch—not about the weather, the road conditions, or his wife, and not even about the cutbacks that have forced us to drive the snowplows without a wingman.

After we've mounded the earth and tamped it down over the young dog, I toss the shovel into the truck bed and step up into the cab. Mel has the truck in gear.

"Teach me how to pray, Mel," I say.

Without turning, Mel lifts a gray eyebrow.

"You pray to real things, like animals. I need you to teach me."

His answer comes like it always does, after a long pause. "Don't pray *to* animals. Pray *for* them." Now he half turns, almost facing me. "To give thanks."

I want some of what he has; that steady sweeping gaze over

the land, the ease with which he dangles his fingers through the
steering wheel, the slow nod when one of the good old boys
at the yard calls him *Chief.* "Is that what makes you peaceful?
Praying, I mean."

"Peaceful?" he says, as if trying out the word.

"Yeah," I say. "How does it start? It sounds like bonjour."

"*Boozhoo,*" he corrects. "We say, *Boozhoo Gzheminido.* Means,
Hello Creator."

"The other things you say—after that?"

Mel nods, returns his gaze to the road. "*Mshkiki nini
ndizhinikaaz,* is how I start."

I try out the words but they feel like pebbles in my mouth.
And it looks as though Mel is trying not to smile.

"What?"

"You said, 'My name is Strong Earth Man.'"

"Well, I like that. How do you say, 'My name is Strong Earth
Woman'?"

The smile that was forming vanishes.

There are these times when I feel I've stepped over some
sacred invisible boundary. It's in the density of his quiet, as if
all the light has been sucked into a vacuum. "What did I say?"

I lean my head into the window and see through the outside mirror that we've done a fine job. Not even a ripple in the
gravel remains to mark the spot where the dog is buried. In the
beginning, I'd try to insist we find the owners, but if the animals
aren't close to a house, the mandate is simply to bury them. No
time to go calling door to door.

"Mel, what should I say?"

Easing his foot from the brake, Mel turns the truck back
onto the road. "Just your name."

"Can't I have a cool name too?"

We're on the road heading south, on the lookout for roadkill, bent signs, and potholes. Sun comes hot and thick through
the heavy leaves of maple, oak, and poplar. When Mel doesn't
answer, I turn to look full at him. "Mel? How do I get a name
like that?"

His eyelids lift and it seems to take some effort for him to focus. He blinks. The fingers dangling from the top of the steering wheel tap at air.

I've screwed things up; the long silence makes that clear. I want to apologize but I'm not exactly sure for what. "Okay, so no special name, okay. So how do I say it with the name I've got?"

The hard line of Mel's jaw softens. "You say your name, then *ndizhinikaaz*."

The sharp sound of my name, *Brett*, is jarring when followed by the warmth of the Ojibwe syllables. I want a name that's tough and wild, like Cougar Woman. But given that the man I live with is much younger than I am, it might not be the best choice. And given that my request has been met with Mel's inscrutable silence, I decide not to push it. After a second attempt at Brett *ndizhinikaaz*, I say, "What do you say next?"

From under his eyelids, Mel watches ahead through the sun-stained windshield. "I say, *Rama ndoonjibaa, waawaashkeshi doodem*."

This invocation flows like a song, warms me right into my belly, where it's been cold for some time. "Does that mean, 'I'm from Rama'?"

Mel nods.

"And the rest?"

"My clan."

"You have a clan? What kind of clan?"

"Deer."

On the far side of the road, guard posts list toward the ditch, their guide wires stretched tight. "There it is," I say, pointing.

"I don't have a clan," I say as Mel swings the truck around in a smooth U. "So, what would come next for me?"

"Just where you're from, then *ndoonjibaa*."

"Where I'm from?"

"Where your heart is," Mel says.

"But they're not the same place," I say.

For the rest of the afternoon, Mel and I are mostly silent. Once when I asked him why he never asked questions, he told me if a person wanted to tell a thing, they would. When I said that inquiring after the well-being of people you care about was supposed to be the polite thing to do, he just shook his head. I get it now. With Mel the quiet is comforting, easy.

I put on my sunglasses to combat the sun glare through the pocked windshield and content myself with watching for potholes to fill and signs to straighten. "I read somewhere that it's going to be a mild winter," I say.

Mel glances out his window.

"Late start," I say. "Would be good."

We have the windows open. Neither of us likes air conditioning, even when it's this hot. A few strands of hair have broken loose from my braid and whip across my mouth. I don't want to think about winter, because when I close my eyes I see snow, ice, sand, and brine. There's a dark empty road and an almost empty hopper and me, alone at three in the morning, stuffed into my padded coveralls, the drone of engine, the steady scrape of blade, lights—in my rearview, blue, red, white—coming down that hill on glare ice. Ahead, at the low dip, a little blue car revolving like something at a fall fair.

I'm used to waiting for Mel to answer. When we first started riding together, I'd fill in the quiet by answering for him or asking more questions. Because it finally registered that he rarely answers multiple questions, I've trained myself to wait. Now I like the waiting. It's as if the world stops just then and my mind goes still too.

A slow smile forms on his face. "Once, Web, my older brother, told me we were in for a cold winter. He said you could tell because the caterpillars had thick coats." Mel scratches the sparse stubble on his chin. His smile fades. "I laughed. I thought he was joking."

"He wasn't? That's how you can tell?"

Only Mel's eyes move to take a quick look at me. "Maybe," he says, flicking on the turn signal and spinning the wheel to the right.

"How do the caterpillars look this year?"

His smile is a smaller version of the one a moment before. "It's still hot. Maybe check in September."

We replace three road signs perforated with bullet holes, cold-patch half a dozen potholes, remove a fallen ash off a county road, and pull a mattress from a ditch.

No more dead things today.

Back at the yard, Mel tips the brim of the ball cap that has replaced his hard hat and we get into our respective vehicles—me in my Yaris, he in "Pony," his Dodge van that he's snazzed up for camping at powwows.

I don't talk about dead animals to Cole. He's a sweet guy with soft hands, except for the calluses on the fingers of the left one. When I get home, I find him on the ottoman by the window. His shape is dark against the yellow afternoon sky, the sun sparking through his hair like new pennies. In the kitchen, I strip off my work clothes and sort them for the wash.

Cole likes to sing me songs like "My Girl," and "Ain't No Sunshine When She's Gone," but he also writes music for my poems. He's in a band that plays at weddings and once a month at a local pub. He's threatened to sing my poems onstage, but so far I've been able to discourage him.

Beckett pads over to me, his nails clicking on the parquet, and pushes his head against my leg, fur crinkling above his eyes. I squat and scrub behind his ears. He bows to bat me with the top of his hard skull.

Beckett is sleek and calm. Cole and I scanned dozens of breeds before choosing a smooth-haired fox terrier. There were many wire-haired ones available, but we had to go to Missouri to get Beckett. On the drive down, I counted fourteen deer by the side of the highway. For large animals like deer, moose, and bear, we use a forklift. That is, if they haven't been gone too long.

After changing into a clean shirt and jeans I come into the living room. "Listen," Cole says without turning around. He strums a G and hums. He doesn't need to do this; he has perfect pitch. Not like me. When I sing, which isn't often, I have to close my eyes and imagine no one is there. Like after the fire when my cousin Dylan left my room, I'd lie on my back and sing made-up songs for Goldie and my daddy.

Cole's warm voice streams into the room. I sit with my side nestled into his back. I think about leaving all the time. It's one thing I do very well, but there's always one thing or another to put off the leaving. Cole's hands for one thing. His mouth for another.

He likes old songs, particularly folk songs from my parents' time. He's singing "Fire and Rain" now, which is nice. I close my eyes, letting the vibration from his ribs move mine. But right after the part about things in pieces on the ground, he stops singing and turns to me. "Let's have a baby," he says.

"Cole," I say, trying to breathe some air back into my lungs.

"We could. It's not too late." He looks so earnest, so innocent, so trusting. He wants to assure me that I'm not too old, as if that's the reason.

"Is the air conditioning on?" I say, unbuttoning my blouse.

Stroking my upper arm, Cole says, "You'd be a great mom."

I catch his hand and bring it to my mouth, kissing the cup of his palm. "I'm sorry, Cole," I say. "We're not doing this."

He draws away his hand to finger the frayed set list on the side of his guitar and drops his head so I can't see his face.

"You want to fuck or eat first?" I ask into his ear.

"I hate it when you talk like that."

I straighten my shirt and push myself off the ottoman.

Cole strums, his gaze floating out through the window and over the roofs of our neighborhood.

Beckett follows me to the kitchen, quiet except for the clicking of his nails. Across the counter are four small plates littered with crumbs, two cereal bowls with gluey flakes, a coffee mug with congealed sugar, a yogurt cup, and a glass tumbler stuck with bits of pulp.

"Cole…"

"Norah called."

I stretch out of my crouch. I don't want to think about Norah, not her flushed hopeful face and not her crumpled one either.

"She wants you to call," Cole says when I don't answer.

"She has my cell number," I say.

Beckett's eyes track from mine to his dish. It's still half-full of dry food.

The guitar strings twang as the wood's hollow sound reverberates against the wall. I set the dishes into the sink, turn on the tap, and squeeze out dish soap in a green line. Beside me Beckett sits, shifting from paw to paw, the skin lifting over each eye into alternate wrinkles. I turn off the tap and reach under the counter to dig into his bag of treats.

The guitar is quiet, and now Cole is leaning on the archway to the kitchen, one thumb hooked into the front pocket of his jeans.

Beckett takes the chicken-cheese strip in one gulp.

"You should call her," Cole says, moving close. "What's with you two anyway?"

"I'll call her," I say, although I'm not sure I want to. It's been sort of strangled between us ever since she had her second miscarriage. I brought her flowers, but I couldn't stay with her for long. We've both created ghosts, their breath like those tiny white flowers that show up in sympathy arrangements.

Cole takes my face in both hands. "You okay?"

I kiss him hard, pushing my tongue into his mouth, and drop my hand to his crotch.

We do a quickstep, with me leading and Cole back-stepping, until we fall onto the couch. Hoisting one leg over his thighs, I straddle him and unzip his jeans.

"Well, hello there," I say, running my fingers along the length of his penis.

"Hush, baby," Cole says, reaching for my face with one hand, my breast with the other. "Come here." I love the saw-against-wood sound of his voice when he's aroused. Afternoons are my favorite time for sex. Cole hasn't been up for long, so he's full of young male wake-up horniness, and I'm letting down from the stink of the road, my body aching for release.

It's quick and satisfying.

I propel myself off him, leaving a slippery trail across his belly. "I'm starving," I say.

He doesn't answer. When I turn to ask him what he wants to do about dinner, it doesn't surprise me that his eyes are closed, one arm arched across his forehead, one leg sloping to the floor, his chest with its fine ginger curls circling the nipples in the slow rise and collapse of sleep.

Cole was twenty-two when I met him, squatting in the aisle of Zehrs with a sliver of skin showing between the knot of his apron sash and the top of his jeans, his hair the color of arbutus inner bark.

"Aisle four, about halfway, on the right." He rose. His eyes were gold-brown with dark flecks. "Here, let me take you. It's a bit hard to find," he said, slowing so we could walk side by side. "You like Thai food?"

I nodded, taking him all in. "You?"

"I love all kinds of food. Just put it in my mouth and I'll eat it."

Oh my, I wanted to say, but instead asked him, "What's the strangest thing you've ever eaten?"

His grin revealed perfect teeth. "Frogs. Octopus. Crickets. You?" He indicated a left turn at the end of the aisle.

I gripped his eyes with mine. "Bulls' balls."

He took in a quick breath and then shot it out with a laugh. "No kidding? Here we are," he said, pointing at the shelves of Asian foods. He hesitated, those fawn eyes scanning me in a way that made me heat and swell. "Bulls' balls, eh? Did it work?"

I hoped that the look I returned made him heat and swell. "I guess it did."

"Okay then," he said, wiping his hands down the length of

his green apron. Big hands, smooth skin. "I'd better get back to my spices."

"I'm making cold rolls," I said, reaching for a pad of rice paper.

"Cool," he said, taking a small step backward.

"I could make enough for two?"

Five years later he is still almost eleven years younger than I am.

After finishing the dishes, I rummage through the fridge where I find only a dried-out chicken breast and a bowl of leftover pesto linguine. I begin to tick off dishes from the Indian take-out menu stuck to the fridge when I hear Cole's feet shuffle toward the bathroom, followed by the metallic squabble of curtain rings and the squelch of bathtub faucet.

"Move over, I'm coming in," I call.

When I pull back the shower curtain Cole's eyes are shut, face tilted to the spray, copper lashes against his cheek. Last month when I went to one of his gigs, I saw his beauty all over again through the upturned faces of the sleek-haired, tight-jeaned young women who aimed their phones at Cole.

He smiles, opens his eyes, and steps to the rear of the tub. I stand under the jet, and he begins to lather my back. Sliding his hands through the space between my torso and arms he cups my breasts. As his hands descend, I spread my legs.

"What's that?" he says, sounding alarmed.

"What?"

He points to a viscous brown-red puddle by my feet.

We both watch droplets of water dapple and disperse the blob.

"Mid-cycle spotting," I say. I take the soap and begin to wash him.

"Brett." His voice makes me stop.

"Yes?"

"It doesn't look like that kind of blood."

Swishing the now pink water with one foot, I escort it down the drain.

He points to the inside of my thigh where a dark, almost brown, trickle of blood has begun. "Maybe you should have it checked anyway. Just in case."

When I soap myself, the water runs clear. "I'm fine," I say, parting the curtain to step out of the tub.

Of course I'm fine.

2

Before pulling the lever, Mel sets his jaw so tight that veins show through the sparse hairs there. I hate the brush cutters too, the way they shred the trees, leaving them twisted and raw. Cost-effective and quick, they say.

My cousin Dylan taught me to use a chainsaw. He took me up the mountain, after it had been clear-cut, to get the surviving cedar. Dylan showed me how to limb, buck, and choke the trees, and then winch them with heavy chains so we could drag them behind his Jeep down the switchbacks. "You're a real lumberjack now," Dylan said, planting a warm kiss on my cheek. "A real pretty one. Fancy."

The good old boys on the yard stopped their snickering at a girl with a chainsaw after I cleaned and oiled one and it roared awake with just one pull. Now I'm down in the culvert with a chainsaw getting branches the cutter can't reach. I'd rather be up close with the trees looking me right in the eye than rip them up at a distance. The looks I get for this work from passing drivers bring a hot flush of shame nonetheless. I'd rather them wonder who I blew to get this job than feel the burn of those righteous tree-hugger stares.

When we finish at Road 11, I drop the chainsaw in the back and climb into the cab. Mel doesn't speak and I don't have much to say either.

I don't know how to pray for the trees.

I never meant to stay in this town. I chose it because it was far enough away from the stain left by Mark, my last toxic relationship, but only an hour north of Toronto. Lake Simcoe is pretty but it's a sad facsimile of Kootenay Lake with its sweeping green mountains all around. Barrie was supposed to be a temporary place to make enough money to get farther away.

Somewhere beautiful. East and farther east. As far as I could get. Then farther still. I ache for beauty, but whenever I turn over my hand after touching a beautiful thing, my palms look filthy. Still, I have a sense that if I can penetrate the mystery of death, I'll arrive at beauty or a state of grace that makes this life bearable.

After getting my DZ license so I could drive vehicles with air brakes, I landed a part-time job with the county doing road maintenance. It was good money, I was outside, and I could be gone within a year. But then there was the full-time posting. Then there was Cole. Then, Beckett.

When I get home from work, Cole is still in bed. He's been working nights in the bakery for two years. The warm, slightly sour sleep smell of him wafts through the open bedroom door. Thin stripes of late sun fan out across the blankets; the rest of the room is dark. Beckett clicks across the floor and begins to circle his bed, once, twice, three times, before he plops down with a soft sigh. I stand with my shoulder against the door frame and listen for Cole's breathing—his untroubled breathing—and try to imagine his dreams. The covers rustle like shuffling paper as he turns under them.

"Come here," he murmurs, his long fingers curving in.

As I come to him, he lifts the covers and a cloud of that boy-smell pulls me in.

But after a few moments of lying with my head on his chest, Cole's breathing drops into an even rhythm. I slide off the bed and go to the bathroom. Pulling out the drawer, I stare at the round packet of pills that sits between the tampons and my toothbrush. I hate taking pills, but these are less crazy-making than the ones I took when I was younger. They're called mini pills, as if they're cute. The IUD was so much more convenient. Convenient but ineffectual. I pop out a pill and swallow it without water.

Cole is still asleep when I come back. I lift the covers and run my tongue along his penis. He jumps, swatting at my head.

"Hey!" I sit up. "That's no way to show your appreciation."

"Oh, baby, sorry," he says, propping himself up on his elbows. "I didn't know it was you."

I laugh. "Did you think it was Beckett?"

A smile begins to shape itself on his face but is replaced by the shock of wakefulness. "What time is it?" he asks, leaping off the bed.

"You've got an hour yet," I laugh. "I wouldn't let you be late."

"Oh." His shoulders slump as he breathes out, stopping in the middle of the bedroom. "I thought I'd slept a long time."

"About five minutes."

"Oh," he says again, as if I had said something very wise. He bends to gather up his clothes scattered across the floor and heads to the bathroom.

"I want to travel," I say to his back.

"Cool," he says and disappears into the bathroom. The faucet squeaks, followed by the shishing of water that sounds like bubbling bacon fat.

I glance at Beckett curled on his mat, his ears at half-mast and eyes closed but moving under the lids to the sounds in the apartment, and then go to the window overlooking downtown. Five years is a long time. I open the drawer of my writing desk and slide out my journal.

Don't be such a sissy, don't be such a fool
Open up your wings, let your spirit fly
The roads are smeared with dead things
~~But you can't stop to cry you can't even cry~~
Don't even

The rest of that page is blank. On the opposite page I have written an Anais Nin quote about being responsible for my own heart. Not that I believe Cole has offered his up for the smashing. Not really.

The heart. You can get your heart replaced if it is faulty. I read about a woman who loved opera, ate only organic food, and drove an Audi. After she had a heart transplant she craved

McDonald's french fries, hard rock, and the long seat of a Harley-Davidson. What would someone who received my heart crave? Flight to some tropical isle? The deep thrum of a Mac engine under the scrape and grind of blades? The revelations of entrails? The steady thrust of a young man's hips? Or would they ache for a reunion with a fair-haired sister and a quiet, bearded father who were hazing out of focus?

My pen is wedged between the pages. I write, "My heart is small and tired. It once knew how to love..."

Beside the words, I let the felt tip create loops and tangles. It isn't anything. I draw about as well as I can sing. But my hand continues to move in swirls and zigzags. It stops and the ink continues to leak from the tip, seeping into a blotch, a blossom, a pool of blood.

The Balinese calendar I have pinned to the wall is all blue-blues and green-greens. In Bali, everything is celebrated, including death. Everyone dances and sings and wears brilliant headgear heavy with fruit. Anais Nin wanted to go there to die, but I don't think she made it. Do the Balinese celebrate roadkill? And how might they celebrate a stillborn or one taken out before its eyes even open?

"That's interesting," Cole says, making me start. He's right behind me, the moist heat from his belly on my shoulder.

Covering the page with a splayed hand, I ask, "What?"

"Your drawing. It's good."

When I lift the edge of my hand I see that the ink stain has spread into rivulets that look like entrails and spots of paper show through like eyes.

"What does it look like to you?" I ask.

He touches the page with the tip of a damp finger. "It kind of looks like an animal. Sort of like Beckett."

What I see is not that, but I don't say so. Sometimes, not often, but sometimes, I can keep my mouth shut.

3

I wait for Mel in the truck. With the other guys, I always insist on driving just to show them that driving a half-ton doesn't require a penis or a big belly. With Mel, I can relax, make mistakes even.

A few weeks ago, I let Norah persuade me to attend a yoga class. She assured me it would be gentle. I laughed. "I don't need gentle," I said.

She gave me a sideways look. "Maybe that's exactly what you need."

When we got to the studio, she arranged the mat she had brought for me beside her baby-blue one and squeezed a hot dog-shaped cushion under my bum. "Just go easy," she advised as she floated her lovely white hands onto her thighs. "There's nothing to prove."

Maybe there is, I thought.

It was a beginner class, and all the postures were relatively easy—twists and stretches, forward and back bends, and reaching our hands over our heads. The corpse pose made me twitch. I couldn't get comfortable no matter how deeply I sighed or let my muscles go slack. In fact, I couldn't let them go at all—they just hung on. I realized that the only time I let my body parts release is post-orgasm.

After the class, Norah said, "You're strong, Brett. You can do just about anything with that body of yours." She gripped my upper arm for emphasis. "You're as hard as steel."

"Thanks, I guess," I said, lifting my arm out of her grasp.

She shook her head, "You're just not flexible."

This afternoon Mel and I spray chemicals on noxious weeds. The chemicals have poetic names like *chlorsulfuron* and *aminocyclopyrachlor*. We like this job almost as much as we like strangling sumac and basswood from the verge. Mel and I are the most silent when we do the jobs we hate. I don't think either of us feels particularly flexible.

On the days when we've poisoned or maimed, I go home to shower and change into my running gear and take Beckett along the waterfront to run long and hard.

As I run I think about how Mama walked after the fire. She walked up and down Nelson's mountainside, avoiding Baker Street shops and people, but steady up, up, up and down, down, down, crisscrossing on the horizontal streets, her eyes not quite focused, or focused on something that wasn't there or never would be again. I waited for her on Aunt June's wide wooden porch. From there I could see Kootenay Lake all the way down the slope of Cedar Street. That first year, I waited every day on the porch for Mama to come home, for her eyes to open again, for her to remember that she still had a living daughter, that she still had me.

Then I stopped waiting for her and waited instead to be away. Away from Nelson, from the valley, from the Kootenays. I would fly. I would visit the world. My legs were as strong as Mama's and maybe my will was as well.

In those waiting years, after Dylan stopped touching me, he brought books, and sometimes we'd talk about what I'd read. I was fifteen and punky, *Anna Karenina* open on my lap. "Here, where Levin talks about being nothing more than a speck of mold in the universe," I said, jabbing an accusing finger at the page.

Dylan, with his honey eyes crinkling. "That how you feel?"

"Yes," I yelled, leaping to my feet, clenching the heavy book. I looked up into the mountain night, pointing the book's corner up toward the Dog Star. "She was right—Anna—she did the only thing she could." I needed him to hear, to understand me, to show me what I wasn't able to name.

"That how you feel?" he asked again, but his smile had faded.

Not even Dylan seemed to understand, and I couldn't spell it out for him. "Sometimes," I said, sitting again.

Sirius shone blue between dark peaks. I wanted to go through that cleft. I was desperate to know the other side. To find a thing that was truly alive so I could be too. I was already grasping for "the beauty under heartbreak."

Dylan stopped coming around, so I cut him away piece by piece, drowned him, numbed him away—with drugs, some hard, some soft; with Southern Comfort; and with awkward sex where I was the one to educate. I painted people's houses for money and wrote furious poems about death and sex. *Fuck you,* I wrote, swollen with bravado. I wrote *lick* and *suck* and *thrust* and never rhymed my lines.

When I was seventeen, I went east and farther east. I continued to devour books—the dark poetry of Beckett and Leonard Cohen, the hell of Dante and the heaven of Blake, the sensual writings of Anaïs Nin and Henry Miller, and all of Shakespeare, until I began to understand what I read. I got a job through a guy I met on the train to Toronto. His brother had a contract with the city, and I got to spin *Stop* signs and listen to assholes hanging out car windows to tell me what they'd like to do to me.

The winter I turned twenty, I went to France and walked the streets where the authors I loved had walked. Then I took a train through the Alps into Italy, and spent two weeks in Florence, most of that time in the Galleria dell'Accademia with *David* and Michelangelo's half-finished slaves. In an English bookstore, I found a worn copy of *The Agony and the Ecstasy* and took it to read in the shadow of the *Young Slave*, the one who would never free himself. I spent three days in the presence of those trapped figures, while in the novel, I followed Michelangelo through the dark, stinking streets of Florence and into the forbidden halls of the dead. Flashes of my sister's exposed skull merged with the vivid descriptions of Michelangelo's peeled corpses. But, as always, I pushed them down, burrowed deeper into the investigations of art's mechanisms—the excavation of marble, the dead-slow labor of hammer and chisel, the sweat and the tears. Beauty buried in rock.

After that, I walked the streets of Italy, France, and Spain, taking in the art and architecture of the dead, drinking their life waters—*acquavite, eau de vie, aguardiente*—and sampled various flavors of the Latin male.

Now I run along a lake in a bland town, drink an occasional glass of wine, and taste the juice of just one lover who cares more for me than is good for him.

4

Sunday morning, Norah calls. She invites me for tea. I go because she's my best friend; my only friend, really, if you don't count Mel or Cole.

Norah and Josh live behind the Georgian Mall in a semi-detached with a little square yard in the front and a long narrow one in back. It's the perfect neighborhood in which to raise a family.

We sit on high stools at the island in her airy kitchen. A song is playing. Something about losing and whether or not this life is real. The CD cover lies open. Marianas Trench. A band named after the deepest part of the ocean. A great trench whose depth has never been absolutely plumbed, not far from Bali. It's like a chant now: *Bali*—lush, warm, slow, and forgiving. I was on my way once, but when Mark stalled, I stopped moving and turned around, stayed with him.

The singer claims he's still awake but half-asleep.

Norah stirs honey into a glass mug filled with something herbal. From the nearby playground come the piercing sounds of young children.

"How's work?" Norah asks simply enough, but I'm aware of a coldness in her tone.

That small dog wasn't more than a year old. No one to claim him. "Pretty hot this week. It's okay when we're moving, but the sun gets pretty intense when we have to stop."

"Josh insists that all women road workers are hot blonds," Norah says with a tight laugh.

"Oh yeah," I say, rocking back on the stool. "I'm some piece of eye candy, especially when I'm shoveling roadkill. In my sexy boots and glow-in-the-dark safety stripes."

"It's been hard," she says to Beckett, who is flat on his belly, head between his paws.

"Hard?"

She fixes me with her stare. "Yes, Brett. Hard."

"You mean—"

"Yes, I mean living like this. With the pain. The loss."

When she called to tell me she'd woken to blood-soaked bedsheets, I brought flowers. Instead of taking them, Norah opened her robe to show me her swollen breasts veined with blue. Both nipples leaked thin white milk, as if there was someone to feed.

"I'm sorry," I say. The impatient sound of maple leaves comes through the open window. I turn to watch the wind turn them over.

"I needed more."

"Oh," I say, hopeful at last. "I'm sure you'll be able to—"

She jumps from her stool and takes a step back. "I don't mean that. I mean from you. I needed more from *you*."

Norah's eyes have turned glassy. She stares at me as if I'm the killer. On the counter lies a single blue button the size of my thumbnail. It has four tiny holes. I can't imagine which shirt or blouse it belongs to. The smell of her tea drifts across to me. I hate herbal tea. They all taste like dirt. I like coffee. I can drink it right through the day and still fall asleep right away.

"Like what?" I say. "What could I do? I tried to be there for you."

"I did everything right," she says as if I hadn't spoken. "I stood on my head, took the right kind of vitamins, never sat with a corner or anything sharp pointing at me, didn't tell anyone I was pregnant, not even you, until the second trimester; I didn't rearrange the furniture, nail or stick anything on a wall, didn't cut something while sitting on the bed. I didn't even open, let alone lift, a suitcase or a box." Her voice stops as if it has hit something solid.

"Norah," I say, reaching for her hand. "It wasn't your fault."

The shine vanishes from her eyes and she fixes them on me. "Right. That's right." She snaps her hand out from under mine. "And you show up with some stolen flowers, take one look at me, and then disappear. It's not enough. Imagine how I felt, Brett. I had just lost my second baby. You can't imagine how painful that is."

A puff of breeze snaps the curtain's bottom edge.

"I can," I say quietly.

"How could you?" Nora snaps.

I'm staring out her glass doors to the slope of green that ends at a slide and swings and a small playhouse. "I lost my baby six years ago."

There's a suck of silence. Norah says, "You never told me."

I can still breathe. "I don't talk about it."

"You could have told me." Her voice has lost its metallic scrape, has become tender and sorry.

I shake my head. "I had an abortion."

The kitchen floor sags in the silence. The playground children have stopped their shrieking. My cup has gone cold. Maybe the button was intended for an infant sweater.

"An abortion?"

I nod.

"An abortion?" she asks again, tipping her head forward as if to hear better. Her glass of tea floats with leaf bits.

Keeping my eyes on the suspended leaves in her cup, I say, "Mark didn't want it. We were over." I want to tell her that I wish I'd chosen differently, that it hurt worse than I could have imagined, that I held a child corpse in my dreams where my baby became my sister, her face black, her blond hair singed. But I stare into my chilled cup and stay silent.

"How could you?" Norah says.

"I'm not a mother, Norah." Then, quietly, more to myself than to my friend, I say, "I can't bear children."

Norah gives the granite countertop a hard slap. "Don't talk bullshit, Brett. Of course you can 'bear' children." She gulps in little spasms, as if the words she searches for exist outside of her. Finally, she says, "This is just bullshit. Bullshit. You don't know what it is to lose a baby. You didn't 'lose' a baby; you, you..." She swallows, then whispers, "...*killed* one."

"Jesus, Norah. I was just trying to—"

"Does Cole know? Does he know what you did?"

"No, he doesn't need—"

Thrusting out her palm, flat like a traffic cop, Norah says, "Enough. I've heard enough. There is nothing the same about what you did and what happened to me." Her hand drops to her cup, which she picks up and dumps into the sink's mirror-clean steel. She watched the liquid swirl into the drain.

"I'll go," I say, bending to retrieve Beckett's leash.

The next song has begun. Something about another day spent away from someone.

Beckett stands at attention while I fasten his leash, his eyes flicking from the door to me.

Outside, cool wind pushes at me with the whisky smell of leaves. I glance up and down Norah's street, its perfect little children playing in its perfect little gardens.

When I get home from work on Monday, the kitchen counter is wiped clean, the smell of basil and garlic sweetens the air, and candle flames waver in the middle of the set table. Beckett stands like a maître d' beside the table. I drop to the floor, pull his head into my lap, and ruffle his fur.

"Wine?"

Cole has on a white T-shirt and faded jeans, tight and low-slung. In one hand he swings an open wine bottle and in the other he lifts a wine glass, the expression on his face so proud and vulnerable I ache to imprint this image on the backs of my eyelids so that wherever I go I will have him just like this.

"Yes? Wine?" he says again and begins to pour. "I made your favorite." He gestures toward the stove. "At least I think shrimp's your favorite." Setting down the bottle, Cole extends his hand to help me up, then places the glass in my hands and holds both of them with his own.

This isn't the first time Cole's cooked for me but there's a dangerous, recognizable glow about him.

When I sit in the chair he's pulled out for me, Cole places

himself across the table to watch me eat, smiling whenever I meet his eyes. He pushes food back and forth, the fork's edge clinking and scraping against the stoneware: clink scrape, clink scrape.

I set down my fork. "What is it, Cole? Go on, spit it out."

"How's the shrimp?"

"Delicious, thank you." Once, when we'd been together less than two months, he asked me to marry him. My response shocked him and I still feel monstrous for having laughed.

Whatever I touch breaks off in my hand.

"Stop staring at me, Cole. I'm not about to disappear if you look away." He looks startled and a little hurt. "I promise," I say in a gentler tone and his face relaxes. "I saw Norah today," I say, hoping this will distract him.

"Cool. How's she doing? Better, I hope."

"She's upset."

"She has every right to be," Cole says, spearing a shrimp.

"What?" I give my plate a little shove.

"It can't be easy wanting something so bad, thinking you got it, and then losing it." His eyes are on me.

I look down at Beckett who is also looking right at me. Everyone is so hungry. "Oh," I say. "Of course."

"It isn't too late, you know," he says, raising his wine glass. "For us."

"Too late for what?"

"I know what you said, but..." Here it comes. "We could have a baby. Just think about it, is all I'm asking."

"I told you." A fire bursts up from my belly, coloring everything red. My shrimp look like fetuses. I screech back my chair and I hear Cole saying my name, but I'm underwater and a weight like stones pulls me deeper.

"Brett, stop." The word 'stop' is a knot at the end of a rope. I reach for it. "Stop it," Cole says again. He's at my side pulling me hard against him. Directly into my ear he says, "It's okay. It's dropped. Forget I said anything." Cole picks up a piece of my hair and places it behind my shoulder, runs his hand along my arm, catches my hand, and brings it to his mouth. I let him kiss my hand and then my mouth. Sex cures everything. We leave our half-eaten food congealing on the table and do it on the living room rug.

My orgasm comes from a long way off, shudders up my legs and along my spine, ignites my arms, my hands, and lights up the inside of my head. As it subsides, the shuddering becomes another thing. It isn't that sweet cry of release and delight; this is different and I can't stop the swelling of it, the rolling, pitching, dropping of it. There's nothing to hold on to. I'm on my knees rocking back and forth, and I know he's there but I can't feel him anymore, he might be a dream too, through smoke and fire and burning things—Goldie, Goldie, my daddy, Norah's baby, and my dead baby. Mark was right—I'm too tough and too needy all at the same time.

"I'm sorry." I'm choking and everything is wet—the rug, my hands, my hair, wet with semen and snot—and now I feel Cole's hand on my back and I hate him because he thinks he loves me, stupid Cole. Stupid boy. Stupid, stupid. I sit up, swiping back the wet hairs stuck to my face.

"Babe?" Cole sounds scared.

He should be afraid.

"You're bleeding."

The blood smeared along my leg and on my foot is brown and sticky, not like menstrual blood.

"You have to see the doctor, Brett. You're going to get this checked. You hear me?"

I want to call Norah. I want to tell her about the blood. I want to put tequila and lime juice in a blender, put our feet up on the railing of my balcony, and have her tell me there's nothing to worry about so we can get back to talking trash. Like old times, before Cole and before Josh.

The afternoon I met her, Norah was folding pale blue lace underwear in the glare of the laundry room's fluorescent lights while I stuffed jeans and shirts and my plain cotton underwear into a canvas sack. "You're new here?" she asked. "Third floor?"

I pointed at the neat stack of lace. "You fold your underwear?"

"I've always wanted hair like yours," she said, hooking her own fine wisps behind her ear. "The blond is natural?"

I nodded, picturing my aunt June with her head like a brush fire. "Couldn't imagine dying it."

"Do you ever wear it down?"

"Not often. Gets in my mouth. Strangles me in my sleep." I hoisted my bag.

"Oh! Yes, of course. Too long to have it loose when you go to bed…" Norah tucked a silky crotch into a blue fold.

"I know, totally gets in the way when you're giving head, right?"

Sometimes I apologize for the things that fly out of my mouth. Mostly, I don't. But instead of looking shocked or disgusted Norah laughed, and we were instantly friends.

As I turned to leave, Norah reached out as if to touch my braid, but then yanked back her hand. "Oh, sorry!"

"You can touch it," I said, laughing.

"No, no, I can't. It will fall out if I do," she said, burying her hands inside her sleeves.

This made me laugh harder. "Seriously? I've had a few people touch my hair, and as you can see, it's pretty much intact."

"It's the envy," she said in a low voice. "Because of the envy." That was my introduction to the whims of Norah's belief system.

I never know when a step I take or a color I wear on the third Tuesday is going to break my teeth or bring the four horsemen. Growing up with my aunt June has given me a high tolerance for wackiness, but June's predictions and appraisals are rooted in relatively concrete things, like planets and stars and picture cards that illustrate actual obstacles. Norah's precision may not be founded in logic, but I like the chaos of it; how a thing so plain or innocuous, like keys on a table, could change the course of one's life. We are unlike in most ways but, like Bert and Ernie, our friendship has endured. Norah makes sure I wear the right colors, don't walk under ladders, keep clear of black cats, even the ones with white diamond shapes on their chests, and never, ever break into song with a mouthful of pasta. Me, I helped with her wedding, threw her an exuberant shower, complete with an extremely hot male stripper who wasn't even gay. And I was as there for her as best I could manage both times she miscarried, bringing soup and those fey flowers from roadside ditches. But it wasn't enough and now she's gone too.

I can't call Norah. I call my doctor.

5

I hate these paper gowns that don't close. Might as well give me a paper towel and call it discretion since it's open at the front and the so-called belt ripped when I pulled it. There's a quick rap at the door. This guy's going to stick a metal duckbill up my vagina and have a good look up there. But he knocks first.

"How are we doing today?" he asks without looking at me. He's older with less hair and baggier eyes than the last time I saw him, which is I don't remember when.

"So…" He flips open a folder. "Brett. What can we do for you today?"

I want to say, *Oh, just a little off the top*, but I can't stop shivering.

"Looks like we haven't seen you in six years." He looks up at me.

I nod. That was the last time I saw him. I probably have less hair and baggier eyes as well.

"Guess you need the works, then?" He can be jovial because he's wearing clothes.

"I've had bleeding," I manage.

"Spotting?"

"No. Blobs of blood after sex."

After summoning his nurse, a little round woman with a toothy smile, he says, "So, let's have a look." He wiggles his fingers into blue stretchy gloves and lets the cuffs snap. "Scootch down right to the edge." *Scootch*, for god's sake. He lays a sheet across my thighs for modesty. The nurse stands at the door with the kind of look you give a child about to get stuck with a needle.

From under a square of green fabric he picks out a silver instrument, runs his finger along my slit as if he knows me, stretches open my labia, slides that hard, cold thing up inside, and switches on a lamp as he swings it between my legs. The heat from the light contrasts the iciness of the speculum. "Just a little pinch here," he says. As if he knows.

I don't tell him it hurts like hell, like the worst cramping, that the speculum is pinching the tender skin inside my vagina. I just breathe deep and stare at the dots on the ceiling, listen to the crackle of paper under my butt and wait for it to be over.

"I'm just going to take another swab here, just to be sure," he says, his voice different now, not so jaunty. He slides the speculum out and I feel goo seep out after it. I start to sit up, but he says, "I'm just going to feel your ovaries here." I lie back down and his fingers swoop up into the place where the metal was, his thumb resting close to my clit. I feel my vagina contract at the contact and my face flushes. This must be how men feel when they get an 'inappropriate' hard-on. "Any pain here?" he asks, his fingers poking and rolling around my lower belly.

"No," I say. "Just uncomfortable."

"Okay, I think we're all done here," he says. "I'll get these to the lab and give you a requisition for some blood work." He swipes me with a paper towel and scrunches it by my bum as he stands, sending the wheeled stool squeaking back to the wall.

"Did you see something?" I ask. "In there?"

"Can't be sure. Call in a week—we should have the results by then." Rolling off the blue gloves, he balls them up and tosses them in the trash. "Have a nice day," he says and pulls open the door.

I'm off the table, reaching for my coveralls before the door closes behind him.

The dream of Bali rises again behind my eyes with color more vivid than the maples which have already begun their showy death dance of splotched red amidst the green. Mark didn't want to go to Indonesia; he'd had enough of the east, so we came home, took our stuff out of storage, and both got jobs with a contractor—him as a drywaller and me behind him, painting. I wanted heat and air heavy with scent, not slush and frozen ears. *Do whatever you like*, Mark said. *Suit yourself.* I would have suited myself. I would have gone without him; that would have been easy, but he'd planted his seed and that changed everything.

On Wednesday, Mel and I scour the roads for bent signs, batteries, television sets dumped in ditches, and dead things. A splayed skunk, its black and white fur like a negative of Beckett's white and black fur, has stopped us on 27. I crank open the truck door and slide out onto the graveled shoulder. "Doesn't stink," I say, picking up a shovel.

"Hit in the head. Didn't die afraid."

I stomp the edge of the shovel into the tangle of grasses and stand on it to drive it in. "Just surprised." I smell the honey warmth of sweetgrass. There's nothing like its perfume in the depths of summer. They grow in single blades, not in bunches or clusters. I can never find it, but Mel always goes straight to it, turning the delicate blades to show me. *See there? How it catches the light?*

I like to keep a small braid in the cab to help with the bad smells.

Mel tips the shovel to release the black and white creature into the hole I've made. A plume of stink erupts, making me jump back.

"That." Mel waggles a finger at the space the smell fills, its vapor visible in the fall heat. "That juice. When everyone on the reserve was dying from Spanish flu my great-great-grandmother had my great-great-grandfather trap a skunk. She made a tea with that juice and gave everyone in the family that tea."

My stomach does a half-turn. "Let me guess—they all died."

"Nah," Mel says, making that familiar wave-like motion, as if coaxing the smell to penetrate. "Not one of 'em got sick." Mel knocks back the brim of his hat and takes in an extra deep draft of the heady air. "Just breathing it in can help heal you."

I've often wondered why whenever we find a skunk, Mel takes deep breaths. I thought he was just crazy for the smell.

Back in the cab, Mel pops shut the door and bounces the keys in his palm.

"Was your great-great-grandma some kind of medicine woman?" I ask.

A bit of gold shows at the edge of his smile. "All women are medicine women."

I like to picture his family wearing elk and doe skins, their hair in long, oiled braids, praying in a dark, smoky circle, even though over the years I've worked with him I've learned these things: that he shared regular head shaves with his brothers after being sent home with lice on the "bug bus"; that his family of nine ate plates of white beans standing at a card table while his father slept off the drunk from his last paycheck; and that he shared a single mattress with four of his siblings. They didn't sleep on bearskins in a cozy wigwam but crowded around a woodstove on an icy floor in their uninsulated shack.

Mel's right hand, surprisingly smooth and unblemished, is draped on the steering wheel, brown fingers in an easy gallop to the song on the radio, which happens to be the same Marianas Trench song I heard at Norah's, "All to Myself."

It's never enough.

The singer's voice reels up and down, in turns plaintive, desperate, and demanding.

I wish I could breathe.

Mel is quiet. Not a vacant or distracted quiet, but one that seems to be listening. Maybe it's just simply quiet; no mind noise in the way, no inner chatter messing up the landscape. It might be his lineage, a tracker in his blood, but it's invariably he who spots the roadkill before I see the dark anomalies at the roadside. Skunk. Coon. Porcupine. Dog. Rabbit. He says the names of the dead things in English, but then like an echo, he names them in his mother's tongue. *Zhgaag. Esban. Gaag. Nimosh. Waabooz.*

Cole once told me that if you're going to be an artist you have to love dark things. He wanted to name the dog Rimbaud but it

sounded too similar to Rambo, and that wasn't the image either
of us wanted to conjure. Samuel Beckett understood darkness.
We'd already named Beckett when I read a passage from *Malone
Dies* to Cole about darkness and how it thickens and accumu-
lates before bursting and drowning everything. Cole had wanted
to change the dog's name after that, but I reminded him about
artists. Not fully convinced it was a good idea to put all that
onto a happy little dog, he did, nonetheless, allow that Beckett
was a cool name.

I don't *love* dark things, although I live there somehow, but
I'm nowhere close to being an artist. Cole makes dark things,
but even a song he wrote about Norah and Josh losing their
babies sounds beautiful. He sings the dark like thick cream.

What I do is search carcasses for something like meaning
or hope or redemption. Hoping that in decaying bodies I will
find an answer or a reason, that in the digging of holes and
dropping in of bodies I will know what death is. That it might
become a friend. With each new dead thing I experience a flip
inside, almost a thrill, as if I am that much nearer to a truth. If
I can come close enough to name organs, smell rot, put my fingers into the stiffness between muscle and bone, fall into their
blank eyes, I should have my answer, my freedom. It isn't that I
expect to find my sister or father or even my discarded child in
these shallow graves, but to uncover the thing that death offers,
what it knows. The organics of death I understand—crows and
turkey vultures chased from entrails, flies and maggots, crushed
bones and twisted heads—but there's a secret locked in there
and I get close, but never close enough.

I close *A Season in Hell and The Drunken Boat* after copying a
quote into my journal: *Whatever it is that binds families and married
couples together, that's not love. That's stupidity or selfishness or fear. Love
doesn't exist.* The words blur a little. I call Beckett but he's already
beside me, his truncated tail buzzing. *The Dawns are heartbreak-
ing. Every moon is atrocious and every sun bitter.*

Cole follows us down the dank stairs to the street. He rarely joins me when I walk the dog, but today he was awake and dressed when I got home, and he took me to the clean kitchen, proud as a cat with a mouse in its jaws.

The leaves' red and orange reflections shimmer like a computer gif in the quiet lake. Beckett walks between us, his eyes darting back and forth from Cole to me. It's too hot for September; more like that mid-July pressing-down heat where every breath's a struggle, asphalt stays soft in filled potholes, and the reek of dead animals sticks to shovels, gloves, and boots.

Fitting a rubber ball into the ball launcher's cup, I say, "He's usually into the grass and back again a dozen times before we even get to the curve."

"He likes this, that we're all together. It feels good," Cole says with a satisfied sigh. "Like we're a real family."

The launcher hangs limp in my hands. Beckett leaps in the air, his white and black body twisting.

Reaching for the bobbing launcher, Cole says, "Here. Let me. Come on, boy."

Cole casts the ball like a fishing rod, sending it sailing into the rushes. Beckett does a little horse-type prance, rears up, and then shoots off into the thicket.

"You don't need to try so hard, Cole. Just relax, okay?"

He sucks in his breath. "Maybe you're the one who needs to relax. We're just having fun here, like normal people."

My laugh sounds like a misfiring chainsaw. "You've always known I'm not normal." I shift into my left hip. "Not big on the whole family thing. Kinda puts me on edge."

He gives his head a shake. "Well, for once it'd be nice to, you know, discuss things like grown-ups? Together. Figure things out together. Plans, you know? Without you freaking out? Maybe travel, like you said. Shit like that. Just talk, you know, like humans?" He's waiting, it seems, for an answer.

As if I have one.

"Cole," I say, compressing my voice in an effort to sound reasonable. "My head's just a bit messed these days. I'm not sure what's up. But I need a bit of space to sort it out."

"What?" His head jerks like Beckett's at the sound of the leash. "What are you saying? What space? Just say it, for fuck's sake." His freckles blaze. "Don't mess with my head."

"I'm not."

"What then? Speak, Brett, please."

The lake water dulls. The dry grasses go still. My soles have begun to burn. Cole's green shirt has darkened under the arms and at the collar.

"I'm not trying to fuck with your head." I shut my eyes and take one sharp breath. "I don't know what's wrong with me, okay?" I didn't mean to yell, but Beckett crashes through the reeds onto the walkway, his mouth empty and his eyes bright as cherries.

"Where's your ball, boy? Go get your ball." Cole turns his back to me and makes to go into the tall grasses, but Beckett has lost interest in his ball and bounces from me to Cole, his tail stuck up like a little flagpole.

I take the launcher from Cole and make a wide arc ending in a snap. Beckett falls for the fake and bounds off like a jackrabbit.

"So, what kind of space are we talking about, then?" His gaze follows the dog.

"Just time, Cole. I just need a little time." The truth is that I don't know how to leave and I don't know how to stay.

6

I have some bad news, I'm afraid," says Dr. Melnyk. He places his hand on the paper in the open file as if it might fly up and out the window.

"It's from the abortion, isn't it?" I manage. When the receptionist called the third time, saying that I had to come in, that she could not and would not give me the results over the phone, I figured it was bad. Ripped scar tissue or something.

"I doubt that," he says, smoothing the sides of the file now with both of his hands. I watch those hands; the left one's ring finger has an indent where the skin is pale. "You have abnormal cells. Cancer, actually. Carcinoma in situ. Cervical cancer."

The doctor wears heavy glasses that have slid down his large eastern European nose. His dark office is close, dust clouding the air between us. He is so wrong. Why does he have both a tiny metal crucifix and a Buddha as big as my thumb side by side on his cluttered desk? That's either egg or toothpaste on his striped tie. It's not even knotted properly, just a tight crooked knot as if his grandson had tied it. My chair must have been made in the Middle Ages with its sharp edges sticking right into my bones. Why did I come here, anyway? He obviously doesn't know his ass from a hole in the ground.

"It's probably just dysplasia," I tell him. Norah had that and she had a cone biopsy—a little day-surgery and she was fine.

He clears his throat. "No, Ms. Catlin. Brett. You have cancer."

I sit forward. "Just day-surgery, right? No big deal?"

He slides his heavy glasses up the length of his nose. "The treatment for this type of cancer is hysterectomy."

The Buddha's hands stick straight up in the air like mountain pose in yoga, his fat little face so self-satisfied. The air in the room has grown so dense I'm breathing in dust. "Hysterectomy? You mean like take everything out?" My sweet pink organs in a pickle jar? *Not.*

"Perhaps not everything. The oncologist might consider just the uterus."

Oncologist? "Just?" I'm staring at him hard enough to make him disappear, but he won't. The doctor just sits there with a sorry expression, a touch worried as if I might sweep the neat stacks of paper off his desk.

"I don't think so." I stand. "Thanks, but no thanks." There's no window in this room. The door behind me is closed. I unzip my jacket and zip it up again as I continue to stare at him. He's either going to tell me he's made a mistake or he'll find another way to fix this.

"I can send you for a colposcopy. This isn't pre-cancer, Ms. Catlin. Brett. Either way…" He's looking at me over the top of his glasses.

My head lifts off my shoulders. "No," I hear myself say.

"You don't have much choice, I'm afraid." He pauses, scans my face, draws in his breath and holds it for a moment. "May I ask you something?" Without waiting for an answer, he continues, "You had a therapeutic abortion six years ago. You are thirty-seven years old. This will save your life. Why are you so adamant?"

It might be a good question. It *is* a good question, in fact, but all I see right now is a wall of black. A wall of black isn't an answer. "I don't know. I just know that I can't." My hand searches behind me for the doorknob.

"I'll get Marianne to make you an appointment for a colposcopy," he says.

"Whatever the hell that is," I say.

"It's a way to get a better look," he says. "At your vagina and cervix. To evaluate the severity."

I walk out into a world where mothers push babies in strollers along the lake's edge, drunks stagger out of bars, and narrow shop windows display red dresses on mannequins with no heads.

"I have cancer," I say, testing the feel of the words on my tongue. They taste like air. Like nothing. Like a lie someone told and no one believed. How could I possibly have cancer?

7

I walk. The restless lake is molten steel, perpetually lunging for shore, grabbing for me, hoping to pull me under. I walk north.

After the fire, Mama and I stayed with Aunt June in Nelson. We just moved, as if we wanted to; as if it were a simple change to an easier life. Everything still smelled of smoke—even the new yellow-and-green-flowered sheets Aunt June had bought, washed with lemon soap, and hung on the line. I slept in Dylan's bed and Mama was supposed to sleep in Donovan's, but she never did. Every night I'd hear the low murmur of Aunt June telling Mama to sleep, *get some sleep, drink some Vervain, chant, om mani padme om, but just get to bed*. Then there was silence hard as stone, punctuated only by the occasional tap tap of Mama's pipe on the green alabaster bowl June had given her.

A month after the fire, June took Mama for a "girls' getaway" to Vancouver Island because Dylan was home for reading week and could watch me. I guessed Mama agreed so she could get away from me, because whenever she looked at me, her face got hard.

Dylan stroked my hair, gave one braid a little tug, and put a gentle kiss on my forehead when he sent me to bed, reminding me as he stood in the bathroom doorway to brush my teeth, even the back, back ones. But after scrubbing my face with goat-milk soap, which I'd been doing every morning and night since the fire in hopes of washing away the smell, Dylan took my face in his hands, said, "Good night, sweetheart," and kissed my cheek. "I'll come tuck you in in a little while."

From my bed, I heard the suck of rubber gasket and the rattle of jars in the fridge door, followed by the pop of the beer bottle lid. I listened hard, losing the sound of him when he closed the screen door and went out to the porch. Dylan didn't smoke cigarettes, so I pictured him out there in the fall night naming stars between the mountain peaks, the way his mother had taught him. Maybe he was thinking about his cousin Goldie and his uncle Ed and wondering if they were up there in a constellation. Dylan's kisses had dried, but I still felt his lips and the warmth of his hands on my face. I liked the way my cousin looked at me, as if I was really there, and that seeing me made him glad.

Finally, the bedroom door creaked open, letting the red-gold lamplight flow through the opening. "You asleep, little cuz?" Dylan whispered.

"I'm waiting for you to tuck me in," I said.

The bed dipped as he sat. His face was mostly in shadow, but to me even in the dark, he looked just like Don Johnson.

"I came to give you a goodnight hug," he said, leaning down into my outstretched arms, his shoulders like wings. I smelled beer and something sweet like incense.

"Are you going to sleep in Donovan's bed?" I asked.

Dylan raised himself on his hands, now on either side of my head, and looked down at me kind of like the way Daddy looked at me when he tucked me in, but different. A special kind of different.

"You're real pretty," he said, holding my braid as if weighing it. "Fancy."

"You have nice hair too," I said.

"Shh, now. Would you like me to get in with you? Keep you company for a little while?"

Lifting the covers, I slid over to the wall.

"I'm just going to take my sweater off," he said. "It's a bit hot."

The warmth of his body penetrated right through my pajamas. "Would you like a little back rub?" he asked.

"That feel nice?" he asked a few moments later.

"Yes," I said, remembering how Daddy's hands felt when he threw me over his head, and I thought about how the morning before the fire, a shadow had made me look up. *What kind of bird is that?* I asked Daddy.

Daddy had shielded his eyes with his hand like a visor. *That's an eagle, honey. They fly the highest of all the birds. It's a special sign to see an eagle.*

"You like that?" Dylan asked into my ear.

"Yes," I said.

Dylan's hand smelled of lavender, the way Mama's did after she came in from the garden.

"Just close your eyes. That's it, just relax now. Good. Good girl. You are so pretty. Do you know how pretty you are?"

Daddy used to tell me how smart I was, but nobody ever said I was pretty. Dylan stroked the skin on my chest, lightly grazing my small version of Mama's nipple where Goldie used to nurse. I could see Goldie's shiny smile and fat cheeks when she sat up after nursing and smell the sweet powder smell of her.

I'm not dressed right. My jeans weigh heavy as if they are soaked. I miss my mother. I want to call her, tell her I'm sick, have her tell me that I'm not really sick, but whenever I've called her, it's as if the phone wire is laid across the prairies and mountains that separate us. I can barely hear her and it's clear that she cannot hear me.

It wasn't only Dylan's fingers that made all the bad things go away. His mouth too. Those little bumps on my chest had nerves inside them that could light up and catch fire, a crazy good fire, when he put his mouth on them. There were so many places on my body that I hadn't known existed, and Dylan took his time introducing me to them. Places behind my knees, inside my elbows, the back of my neck.

He always saved the best for last.

This is what I think about as I walk. Dylan and all the good parts. Not the part where he told me we had to stop. Not the part when my blood started and we ended. Not about what's going on inside me now.

When I get back to the apartment, I press my back against the closed door and shut my eyes, my arm bent up behind me, my hand reaching for the knob. Not even Beckett comes to greet me, no click of his nails, no sliding stop, no hopeful looks from door to treat cupboard. Street sounds could be coming from the moon. I try to will myself forward, propel myself into the living room or the kitchen, to pick up a dishrag, mop the floor, write a letter, call Norah. *Call Norah.* My cell phone is dead. The regular phone is right there, poor phone, no one ever uses it anymore. I should cancel the service. I could do that right now—pick up that perky little receiver and end its life by calling Bell. It's easy, something like BELL123. I could do it.

"Beckett," I whisper.

There's a stirring in the bedroom; a rustle, a click, followed by a soft moan. Then the tidal sound of duvet pushed across the bed and dropped to the floor. I follow the sounds as I imagine them—Cole's sleep-drenched body rises to sitting, long legs turning, smooth bare feet landing on the rug, the push of his knuckles against the mattress as he stands. "Brett?"

When I open my eyes he is not where I thought him. He's in the darkened entrance to the bathroom about six feet away. He's wearing his boxers with the little red Hot Stuffs holding flaming pitchforks. I should never have bought them.

"What are you doing?" His throat is thick with sleep. "You okay?"

I could lie. I'm relatively good at that. But I'm better at just not telling than out-and-out lying. But still. He's waiting.

When my dog looks up at me he might be quoting his namesake: *Don't wait to be hunted to hide.*

"I…" I begin, but instead of forming a sentence, I sink down against the door, my arm still twisted up behind me, until my bum meets the floor.

"Speak." Annoyance has cleared the muck of sleep from his voice.

When I say nothing, he crouches and brings his face close. The sour-sweet scent of dreams hovers around him. When he opens his mouth to speak, I recoil at the stale smell.

"What's going on? Where have you been?" He gives my chin a firm tug.

Jerking away my head, I launch myself to my feet.

"Hey!"

From my height I look down on his naked shoulders, his flattened hair, the crouch of a beggar, and I tell him, "I have cancer."

Beckett tucks his tight little body into a sit. His eyebrows lift one at a time. Cole stays in his crouch right down there beside him. Like a beggar left so long in the Bombay sun that he petrified.

I speak to this paralyzed sadhu, this man I never intended to stay so long with. "The blood. It was from a tumor," I say.

Then I go into the kitchen and take two peaches from the bowl on the counter.

My boyfriend's name is Cole, like the old king who was a merry old soul. He uncoils and comes to stare at me across the kitchen counter, but the stare reaches only as far as, say, the coffee pot, and drops off there and splatters on the counter. I have a peach in either hand, hefting them like ass cheeks, breasts, or testicles, or like peaches. *My sweet little peach.*

It's quiet in here aside from the sound of a voice I think is mine, saying these words: *I guess it's payback.*

Cole, with soft reddish hair that lights up in the sun, speaks, but like his stare, the words don't quite make it across the counter. His face is screwed up, squished like a crumpled road map. "Chemo?" This word barely sounds like language. It sounds like choking.

I shake my head. Lift one peach.

"Radiation?"

I lift the other peach. "Don't know yet," I say. "I'll figure it out."

He's coming around the counter, coming at me with arms like a turkey vulture, and I can't step away fast enough. He has me. His voice rises in space and lands behind my ear. "We'll get through this."

I open my hands and the peaches land on the floor: *plop, plop.* I reach through the open slit between winking red devils, reach for the solid warmth of the treasure Cole keeps in there just for me, but he swings his hips away and slaps my hand. "For fuck's sake, Brett."

The apartment falls quiet as a power outage.

"I'm going back out," I say, at which Beckett does a spin and dashes to the door.

Cole's wide awake now. "You can't just leave." This is more question than command. "Talk to me. What are our options?"

"Our?" I press my foot into a peach. Its flesh oozes through my socks and in between my toes. "You didn't sign up for this, Cole. It's not your fight."

His eyes close. How can anyone's eyelashes be so long? The smell of ripe peach, sticky with sun, wafts up from the floor. "You're wrong," he says at last. "I did sign up. Now tell me what the options are."

"Fucked if I know. They want to cut me open, okay? And I don't want to be cut open. That's all." I move toward the door. "I'll figure something out. My aunt knows things."

"What?" A peach squelches under his bare foot. "You can have surgery? Jezus, why didn't you say so?" He's behind me. I can smell his breath. I can smell his sweat. "So you're not going to die, right? They can take it out, right?" His hands press into my waist. They press until the fingers make runnels. The weight of his head sinks onto my shoulder.

"I need to run," I say and dip away from him to go change into running clothes.

I fasten on Beckett's leash and don't look at Cole as we pass him standing in the hallway with his open mouth and sad eyes.

Once away from traffic, I let Beckett free. He keeps pace with me once I hit my stride going north along the path. The lake is calm and dark, clusters of geese rip its surface as they land, braying at each other like bitter old women. The path is lit in regular pools by streetlight. As soon as the sun disappeared, the wind died and now cooler air pushes in.

That first summer without Daddy and Goldie, we'd go down

to Kootenay Lake, Mama and Aunt June drinking cups of lemonade by the concession booth while I pushed sand around and listened to other children shrieking and splashing in the water. It was the little ones I couldn't watch. I hated them for being alive.

The path veers sharply east and passes under finer homes. Boats lift and tug at their ropes at the edge of the water. I want to untie their moorings, set them free into the open lake. But even the open lake is finite, enclosed. I suppose they might find the mouth to the waterway that would eventually lead to open sea. It's just so easy to get lost along the way, to end up ripped open on jagged rocks or to drift for days without making headway.

Beckett squeals and jumps forward, bouncing like a rabbit into a thicket near the water.

"Beckett!" I hurry after him.

One, two bounces and he plunges into the tall grasses and emerges with a black creature clamped in his jaws.

"Drop it!" I shout, but Beckett shakes the animal as if it were a stuffed toy. White streaks in its black fur tell me that it isn't a cat he's caught.

I scream, "Down, Beckett, down. Drop it!"

Beckett's jaws open and the skunk tumbles out. A pissy burnt-coffee smell lifts out of the grasses. My eyes tear and I slap my hand over my mouth. Beckett spins and races back to me. We run along the pathway, Beckett just ahead. We keep running as if we could outrun that smell.

After putting Beckett in the bathroom, I drive to the grocery store. When I walk in through the swoosh of automatic doors into the ice-cool, all heads turn toward me, their faces in an array of shock, disgust, and amusement.

I'm putting the last of three large cans of tomato juice in my basket when Cole appears at the end of the aisle. He starts to laugh but stops by the applesauce about ten feet away.

"Beckett?" he calls down the aisle.

I nod. I had hoped that at least I'd stop smelling it after a while, but it continues to waft around me, just as the singe of Goldie's hair did.

Cole takes a few steps and stops two feet away. "A rose by any other name..." he says.

It's intolerable—my smell. I have to get out of this cold store, out of this town, this country, out of sacrificial animals, out of my own skin. "I've got to go," I say without looking at him.

Cole takes a long step back. Waving a hand in front of his face, he says, "Good idea."

I nod, keeping my head down. "I have to get out."

"So you said."

"Bali," I say.

"Bali? That's extreme," he says. Then he brightens. "What about a week in Mexico or Cuba? That'd be cheaper."

I grip the handles of the basket until I feel them cut into my palms. "I don't want to go for a week. I want to go forever."

There's a pause before he laughs.

The air conditioning blasts in the too-bright store and my basket is too heavy. There's a crescent-shaped splotch of something creamy on Cole's apron. Behind him, a woman with slitty eyes and lank gray hair absorbs herself in a label on a jar of pickles. He is so beautiful, so kind, so young. I can't do this. I can't go and I can't stay.

"One can dream, right?" I offer a laugh I hope sounds genuine. "When your first album goes platinum, okay?"

His whole body softens as he lets out his breath. "When you're all better we'll go." Before his hand reaches my arm he retracts it. "You'd better go get cleaned up." His laugh is relieved, grateful.

I'm starting to feel a bit nauseous. Maybe it's the skunk or maybe it's on account of whatever's festering inside. "We'll talk when you get home, okay? I promise—we'll *discuss* options." I stretch my mouth into a smile. "Like grown-ups."

The thin woman with the pickles hasn't moved.

When I lean in to kiss Cole, he takes a step back. We both laugh. It's a good feeling.

The pickle woman sticks her thumb up in a sign of approval.

"There's a lot of sugar in those," I tell her. "Maybe try kosher dills."

The white of Beckett's fur has been stained pink from his juice bath. When Cole comes home we both still reek. He's in the kitchen pushing jars and containers around inside the fridge. He won't find anything he wants to eat. In a few moments, he'll come into the bedroom to ask what there is. He's a better cook than I am, but after his shift he turns into a helpless boy. I usually cook him an omelet or warm up leftovers. This morning, the contents of the fridge might as well be the contents of my suitcase.

Picking up a pair of my panties, I study the way the lace has started to come undone at the seam and debate whether to toss them. "I won't bear children," I say very quietly. Goldie squatting in the garden, her pale face smiling up at me. "I can't bear them."

"What are you talking about?"

Startled, I clutch the panties to my chest. "You...you want a baby."

Cole regards my hands, his forehead creasing. "Yeah, thought you'd be a great mom." He reaches for my panties. "But babies don't matter. You matter."

"I never meant to stay so long," I say.

"Things have changed. I get that." His feet begin to shuffle back and forth, fast then slow, then fast again. *Shush,shush, shush, shushshushshush, shush.* "Look, I don't need..." He hesitates. "It's not like I *needed* a kid." The movement stops. "I just thought that you...that we...that if we had a kid—" His struggle is obvious. "Have the operation. We'll be fine. There's always adop—"

My belly spins like a car on ice, my hand trembling on the emergency brake. "We're not going there, Cole!"

"Not going where?" His freckles blaze, then fade just as

quickly. "Okay, all right. We drop the baby thing, all right? Let's just get you well. There'll be lots of time after—"

"I can't think about operations right now." The ghosts aren't his. This is my doing. I drop the panties and pull out a white cotton blouse to examine for lightness. It's very hot in Bali. "I don't want to cause any more damage."

"Damage?" Cole rips the blouse from my hands and snaps it to the floor. "You have to stop talking bullshit."

Lunging after the blouse, I yell, "I'm sorry, okay? I just can't do this, this *together* thing. It's not right." What isn't right is for him to watch me die. Better just to break his heart. Cut the head off the chicken. Then once he's over the anger he can find someone younger, healthier, whole.

Light filters into his eyes and his entire face softens. His grip as he draws me close is firm but he's not hurting me. "Hey, hey," he says, his breath touching the fine hairs of my cheek. "We all have skeletons or whatever shit, but you can't run away from them." Out of the corner of my eye I notice that Beckett has left his bed. "Brett, look at me, please."

I scan the room for Beckett.

"Please," he says again.

I meet his bare eyes and wish I hadn't.

"Let's do this, all right?" His warm mouth presses a kiss on my forehead. "We'll figure it out. However you want. But we're doing this together." He draws back, holds my gaze. "Got it?"

We're almost the same height, his belly warm against the hard surface of mine. Even though I have no idea what together actually means, I whisper, "Got it."

We go lie together on top of the covers, my back nested into his burnt-sugar smell and I watch the sky surrender its dark pink and orange to the flat blue of day. The weight of his arm on my waist used to feel like an anchor but now it feels like stone, smooth but just as capable of holding me under.

At work the next morning, Mel opens the driver's side door and stops. "*Zhgaag?*"

"You can still smell it?"

Closing his eyes, he takes a deep breath. Maybe I should have buried my face in Beckett's fur instead of trying to wash it all away.

I want to tell Mel about the cancer, but I can't seem to open my mouth. We ride in silence on the 400 which is stockpiled with cars headed north for a last whack at a cottage weekend. Leaves bleed into reds and golds this hot Friday morning. Mel's got the radio tuned to *The Dock*. I've been skunked. My best friend hates me. My mother lives on another planet. My sister and father are dead because of me. And I have cancer. *Payback*.

"Turn that up, will you?" Mel points to the radio with his stubbly chin.

It should be Del Shannon singing "My Little Runaway." That would make me laugh. Or possibly cry. The song he wants louder is Tom Petty's "Freefalling," and I sing along, loud, and then louder. "I'm FREEEEE FREEEE FALLING." I buzz down my window and sing out to the highway jammed with blinking brake lights.

"You like this song." Mel gives me a sidelong glance. He's so droll I want to kiss him on his old geezer face.

I answer by opening my mouth wide and singing even louder.

We're stuck in traffic hell. "I'm freeeee," I sing to a stone-faced driver with children and old people jammed into his car, kayak strapped to the roof, three bicycles bouncing on the back.

My window slides up and I'm faced with the ghost of my own face.

"Good song," says Mel in a sad, kind voice.

I'm not sure how Mel knows my bullshit. He just does. I go on singing, but we keep the windows closed.

Eventually, we turn off the highway, and on the Third Line heading east, a streak of gold-brown crests the far side of the culvert and slides into the underbrush.

"*Ma'iingan*," Mel says in that growly voice he uses every time we spot an animal, dead or alive.

"Oh," I say, sitting forward. "I've never seen one."

"They don't usually get hit."

"Too smart?"

Mel touches the lump of the pouch he wears under his shirt. "Strong medicine, wolves."

"I only remember hearing coyotes in the Kootenays," I say. "At night, especially. Once, my cousin Dylan took me up a clear-cut mountain to harvest some dead cedar, and a whole family of them were wailing like lost souls. I'd never heard anything so mournful. My cousin had to buy me ice cream to stop me crying."

Mel listens. As always, it seems that he is hearing something besides what's being said, something more interesting than the words.

I say, "What is wolf medicine?" I imagine something about their ability to survive despite human idiocy and bloodlust. Mel's good at slicing into the heart of things and making what is complicated sound so simple.

"Family," he says, turning to regard me fully. "They take care of each other."

"What about lone wolves?" I say, feeling the crackle of an itch start around my belly button. "How can they take care of each other then?"

"They look for family. To make one."

"Well, good luck to them," I say, a sour taste seeping in under my tongue.

Again, I sense Mel studying me.

Letting out my breath, I feel my shoulders sag. "I'm not so good with the family thing, I guess."

"Family can hurt or heal." Mel's head dips. "All depends."

8

Our days move from one to the next in a similar pattern to the way they've passed for more than five years. The weather has turned, the promise of winter on its breath. Cole works nights, practices with his band twice a week in the afternoon and some weekend days. He's had two gigs this month, one in the café where a neighbor of ours works, and one in a sleazy bar that pays them in beer. Our life looks similar but now there is an undertow to that surface flow. We haven't discussed "it" except in the brief exchanges when Cole asks if I've made a doctor's appointment to which I answer either "Not yet," or "I will." With an uneasy acceptance, Cole doesn't pursue the issue.

I didn't tell him that I went to the specialist. I saw it—white and glutinous on the colposcopist's screen. Now I know what a tumor looks like.

Bali is far enough away that no one will have to watch my sorry ass die and I won't be tempted to run back home. I'm searching on the internet for visa information. If I'm going to die, I want to celebrate in a good way under a different sun. The whole village will be in the street with fruit on their heads singing and dancing with my ashes in a beautifully painted urn on their shoulders.

Goldie and Dad were never celebrated, never even properly mourned. The ashes went downriver and everyone, including Aunt June, went silent.

Coming back from the colposcopy appointment, I sit down at my laptop to search for information. Cole is doing some research of his own at the desktop. I find out that I could get a visa when I land in Indonesia, but it would be for only thirty days and after thirty days I'd have to renew for another thirty. And then I'd have to leave. Two months is not long enough.

It might take years...The only option for a long-term visa is to have a sponsor, but I don't know anyone in Bali. I consider Thailand. Or I could go back to India. I've heard that there are amazing healers in the Philippines. Maybe I should go there. Maybe they'd be able to fix the rest of my mess as well.

Cole turns from the desktop screen. "It says here that women who have sex early and have multiple partners are more likely to get cervical cancer."

This lands like a punch, but I'm adept at recovery. I can walk and talk and breathe just like a normal person. "Great. That really helps."

"I didn't mean it was your fault or anything. Just that it explains why..."

Luckily, my body breathes on its own. "That's how it sounds."

"You aren't listening. I said—"

"I heard. Statistics won't help unless they can make this go away."

Cole powers off his computer and joins me at the window where I am looking over the lid of my laptop to the gray and brown city and the freezing water beyond.

"It's not going to just go away."

"But I can," I tell him.

"You're not going anywhere, Brett. Not until you're better."

Will I ever be better? "We'll see about that," I say, stepping away from him and his concern. I don't want to argue. Best to just keep it all tucked in.

Cole puts a heavy arm across my shoulders. "As far as I can make out, the success rate after a hysterectomy is good." He presses me close, the way he pulls Beckett in when he's retrieved a ball. "And you don't really need your uterus, right?"

My hands ball into fists. "Yeah, who needs an old sack of flesh if it's not going to earn its keep, eh?"

Cole releases his grip. "You misunderstand everything I say, Brett."

Sex should fix this tangle we're in. I stand up, take his hand, and lead him to the bedroom. After his pants are off, I kneel

down, take him in my hand and open my mouth. But Cole cups
my head, pulls me up, and gives me a gentle push.

"This time it's just for you," he says, palms pressed lightly on
my shoulders to keep me prone.

This time, though, neither his hands nor his mouth ignite
anything but the image of the shiny blob pulsing on the deep
pink of my cervix. I'd assumed the position, had a white sheet
draped over my bent open knees, and watched the reasonably
attractive doctor's fair head dip out of sight. "Just a little pinch,"
the colposcopist said, which, as always, was a big fat lie.

Lifting his head from between my legs, Cole studies my face.
"You're very quiet," he says.

The face of the doctor and Cole's jam together. "What are
you finding down there?" I say, but it doesn't come out with the
light, amusing tone I'd intended. "Anything interesting?"

Cole crawls up beside me, lifts my hand, and says, "Marry
me." I laugh, not unkindly I don't think, but the red flush of
Cole's cheeks deepens to tomato red. "I'm serious, Brett. I want
to marry you."

He looks extra young, his face too eager. Something metallic
inside presses into my ribs. He's squeezing my hand so hard his
shakes.

Beckett has begun to pace, circling the bed, then turning
and circling in the other direction. "We'll get married in Bali—
wherever you want. You can wear a big thing with flowers on
your head, and I'll wear a white shirt with big sleeves and one
of those skirt things with the little dot patterns. We'll get married in the jungle, or no, wait, by the sea…whatever you want."
He's so close I can smell celery on his breath. "Don't laugh,
please. Just say yes."

I don't laugh. "Just stop it. I can't marry you, Cole." Wringing
my hand from his, I shuffle to the edge of the bed. The squeal
of my bare soles on the parquet brings Beckett scrambling, his
sharp little ears pricked toward the door.

"We're not going out," I say, squatting to give him a scrub
behind the ears. "Come on, buddy, let's get you a treat."

"Hey. We're not finished here," Cole says. "You can't just leave like that."

"I haven't left yet," I say, but my words seem to create cross-currents that cut across his face. "I'm still here, Cole." I come back to him, take his face in my hands. "I'm still here."

I leave him pantless and confused to go sit on the ottoman. Beckett has followed me but doesn't sit or lie down. He stands between the bedroom and me, his tail pointed up, waiting. It isn't likely I could take him with me, so he too, will become half-orphaned. I pat the side of the ottoman and he walks, not scampers, to me and sits, leaning in to have his head stroked.

The ottoman. I called it a hassock, but the saleswoman corrected me. I'm not big on box stores, but Cole had La-Z-Boy stuck in his head like an earworm. Because Cole moved into my apartment, he needed to put down his own stakes, buy things, pee around the perimeter.

He'd pointed to a fabric one with a strange array of flowers and starburst patterns. "My mother would like that one," he'd said. "I couldn't do you on it."

I bumped his arm. "Then find one that you can," I'd said.

He'd chosen a spot for it directly in front of the big window overlooking the lake and we rearranged my dark red Ikea couch and mismatched easy chair to accommodate it. Three months in he was already pulling us forward while I leaned back, but because our hips always met I convinced myself that was enough, that it could stay like that—that the aroma of sex could mask the smell of burned things.

The smell is around me now, more pungent than ever.

Every time Goldie's face appears at a window, or hovers over the face of some child wailing in the supermarket, a hand takes my neck in its bony grasp. It might be her three-year-old hand traveling through space and twenty-odd years, but I know it is my own hand gnarled from years of twisting into itself. Before Norah lost her first baby, she told me that I carry my guilt like armor. That I needed to grieve instead. I don't know what that means. Norah doesn't understand that I might as well have locked the door behind Goldie. How do I unlatch that closet door which is now sealed by fallen timbers and grown over by moss and lichen? No one seems to understand how one gesture, one shove out of a bed, can carve itself so deep on your heart that even the sweetest lover, the kindest touch, only serves to harden the wound and assure you that what you deserve is someone like Mark. *Suit yourself.* Who only liked my mouth when it was servicing him.

I don't know how to bury my sister.

I missed the appointment with the oncologist, or maybe the oncologist missed the appointment with me. In any case, it didn't happen. Instead, I went to the post office with my passport renewal application and paid the extra fifteen dollars to have them verify the details and zoom it through. There's an option for a ten-year passport, so I chose that in case I live longer than five years.

At home, Cole comes to sit beside me, both of us like lost people staring out to a hostile sea. I let him gather up my hand and hold it in his lap. Crickets chirp. I chose that ringtone because the sound of crickets usually calms me down. This time, though, it just annoys me. Cole gets up to retrieve my phone from my jacket pocket, hands it to me. I glance at the caller ID and set it on the floor.

"Hey, that's the hospital. You better call them right back."

"Why?" I say, feeling prickly. "They aren't going to tell me anything I don't already know."

"Maybe they are," he says, swiping up my phone and pushing it at me.

"Like what? *Oh, Miss Catlin, there seems to have been a miracle.*"

Cole lets out his breath in a controlled sigh. "Just call them, okay? You never know."

"No, that's right, you don't."

"Take the fucking phone, Brett."

I shake free his hand and leap up. I know I'm going off again. The only thing that helps is running. As if I could hit a speed fast enough.

I push my weight into my feet, but I have no feet; my shoes are empty sockets. I stomp as I run. *Stomp, stomp.* The reverberation is distant like far-off thunder. Gravel slips under me but between the sound and my body there is nothing.

Beckett halts, his nose pointed toward the lake. From behind us come rapid footfalls—Cole's gait: *step-step, step-step,* like a regular heartbeat.

Hunching up the shoulders of my jacket, I pull the zipper up the last centimeter to my chin, grab the sides of my hat and jam it down over my ears. I run, feet or no feet. The body knows how to run. No scrambling dog beside me now. He's turned back. Cold air on exposed cheekbones and eyelids, copper in my mouth. Somewhere there are arms pumping, legs lifting and striking, feet flexing, and toes gripping. The lake is an ocean, the trail is a highway, I will run and run until I reach the lip of the world and then I will jump.

"Brett!"

He's closer than I thought. I am an engine, a freight train, a rocket.

"Stop. Damn it, Brett, please stop."

I am burning. My thighs are on fire, my feet unstoppable, blood in my mouth.

A flash and a blur of blue cotton shirt as Cole passes, wheels, and stops dead. I crash into him. His arms encase the wreckage. There's someone left alive and she's fighting. Fighting for air, fighting to free herself, twisting out of his grasp, teeth ready to gnaw off her own arm.

"Stop," he yells.

But I don't stop. I kick. I bite down hard.

"Fuck," Cole says, yanking away the arm that has tried to hold me. He shoves up his sleeve revealing a fine white arc in the shape of a smile with a single dark red pearl forming at the corner.

"You bit me."

I'm stuck with sweat. "Let me go."

Cole goes on staring at his arm where the blood sits like a bead, not gushing or flowing; it just perches there among the gold-red hairs on his arm. It could be another freckle, a beauty mark, or a tumor.

I jut my chin at the smiley mark. "You shouldn't grab me like that."

"You're a fucking madwoman, you know that?" He shakes down his sleeve and begins to rub both arms. "Look, you've got to understand. Just stand still long enough to fucking listen. To hear." He bends at the waist, panting. "You can't keep running. You just can't." Straightening, Cole continues. "I looked it up—the surgery. This kind of cancer, the one you've got, has a great recovery rate after having a…a, you know—the operation." His gaze whips back and forth from lake to me, from me to the road. "It's not that bad."

True. It could be worse. I could be crushed by a burning timber or die gasping for breath with collapsed lungs. Cold air from the lake has dried my sweat. "I'll call my aunt."

"Your aunt June? The crazy one?"

"She's a healer. She knows things." Beckett spins in place, his tail buzzing. "She can help me."

Cole shrugs. "So, get her to help then, but book the damn surgery!"

My lips knot. "I gotta keep moving or I'll cramp up."

Two women runners approach in black stretchy running gear striped with bright greens. They're fast, swooping out to either side of us as they run pass. Their breathing makes a solid sound that stays in the air. I lift my hand, but there's nothing to touch.

"I'm cold," I say.

"Me, too. I'm freezing, so let's go home," he says. "I'll run with you."

When we get home I've partially regained my sanity. I go sit on the ottoman to look out over the water. I want it to be blue. I want it to be salt. Beckett's fur is cool and damp. I unclip his leash and wind the smooth red of it around my left wrist.

I have cancer. Cancer has me. Cancer is my friend. I pick up cancer's hand and begin to dance. Like the pivot of a Bobcat digging up dirt and spinning to drop it elsewhere, I take my cancer for a whirl. I must love my cancer. Otherwise, I would let them shave, skin, and excavate me just like that. Because it's not that bad.

The unmanned trucks idling in the lot look more abandoned than prepared for work. Mel isn't in the office, at the coffee machine, or in the yard.

"Seen Mel?" I ask Tom whose buggy sleepless eyes remind me of a tarsier I once saw at the zoo.

"In the dome," he says, pointing.

I push out the door. "But it's too early," I say before the door closes behind me. I don't want Mel to be mixing, don't want to think about plows and ice and stupid cars trying to pass on icy roads. I just want the comfort of Mel, his quiet, his peace.

In the sand dome, I find him, a cigarette at the corner of his mouth, kneeling in front of a loader.

"We're going out today, right?" I ask.

"I'm on maintenance," he says.

"But…" I don't really have an argument. I know cold is coming, snow is coming, freezing rain is coming, and the fleet has to be ready. "You're not a mechanic." Which is a stupid thing to say, since we're all trained to clean and maintain the vehicles.

His forehead almost touches the gray cement, and his gloved hands at either side of his face make him look like he is making *salaat*, the Islamic prayer. "True," he says. He still hasn't turned to see me.

I realize with a start that I haven't even said hello. "*Boozhoo, Mishkiki Nini*," I say quietly.

"*Aaniin*," he says, turning now to give me a brief smile. Taking the cigarette from his mouth, he grinds it into the cement and slips the butt into his breast pocket. "Just Mel is good," he says, pushing against his thighs to stand.

"Oh," I say, feeling stupid again. "You don't want those rednecks to know the other name?"

He glances out the door to the yard where this shift workers mill. "The spirit name is for ceremony. Prayer."

"Sorry," I say. "I'll remember."

He nods that slow single nod and says, "Caterpillars got heavy coats."

"Oh," I say, taking a step back. "Oh." I glance behind me past the row of trucks and plows to the field beyond. As if I could see those black and orange bodies inching up stems. "We're in for it, are we?" I scuffle a laugh, but Mel's attention has returned to his task.

I have to go back to the office to see who I'm riding with. Luckily, it's Tom. His silence is different, kind of dense and defensive, but at least he's quiet. If I'd been quick, I'd have been in the driver's seat before him, but by the time I get back to the yard, Tom is waiting with the engine running.

The roadkill today is mostly raccoons bloated with corn. My prayers are spoken in my head. Tom digs the hole while I pray and shovel up the carcasses, their blood nearly black against the gray road.

It's the mother with her two babies spread across two lanes that makes me pray out loud. My voice is hoarse, but clear enough. I say, "*Boozhoo Gzheminido.* Brett *ndizhinikaaz.*" I don't remember the next bit, about where I'm from or where my heart is, but I remember, *esban*, so I say, "*Miigwech, esban*," and hope that will be enough.

I can't read Tom's look. Maybe he's too tired to comment or ask, but it's the kind of look I sometimes get when I say *fuck* or *cocksuck.*

My passport arrived by registered mail a week ago, the photograph looking vaguely sinister, but even in the studio's strong light I didn't look like someone about to die.

Cole appears to be sleeping, so I lift the stack of fliers on my desk without ruffling the pages. Gone.

"Where is it, Cole? What did you do with my passport?"

Cole half rolls toward me, an arm covering his eyes. "What?"

"Where did you put my passport?" Brochures featuring pictures of meditators under heavy green fronds shake in my hand.

"Didn't touch it," he mumbles and rolls away again.

Flinging the fliers across the bed, I stamp my foot hard. Pain zings up from my heel up into my hip. "It was here." I jab my finger at the desk. "Right here, Cole."

He doesn't turn. "Not my problem."

I want to tear out his flattened hair, his sleeping eyes. "It's a crime, you know, to steal a passport." I can smell myself.

With deliberate slowness, Cole begins to move. First one leg, then the other, an arm, then finally, his head lifts from the pillow. "That so?" he says with a trace of amusement.

"It's not funny. What did you do with it? You can't keep me here, you know."

"*Keep* you?" He's wearing those boxers.

As he shuffles toward the door, I notice that all the devils on his ass have faded to pink. They're almost five years old. I can't recall the last thing I bought for him. Guitar strings?

"Where are you going? I'm talking to you."

Without pausing, he says, "No, you're yelling."

"Well, fuck you, then." This I don't yell. I yank open my desk drawer and rummage around in the papers there, but I'm sure I didn't put it in that drawer. I stay in the room, because I actually know I'm a bit crazed, and the urge to physically attack Cole has to be suppressed. As powerful an urge as it is, I'm aware that this isn't about him.

Sounding both far away and close, his voice comes through the bedroom door. "Brett, come here."

"Why should I?" But I do go into the living room and then to the hall where he is standing by the telephone that we never use anymore, staring into the open drawer of the small wooden table where we drop our keys. Beckett, sensing movement by the outside door, has scrambled up and stands ready, his tail vibrating.

"This what you're looking for?" Cole asks.

All the vinegar and spit is sucked from me. "Oh." That's the only sound I make: "Oh."

"Say sorry," Cole says lightly, like it's been a game. He can do that, make like he doesn't notice when I'm boiling, as if I've just inquired as to whether he'd like chocolate or vanilla.

Picking up the dark blue booklet with the gold coat of arms. "A MARI USQUE AD MARE." He offers it with a small bow.

"Cole." I set down the passport, giving it a little pat. "You didn't deserve that."

"I know." His smile is more of a straight line than an actual smile and makes me feel even more like a shit. His shoulders round forward as he goes back to the bedroom. Beckett's groan when he realizes we're not going for a walk sounds almost human.

When I lie down behind him, Cole's skin seems to contract. "Hey," I say, pressing my breasts into the flat bones of his shoulders. There's no mistaking the recoil.

"I can't." His voice is distant and very flat.

"I am sorry, Cole. I really am." Reaching over the crest of his hip, I dive my hand under his loose waistband.

I might have tickled him, but I'm pretty sure it was a flinch.

"It's not that," he says. "It's okay."

"You are a saint," I say, enjoying the warmth of his stiffening penis under my hand.

But his fingers circle my wrist and pull me away.

"Hey!" I snap into a sitting position. "It's me, baby."

"It's the blood."

"Blood? What blood?"

"You bleed when we have sex."

"Not every time," I protest.

"I don't want you to bleed."

Throwing myself onto my back with a thump, I spread my legs. "Go down on me, then." Cole rolls over and covers me with the duvet. "Come on, Cole, you know we'll both feel better. Don't you want me to feel better?" I'm fighting to keep my tone playful and sexy when inside I feel damaged and rejected. Scared too.

"That's all I want," he says thickly.

"Well then?" But I've lost my nerve, so I fling my legs off the side of the bed. Beckett squeals as my feet land on his ribs. I take the laptop into the living room and begin to search for cures that don't involve knives.

I'm living with my feet in different worlds—one foot is in a world that wants me to stay, to live, and to love, while the other foot is already running toward a beautiful distant world where I will die alone.

In the afternoon I line up my vitamins and minerals and chop my vegetables. Aunt June was thorough in her recommendations for my sick friend, "Norah," so I've spent a bundle at the health food store. I've ordered the special hydrogen peroxide from the US, stopped drinking coffee, and drink instead a lineup of herbal teas and smoothies. I've also sourced cannabis oil which seems to be the cure of the moment. It looks as though I'll be spending most of my paycheck on supplements. And coffee. Not for my morning pick-me-up, but for my liver via my butt. So I'll have to get an enema bag and a juicer, go for infrared saunas, and think happy.

I've made a list. It's a long list.

When the oncologist's assistant called to attempt to persuade and reassure me about the surgery, she'd said, *Don't worry; your husband won't be able to tell.*

Seriously? I said, holding the phone away from my face.

Yes, really, she said, all chipper. *He'll never even notice the difference.*

I'm pretty sure that I would, I said.

"Where's the ice cream?" Cole calls with his head inside the freezer.

"I threw it out."

"Wait. What?" Slamming the freezer door, he stomps into the living room. "You threw it out? Did we have a power outage? Was it green and fuzzy? Why would anyone throw out an almost full container of Jamoca Almond Fudge?"

"We can't eat that stuff anymore. Cancer thrives on sugar, apparently."

Cole drops onto the ottoman and picks up his guitar. In the afternoon light, its wood is the color of buckwheat honey. "'We'? Since when do 'we' have cancer?"

I can't blame him for being pissed.

As he tries the G string, he continues, "Tea and mushrooms aren't going to make it go away, you know. And I doubt that sticking pot up your pussy is going to help unless it also makes you high." He stops tuning and rests both arms on the curve of his guitar, his upturned face pinked by the late sun.

I'm not sure any of this will work, not sure I even want it to. I'm tired and empty, afraid and empty, sorry and empty. What I would like to tell him is that I love him, that I'm doing this for him, for some distant family we raise together. If I were capable of loving anyone, I'm sure it would be Cole.

"You make me high," I say, which elicits a flicker of a smile.

"Brett," he says, setting down the guitar to lean forward, arms resting on his thighs. "Thing is, I don't want you to die. You get that, right?" I open my mouth to protest, but he puts up a hand. "Sometimes, I think that you do. Want to die." He waits.

I wish I could say things that would light him up, make the newly formed webs of lines on his forehead and around his mouth smooth and fade. But he's hit the nail on its lethal little head, and the truth of it makes cuts inside my mouth. I'm afraid if I open my lips blood will pour out.

"Do you? Want to die, Brett?"

The blender whirrs to life, smashing avocadoes and kale into a riot of red berries and oat milk.

Beckett's feet scrabble under him as he jumps up.

Over the blender's roar I hear Cole's powerful voice. "This

isn't just about you, you know." He's risen and come across the living room to the kitchen counter. "Turn that fucking thing off, Brett. I'm talking to you."

I watch the green swirl into red, the red into green, the roar of the machine soothing. I don't want this conversation. I am inside the blender, all the edges of me beaten off and made smooth.

Cole's hand shoots out to jab the stop button. "You." One word, hard and brittle as glass. His chest rises, falls, rises and falls again, quicker this time, eyes locked on. Even Beckett sits. "Are the most selfish, self-absorbed person I know. You go on as if there's no one else in the world. You're sick and there's a way to get better and you don't take it. Why? You're doing all this healthy stuff, but I wonder if you really believe it will help. It's as if you're just going through the motions. I mean, have you even considered me? That *I* might want you to live, that I don't care if we have kids, that I just want you? It doesn't seem like it, that's for damn sure." He pulls in a breath, and before I can respond, he resumes. "You know, you tell me things like how Norah's upset, but have you really tried to understand what she's gone through? How devastated she was? How bad she wanted a baby and lost two? That she needed you there with her? And you weren't. You just weren't, were you?" I begin to speak. "No, no. I'm not finished." He holds up both hands as he comes around the island to where I'm standing. "You just need to shut up and listen.

"And sex…You think I don't know that you use my dick like a soother?" He makes a chopping gesture toward his crotch. "That it's your way to avoid anything you don't like? You don't think I notice things. You assume that because I don't react, things don't get to me. The way you talk to me. I know how you see me. Inferior somehow. Not quite in-the-know. I see it, Brett.

"And maybe you're right, maybe I am those things because I do love you anyway. I just love you. I want you to stay. Alive. And if that makes me some poor slob pussy then so be it." He sucks in a breath. Again I try to speak. "No, you still have to shut up. I'm talking. I'm not stupid, Brett, and it makes me crazy that you think I am, as if I'm too young or inexperienced to 'get it,' but here's the truth: I feel you. Every bit of you. And if that's too much for you, then too bad. I even know when your period's coming, you ever realize that? How my own gut cramps just before yours starts?"

Whatever shape my face takes at this last statement makes Cole nod, his eyebrows lifted so high his eyelids stretch flat. Then his chest collapses as if the wind has been knocked out of him. "Here's another thing, oh golden girl of dead things, I think I know why you like that job so much. I don't have the exact words, but I get you. I know it's somehow connected with your little sister and your dad—"

"No!" My hand lashes out and claps over his mouth. "Stop."

Cole catches my wrist and presses my hand hard to his mouth, holding it there. His eyes close. Not squeezed shut, but light like leaves. Beckett begins to whine. Under the window, a car honks twice, pauses, then a long third blast. I can feel Cole's teeth through his lips, feel the sliver of a gap between the front ones. The hardness of them feels like pebbles under the softness of his lips. The moisture from his breathing collects inside my palm.

His eyelids lift and he is looking right through my eyes, into a place I never wanted him to see. I try to shut my eyes but I can't. They are burning dry but the lids won't descend. His mouth is so still under the hand he holds there. My arm aches.

I whisper, "Okay. You win. I see you. I will make an appointment. I will try to live. Okay? Good? Are we good, Cole?"

My hand rides his head as it slowly moves up and down.

When he lets go, Cole says, "I want us both to win, Brett."

Us.

Perhaps I can allow this *us* to exist. If I stay.

I pull him close and rest my head on his shoulder. His chest softens against mine and I turn his face to rest my lips on his cheek. "I love you, Cole."

I miss the taste of coffee. Its dark promise drifts past as it drips fragrant and smoky into the pot. I want its heat, its roasted chocolate-earth taste, its weight on my tongue, the sweet sting of it in the back of my throat, the warmth through the cup on my palms and fingers. I want that taste of wood fire, Mama's glass percolator with its darkening bubbles, Daddy's sleepy laughter at the breakfast table. The fine hairs on Cole's lips lit like new pennies when, once, his lips leaked morning coffee into my mouth. That.

Removing the pot from its warming pad, I sigh as I tip its contents into the red rubber hot-water bottle I'm now using for an enema bag. The bathroom has been retrofitted with a hook on the shower head to hold the tubing and Cole has rigged a slanted board into the tub so I can lie with my ass in the air. After the coffee has cooled to body temperature, I turn up the heat in the bathroom and set myself up, inserting the lubricated white plastic tip into the correct orifice. There is nothing about this procedure that is pleasant. The rush of liquid into my lower belly makes me immediately want to let go, but I force myself to let the sphincter relax and in the coffee flows. That's the easy part. The tough bit is holding it, massaging the belly so it gets high in the colon and, hopefully, even into the ascending colon. Cole traced the proposed route of this healing elixir on a diagram of a cartoon bowel with such a look of enthusiasm I had to laugh. The first few times I could barely hold a cupful for more than a few minutes, but now I can hold two whole cups for the recommended fifteen minutes. Cole times me, whistling outside the bathroom door while I squirm away inside, and asks me afterward, with the eager bounce of a five-year-old, *How was it?*

I tell him the truth. That I hate the procedure, but afterward I feel all cleaned out. Kind of light inside. Empty in a good way. And maybe as my liver gets cleaned, it will take with it some of those mutating cells that have it in for me.

The tough part is going out. Finding something to take to work that won't have the boys side-looking at me while they cram orange plastic cheese and shiny ham sandwiches on gooey white bread into their fat faces.

One night when Cole's band played at the downtown café, there was not one thing on the menu I could eat: pasta—out, sandwiches—out, any kind of meat—out, and I watched as everyone guzzled glasses of honey-colored beers and blood-red wine, and pretty cocktails all done up with bits of fruit. I ordered a salad with dressing on the side and soda water with extra lime, and tried not to sink into self-pity, which wasn't easy. I want to eat steak and chocolate, and drink myself so stupid I don't have to think about the fact that my best friend hates me, I'm exiled to a planet where the food sucks, and my boyfriend won't have sex with me anymore.

Cole whistles a lot lately, like when he crams chard and parsley into the juicer along with swamp-green powder, or while he brews up a fragrant pot of dark roast organic coffee that I'm not allowed to drink, and as he lines up hillocks of capsules for me to take after I drink my smoothie. He's taken on the role of savior with a vengeance.

This morning he slid a white bowl across the table to me. It looked exactly like sludge; the stuff we dredge off the road at the end of winter, gray goop dotted with reddish orange blobs. "You can add oat milk," Cole offered. "Unsweetened, I suppose," I said, poking a spoon into the porridge's soft belly. Singing that Gibb Brothers song 'Staying Alive' was his answer. Pressing one of the rosy bits against the side of the bowl, I asked, "Why are there carrots in here?" "Taste it," he said. I did, but it tasted like nothing at all. Just that same sludgy texture knotted with gravel. I let go of the spoon and pushed the bowl back. Cole brought down the carton of oat milk with a force that popped open the lid and splashed out white liquid. "They're not carrots; they're goji berries, so just eat the fucking stuff," he said.

This afternoon, when I come home, he's waiting with a new set of vials. "It's a parasite cleanse. Liver flukes. You have to kill the liver flukes. They're what cause cancer."

I've seen my fill of parasites. Hookworms. Roundworms.

Maggots, tapeworms. *Everything is food for something,* Mel says.

Cole's hair seems to be thinning at the front and I noticed the other day when he was arguing on the phone with his mother that the fine lines across his forehead have dug in deeper. Maybe I am self-absorbed but I don't intend to hurt anyone. Whether I leave or whether I go, whether I die or go on living, it seems Cole will suffer.

Norah suffered. I know how fiercely she wants a baby. I've thought about calling her more than once. Every day, in fact. But she's dismissed me. Didn't even walk me to the door. *You killed it,* she'd said.

I'm sorry. That's all I have. *Sorry.*

I haven't asked and Cole hasn't said, but I'm sure he's talked to Josh. He must have spilled the beans about my diagnosis and all we're doing to cure me, and how I refused to let the oncologist have at me. But Norah hasn't called.

Probably all the guys in the band know too. None of them talked directly to me at that last gig. Their eyes sort of swept over me to land on some made-up hottie or to their bottles of warm beer, or down to the set lists.

The site where Cole found the statistics about early sexual activity and multiple partners being contributing factors to cervical cancer also noted that trauma and loss often precede its onset. This makes me wonder if I've been cultivating these little bastard cells since I lost Dylan. Or if they just rallied right after I left the hospital six years ago? What if I hadn't made that appointment, hadn't taken a taxi to and from the hospital, hadn't, hadn't, hadn't?

I'd have a five-year-old without a dad, but maybe I wouldn't have a toxic soup cooking in my sweetest place.

Since I'm on the *what if* train, I have to wonder what if there had been no Dylan? No one to tell me I was fancy, or say words like "beautiful" and "I'm here for you" when the rest of the house was full of emptiness without even a ghost to ruffle the curtains.

I make an appointment with the oncologist.

9

Snow falls and then rain falls, filling the culverts with a pale white haze.

I load the steam jenny and propane tank while Mel changes the truck's oil.

Mel still doesn't know about the cancer. *People say what they need to say.*

It's minus two degrees Celsius as we rumble out to Snow Valley Road. Mel looks extra worn this morning, pale against his jacket's bright safety stripes. Neither of us reaches for the radio, so the subterranean thrum of the engine is the only noise, its vibration like the purr of an enormous cat.

"That skunk juice," I begin, and pause to assemble my question. "Have you tried it? I mean, do you think it really works? Does it work on other things besides the flu?"

His eyes don't move from the road as he speeds from slow to not-quite-so-slow. "Well," Mel says. "I guess that depends."

"You mean on whether you breathe it in or drink it, on whether it's dead already or if you kill it yourself? That sort of thing?"

His forehead buckles in the kind of frown that usually follows with some sort of ribbing. But there's no smile under the frown. He drums his fingers along the gear shaft, clears his throat, shifts in his seat, flicks on the wipers, glances out the side window. "It depends on why a person would ask," he says at last.

"Oh."

We ride in thickening silence until the first turn.

"Well," I say, holding my gloved hands together like a prayer. "What about cancer?"

His jaw tightens. "Never tried it." His lips purse out almost like a kiss. "Maybe should have."

"You had cancer?" I blurt.

He turns to me, confused. "No. No, I didn't have cancer. Diabetes. Not cancer." Then: "My ma. They took both her breasts even though only the one had cancer. Then they put that chemo in her until her gums bled and she was bald as a baby. Wanted to do a sweat for her, wanted her to fast, but she had Jesus, she said, all that Indian stuff was from another time, she said..."

"I'm sorry," I say. "Is she...?"

"With her Jesus, I imagine." The plow does a slow, graceful arc turning left. And we return to dense silence. The sun shoulders away the clouds to illuminate the fine pebbling in the windshield, blinding us.

Pulling down the visor, I ask as casually as I can manage, "How would you trap a skunk?" I'm wishing I'd thought of this, that I'd known before he dropped that intact skunk into the hole. Maybe I could have harvested some.

Mel's laugh is silent, just his shoulders jump a little. "Carefully, Brett, my girl. Very carefully."

"Beckett caught one this summer. It looked like his little brother or something. Would there be more stuff left in the sac after it sprayed?"

"Got me there." He shoots me a quick glance, but he doesn't ask and I know he won't, which is why I keep grilling him.

After pulling onto the shoulder, Mel and I get out and set up the jenny. Soon, hot water shoots through the first culvert, turning ice to dirty water.

"*Zhgaag*," he says, squatting to aim the heater's hose into the opposite pipe. "They named Chicago after them. Lots of skunks in Chicago back then, I guess."

When we get back in the truck, Mel turns on the radio to some news about another shooting. "Funny thing," he says over the announcer's jaunty voice. "The word for skunk and the word for white people sound pretty much the same."

The walls of the oncology unit are painted pink like bubblegum. I wait in my paper gown to be called along with a row of paper-hatted, paper-slippered women. As usual, in these places where we have to strip down to nothing, they crank up the air conditioning. If we don't die from cancer first, we may die from exposure. This is death row, especially designed for women who opened their legs too soon and too often. The magazines are soggy, their covers exploding with pictures of thin big-boobed big-haired women accompanied by proclamations of the diet of the century, while at the corner of each one is a photo of a chocolate or strawberry cake oozing with icing.

We don't talk to each other, each of us trapped by our own shameful disease. My calves begin to cramp so I stand to stretch. The paper belt I've managed to tie into a small tight knot rips and my gown pops open. This whole scene is so ludicrous that I laugh out loud, look at the ducky row of women for a shared chuckle, but they are looking down into their damaged laps or are suddenly mesmerized by smudgy type in the magazines. Phones, purses, anything to identify us as human, have been left in the cubicles along with our clothing.

"Brett Catlin," a skinny nurse in pink-and-green scrubs calls at last. Holding my paper dress together, I follow her out of the pink room into a white room lit white with a TV screen and a square of green cloth concealing those cold silver duckbills.

The oncologist's unfortunate name is Downham. He isn't pleased with me for what he considers my inaction, and not at all impressed with my level of dedication to "healing."

With that LED lamp attached to his forehead, he's some kind of vagina miner. "This doesn't look good," he says with an expression that, even with only his eyes showing over the mask, indicates this is an understatement. Pivoting the screen so that I can view it, he says, "See here?" He points a gloved finger at a familiar white membrane glistening over everything pink. "Whatever you're doing doesn't seem to be working so well."

"Is it any smaller?" I ask, propping myself on my elbows.

He clears his throat, turns the LED beam on me. "Let's get this out of you. Now."

I can't tell if the rumble is coming from outside or inside me. My eyes close and I slump under the weight of an entire truckload of sand. The doctor is saying, "LEEP," but I can't. Even my eyelids are sealed. He goes on talking. "Or, Loop Electrosurgical Excision Procedure, to be precise."

The heat of his lamp penetrates through the sand. My mouth finds words in it. They are: "Not hysterectomy?"

"Since you've refused the surgery, we can give this a try. We might be able to get it all."

"Just the rotten bit?"

He says it like it isn't a big deal, just "a thin, low-voltage, electrified wire loop." He can do it right now and here. No big deal.

My torn paper gown is replaced by a warm cotton one. The next moments blur like a movie running in fast forward. I'm given a local freezing and he gets in there with his fancy instrument, burns away the mouth of my cervix, stuffs my vagina with cotton wool, and sends me on my way.

Done.

I walk out of there with only a piece of me gone.

On the way home, the steering wheel's surface in my hands is like the pebbled ice at the lake's edge. Some asshole in a ghoul mask and a long silver wig flaps his caped arms at me, making me yank the wheel to the left and almost into oncoming traffic. And then I see them—like a bad dream, creatures swarm the sidewalks, bloody-faced, skeletal, shredded clothing, limping, dragging, open-sored.

When I was little, we were fairies, princesses, and gypsies. Mama pinned and sewed my costumes from scraps of her old dresses, the long cotton ones from her early days in the valley: gingham, paisley, and one with small pink flowers. She'd paint my face with rouge and eyeliner and tell me I didn't need a prince to be a princess. After I turned eight, Goldie was with us, so Mama made her a bunny costume and Daddy bounced her in his arms while kids from up the valley trooped in to display their costumes. Pirates. Lumberjacks. Witches. Goldie with her pink cheeks that needed no rouge, and her great blue-green eyes under those long white ears.

These streets teem with the undead. From the seething mass of peeling flesh, open wounds, blackened teeth and eyes rimmed with mold green, emerges a girl of about five wearing a white ruffled dress, her long fair hair adorned with pink and yellow ribbons, strands of plastic pearls, and a stick tipped with an aluminum star. Glinda. The good witch. I've been cruising slowly, taking in the contagion and decay, but when I spy this pretty little witch, I let my foot lift from the accelerator, hearing, for a brief moment, my seven-year-old self giggling at her transformed reflection. When the girl turns, I slam the brake. The car stalls. Her small face is smeared red and black. Blood and soot.

I drive to the lakeshore and park, but I can't get out of the car. I watch as the inside windows fog until I can't see the water or the other cars in the lot or the sky or the city hulking behind me. Resting my head on the steering wheel, I count my breaths, as Norah instructed me to do when I felt anxious. Then, I had laughed at her. *I don't get anxious; I get even.* Now, I'm breathing: one breath, two breaths, three… I need to call Mama.

She answers on the second ring. "What happened?" she says after I say her name.

"I miss you," I say.

"I miss you too," she says. "What happened?"

"Nothing, Mama. I just wanted to say hello."

She laughs, very far away in her valley between two high mountains. "Hello," she says and her hello echoes and echoes.

"You could stay at June's. The boys' room is empty."

"Maybe…" I say.

"Dylan comes up every weekend to cut firewood and tend to things. He's such a good boy. I'm sure he misses you too, Brett."

"I love you, Mama," I say.

"Is that boy still living with you? That grocery boy?"

"He's a musician, Mama. I told you. Songwriter."

"Like your daddy."

My stomach lurches. "Daddy wrote songs?"

Her laugh echoes and echoes. "Don't you remember?" She starts to sing but she sounds like an old woman, like she's ninety—all warbly and wrinkled. "Lala la, she's the finest flower in the field…lala la…" She stops singing. "Remember?"

After I swallow twice, I say, "No."

"Bring your boyfriend when you come."

"Okay, Mama." I swipe my nose with the back of my hand. "I gotta go now."

"Yes, yes, you've got to go. Always going. Going, going, gone."

Cole has been singing and smiling and touching my hair a lot since I had the LEEP procedure. I'm glad he's happy. He *is* a good man. I continue with my regimen, following June's instructions for "Norah," but the diet is so meager I'm hungry all the time. I'm hungry for Cole, too, because even though I'm all healed up, he won't have sex with me.

At work, the guys try not to look like they're staring, but I recognize their looks of pity and disgust when I open my lunch box. One morning as I was leaving the office for the garage, I heard Mitch mumble to the guys, "She's lost her ass."

When I get the all-clear, I'll eat. Steak. Potatoes. Chocolate. Ice cream. I'll get my ass back.

After work on Monday, I head to Dr. Downham's office for a post-surgical checkup.

I slide as close to the edge of the examining table as possible because I do not want to hear that word *scootch* one more time. But when Doctor Downham arrives, he comes to my head instead of between my legs, humming and hawing and cradling a clipboard. "Ms. Catlin," he says, clearing his starchy throat. "May I call you Brett?"

"We've already established that you may," I say, which makes him actually look at me. "We've met," I assure him. *Duh.*

"Right. Of course. Well." He clears his throat again and taps his chart with a pen. "I'm afraid that the margins weren't clear."

"Margins?" I see a page without writing—empty lines—and along the left side a long strip filled with my scribbles, doodles, and random quotes.

"From the *LEEP* incision. We weren't able to get all of it."

I experience a nearly uncontrollable urge to slap his unshaven face. "Why not?" I demand. Damn him all the way to hell.

He shakes his head. "We need to rethink hysterectomy."

"Rethink all you want," I say, lifting up on my elbows.

"Ms. Catlin. Brett. This is serious."

I clamp my thighs to stop the shaking, but they continue to vibrate against each other. I clench my jaw and then, in order to speak, I unclench it. "So? What if I say no?"

The doctor's face screws up in disbelief. Who wouldn't want a hysterectomy? "This isn't a cancer we treat with chemo," he says.

I picture him offering a cookie to that gelatinous blob, but that naughty little tumor just won't be tempted by that delicious treat.

"No," I say, my knees like naked bumper cars. "I mean, how long do I have?"

Frowning, Dr. Downham refers to his chart. "There's no need to think like that. No need. We're not thinking like that. Not at all."

"Just give me a ballpark," I say, turning my gaze away from his tired, very tired face, up to the constellations of dark dots on the white sky. "If I do nothing, I mean."

"That's not really an option here," he says. "We can leave your ovaries, Brett." He pauses, but I don't look at him. "But just to be on the safe side, we can do radiation therapy on your ovaries after you've recovered from the surgery."

That does it. I swing my legs off that vinyl table, ripping the strip of white paper rolled down its hygienic length and leap right past the stool onto the floor.

"That's not really an option," I say, pushing past him and back out into the bubblegum room where the last of the wom-

en wait for him to scrape, blast, and poison every sweet bit right
out of them.

"You need to make an appointment," he calls after me. "See
my receptionist."

Maybe I should offer up my breasts as well. They'll never
feed anyone.

Once I've ripped off the gown and reconstituted myself,
I walk past the receptionist and out into the street. A newspaper swirls in a stiff wind and pages stick in store doorways,
the headline on page three: *CHILD MISSING. POLICE ASK
FOR HELP.*

I pull out my phone, search Norah's number, and stare at it.
A cold push of wind from the lake sends a shiver from the base
of my spine, dislodging the ice that has formed there. I select
the green "Call" button.

Norah agrees to meet me at the pub when she gets off work.
She must have sensed the urgency in my voice or said yes before she realized she still hates me. I have two hours to kill, so
I walk, then I run. I run because I am healthy and strong, not
sick at all. In fact, all this healthy eating and drinking has made
me light and fluid, my muscles more defined.

I have traveled almost ten kilometers when I turn around.
The way back I take at a slow lope, punctuated by stretches of
walking. All the muscles in my legs begin to ping and twitch the
moment I stop. In front of the bar, I grab my heel and pull it up
to my skinny ass. My clothes are soaked through.

Norah is late. Thirteen minutes, to be exact. As she glides in,
with a slim blue leather purse pressed under her arm, blue cut-
glass butterfly barrettes catching her hair on both sides, and a
blue-and-yellow checked jacket nipped in at the waist, it occurs
to me that she is always just a few minutes late—never precisely
on time, but never long enough to get me steamed up. Good
tactic, that, to let the other guy experience the anxiety of waiting, although in this case, she needn't have gone to any extra
trouble. I have to restrain myself from jumping up and knock-

ing her over, the way Beckett sometimes does with children playing in the park. Norah is so familiar, so beautiful to me at this moment that every accusation and harsh word that's passed between us evaporates. She is my friend: known, cherished, and as inextricable from me as my own veins. I need her.

"Girlfriend," I say, raising my wine glass once she's settled into the booth.

Norah leans forward across the scratched wood table. "I've missed you, my friend."

I nod. "And I, you. Hey," I say, straightening my back, clearing something caught in my throat. "Remember that night we got so wasted on margaritas? We sat at this table."

"Of course I do, silly." She swats my arm. "Don't you remember—that was the night I met Josh."

All eight television screens blaze with red and blue figures on a white background, gliding in circles, warming up, getting ready to chase a little piece of black rubber and punch each other in the face. From every speaker blasts Lady Gaga insisting that she was born that way.

"Is there no such thing as a quiet bar in this town?"

Reaching across the table to touch both her cheeks, I say, "Just look at *me*."

She laughs.

I don't.

"You're drinking wine," she says, drawing away from my fingers. "Let's have a cocktail, shall we? A cosmo? A margarita?" She's so festive, so obviously willing to pretend we never fought, so willing to believe this is just a girls' night out that I consider not telling her.

"Oh, I'm not too sure about margaritas. You married a guy you'd met when you drank too many. And remember that time we drank ourselves stupid watching *Sex and the City* until four in the morning?"

"They're both good memories," Norah says soberly, waving over a server with heavy black eye makeup and round black ingots embedded in her earlobes.

"I told you everything that night." I slap the table and hold up my palms, surrender-style. "Almost, anyway. I spilled my guts. I never do that." Everything about Mark. Some things about Goldie and Dad. Nothing about a dead baby or about Dylan.

"So? That's what friends do." She's being earnest. It's hard not to look away. "I told you everything too, Brett." This is delivered directly; no bullshit now.

That night we'd blended up a second pitcher of tequila and fresh lime and put our feet on her coffee table, and after we'd laughed ourselves sick over the guys in Carrie's New York who only wanted to have sex outside, or talked dirty except about having a finger up their bum, or took a crap with the bathroom door open, the talk turned to dreams and hopes and heartbreaks. What Norah told me was that she was an only child because her mother had MS, and that all she longed for was a swarm of children laughing and fighting and scrambling around in the dirt. She'd gladly give up her consultant job for a shot at being a mother, a housewife—anything for a family. I spewed my usual, "The world's going to shit. How can you justify bringing another human into this hellhole with no future?" And she'd laughed, poured me another drink, and fast-forwarded through the credits to start the next episode. "Don't be an idiot, Brett," she said. "Children are what make it all worth saving."

I have to tell her. Right now.

I motion to the server. "Bring us two margaritas. Shaken, not frozen. No ice. Lots of salt." The server nods and slinks off, her hips too narrow to bear children.

I will tell her when the drinks come. Maybe after we've finished the first one.

"So," Norah says, happy now, forearms supporting her as she leans toward me. "Bring me up to speed. What's new?"

"I have cancer."

She doesn't know. Josh didn't tell her because Cole didn't tell him. Men are so mystifying.

Of course she's pissed off that I didn't tell her sooner, but she won't abandon me. It's easier to support someone when the thing that's wrong isn't their fault.

"I've been thinking about leaving," I say. "Maybe it would be better for everyone if I get my sorry ass out of here."

"Leave? For where?" Norah's tongue slides along the glass of her margarita. "You mean after you have the surgery?"

"You know I've always wanted to go to Bali."

"Yeah, yeah, but that scumbag Mark didn't want to go, right?"

A crumb of salt lodges in my throat. "Right," I say, coughing a little.

"Oh, right," she says, looking down. "I am sorry, you know. I was hurting. I shouldn't have—"

"It's all right," I say. "Really." Indicating her glass, I say, "Should we do this again?"

She's grateful, I can tell. Which makes me feel grateful. I order another round.

"So, you won't go? You'll stay, right?"

I shake my head too vigorously and the plasma screens distort the way a fairground distorts from the Zipper ride. Blinking, I whisper, "Cole loves me. I'm trying to let him."

"Let him?"

I continue to whisper. "Yes, let him. And between you and me," I say, tipping my body over the table, "it scares the crap right out of me."

"Well, for heaven's sake," she says, meeting me there at the center of the table. "You love him, don't you?"

"Love is a scary, scary thing, Norah. A very scary thing."

She laughs, that high tinkling sound I've missed so much.

Pushing myself back against the seat, I raise my frosty glass. "This may be the last time I get drunk as a real woman," I declare.

"Oh, Brett, you mustn't say that!" Her glass stalls in the air. "You'll still be able to have sex, won't you?" Her voice drops low. "You can still have sex now, right?"

"I can since I've healed from the LOOP or LEEP or whatever. And apparently even if I have the works taken out my husband won't even know!"

We clink. "You got married and didn't invite me?" Her eyes have lost their focus.

I follow the path of her fingers as she pinches up some salt and pitches it over her left shoulder.

I lift my glass again. "You're drunk, Norah. Plain and simple. Like a skunk."

"Look," she exclaims, pointing with her knuckle at a forty-something guy in a ball cap at the bar. "He's into you. He knows you're a real woman."

The guy has a three-day beard and a pretty sweet profile, a Keanu Reeves look-alike.

"He's not even looking this way," I say, although I'm aware that he has been.

"Are we going to talk about it?" says Norah, suddenly sober and dead serious.

Over her head well-padded men in blue and white and red and black chase each other with sticks up and down a wide, slick surface. The sound system blasts a batch of singers singing about being really happy. "Happy!" they insist.

"I think we need another round." When I speak again it isn't quite a mumble. "It's not right to bring children into this world, Norah. It's not safe."

Pinching up more salt that's fallen from my drink, she casts it over her shoulder, her lips mouthing some habitual incantation, gestures so automatic she doesn't notice my amusement. "We can keep them safe. We just have to watch for signs. You can't stop the wheels of life because some bad things happen to some people some of the time."

Happy.

"Signs? Bad things happen in this world. Bad things happen to children. Children get hurt, Norah. No rabbit's foot or horseshoe or rain dance is going to prevent that."

She swats at the air. "It's not like that here. We have things in place. Safeguards. We're civilized."

My laugh is harsh. "Those safeguards are illusions. Wake up, Norah. Bad shit happens. It happens here, there, and everywhere. This world is a barbed-wire maze of bad shit."

Happy.

"Aren't you just a ray of sunshine? We don't live in a third-world country, Brett."

I fall back against the hard wood of the booth. "It can happen. In a heartbeat."

She waves her empty glass. "I don't believe you. I think you are afraid for different reasons. But if you don't want to talk about it, that's okay; I still want a family. I don't care what you say, I'm not giving up." These last words quaver at the end. As she tips the oversized glass to her mouth, she tilts her head as if to pour back tears as well.

"I need a cigarette."

"That's the stupidest thing I've ever heard," she says after guzzling her drink. "You hate smoking." She sends a knuckle out toward Keanu. "Maybe *he* smokes."

Norah is my good friend. She won't let me drive, said I was too drunk, that my car would be fine parked down by the lakeshore until morning, so she fumbles through her purse, finds her keys, drops them, gets bumped by a twenty-year-old with a faux-hawk and skinny jeans that show the crack in his almost-ass, crouches on the sidewalk in the after-hours frenzy, gets her fingers stepped on by a pointy heel, scrabbles the keys up, and leans against her car while she negotiates the remote to her little blue car.

"Maybe you shouldn't drive either," I say, sage that I am.

"Ah." She dismisses me with a wave of her keys. "You drank way more than me. I'm the DD, and I mean Designated, not Drunk, Driver. You know." She stretches her arms across the car's roof, as if all the reasons in the world are cupped in those upturned palms. "I am the responsible one. Always."

But then we're cruising along, past my street and on to Penetanguishene, where she zooms down her window and says, "Breathe that air. The cold keeps us sober, right?"

The eerie orange from the dashboard illuminates her face, an opal glitter at the corner of her eye.

"You're not crying, are you?" I plead.

"Of course not," she snaps, sniffing. Then she says with violent force, "I just don't want you to leave and I don't want you to die, okay? You can't die."

"I'm not going to die, Norah. Look." I stretch my face into the widest grin I can manage. I turn over words in my swimmy head, trying to put them together in a way that will make her happy for me. When I reach to pull the visor down to have a look at my cheerfully arranged face, I see a flash of white at the side of the road. "Hey! Pull over."

"What?" Norah checks her rearview mirror. "Why?"

"Now. Now. Pull over," I yell, yanking at the door handle. "Let me out."

As soon as the Mazda lurches to a full stop and the doors unlock, I fall out and scramble down into and across the ditch. Norah shouts after me, "What the hell are you doing?"

The fence is easy to climb—I just push it down with one foot and swing myself over. Rustling in the stiff brown grasses makes me stop. "Here, skunky skunky, punky skunky, come on spray me up," I call out.

When Norah finds me, I'm on my knees in a stand of evergreens with my mouth wide open. I'm being patient, waiting for that clever little waddler to raise up its behind and give it to me. I'll gulp it down raw.

"Is this one of those voodoo treatments you're doing?" Norah asks, breathless and more than a little irritated.

"The wisest man in the world told me that skunk juice can heal people."

"Don't be an ass. Who knows what's out here in the woods." Casting a suspicious glance to the sky, she says, "It's not good to be out when there's no moon. Not good. No, no, no. Let's get you home now." She's yanking my arm, vainly trying to lift me.

"I don't have a home, Norah. I have no *ndoonjibaa.*"

She drops to her knees beside me, fingers still wound around my upper arm. The smell of her is warm and fresh, like sweetgrass and sun. In the half moonlight, her skin gleams a translucent blue.

10

The bathroom doorknob rattles, followed by a moment of puzzled silence. "Brett? Is the door locked?" Then, "Why is the light off?" His voice enters by means of the space at the door's bottom edge. "You okay?"

"I'm sick." My bare legs straight out on the cool tile floor, I rest my head on the hard pillow of the toilet seat. All is calm for the moment.

"You were a bit, uh...wasted last night, hey?"

"I just need a minute," I croak, unable to lift my head. Nothing solid is coming out anymore, just bubbling yellow stuff.

Cole chuckles through the slit. "You took advantage of me when I was asleep."

"Really?" A lime-green silhouette against the darkness of sheets. The smell of dried semen wafts up from between my legs. I touch my pubic bone and wince.

"You were wild. I've never seen you that, uh, lubricated."

"It's not funny," I whisper, shuffling to my knees as my gut starts again to pinch and roll. "Sorry," I say, just before a violent retch convulses me over the bowl.

"You want a Bloody Mary?" he asks. "Just this once? Nice and spicy?"

I gasp. "No. Please, no."

"It might help," he says. I can hear the laugh in his voice.

"It won't."

He doesn't move away from the door; his breathing, mingled with Beckett's snuffling, fills the bathroom.

I flush the toilet, pull a towel down from the rack, and wipe first my forehead, then my mouth. The sink is too far away. Evil people with pitchforks are trying to scrape my brains out of my skull. Closing my eyes, I settle back against the wall, one forearm resting on the toilet seat. On the backs of my eyelids, I see Norah's flushed face beside me in that prickly frozen place of runaway skunks, both of us on our knees, and her crying those crushed opal tears. "You have to have that operation, you have to, you can't die, Brett. I need you. You're my best friend in the whole world. In the whole entire big, awful world, you're it." And me, pushing her hair back into that blue butterfly that catches light even when there is none, my mouth settling on hers as if it was meant to go there, fitting like one mouth, and Norah not just letting me, but her tongue wet and soft seeking mine. *Dear god.*

"I kissed someone."

Only Beckett's anxious sniffing. Cole is there, dense as a black hole.

"Cole?"

"I'm here," he says, but he sounds a long way away.

"I kissed Norah."

"Oh." It's a sigh. Maybe of relief.

But there's something else shouldering its way into my vision, to that wavery place I inhabited last night. A ball cap. A three-day beard. A smoke on the street, hunched shoulders, stamping out the cold along with the butt, beer on his breath. *Dear god.*

Cole's tone is cautious; the words come out slow. "Is that all?"

Pushing all my fingers into the grooves above my eyes, I moan. "I'm sick."

"Is that *all*?" Quicker, more insistent. Does he want details or reassurance?

"No."

There's a shushing and a scrambling of paws with little nails that need clipping as Cole springs to his feet and Beckett makes room. It's as if the door is a window. Cole's face is bruised with rage and pain. That's what I do to him. That's how I make him feel. I break everything I touch.

Shaking the doorknob, he says, "Let me in, Brett. Open the door."

"I can't."

"Tell me what happened."

"I kissed a boy too."

He doesn't slam the door, but he's gone so quickly I know he doesn't hear me say sorry. Beckett returns to poke his black nose into the narrow space under the door. He will have to be walked.

After the walk, I make coffee, cram a chunk of Ezekiel bread into my mouth, which is so dry it makes me cough, and down two extra-strength acetaminophen capsules with a glass of my super-duper fortified, energized, chakra-balanced water. This coffee I don't transfer into an enema bag, but rather put it in a cup where it belongs and send it down into my belly, which immediately responds with a welcome gurgle. Warm caffeine floods through my veins the way it should.

My cell phone is dead, so I have to look up Norah's number online, which gives me time to consider what I will say, if I will need to apologize to her as well.

She's not exactly cheerful, but brusque, as if I've interrupted an important task.

"How are you feeling?" I ask, my eyes roaming around the empty apartment, my gaze falling on the backside of Cole's guitar. He told me never to lean it that way—it could break the neck.

"I'm okay," she says, her voice in some other room. "A bit messed up. You?"

"I'm sorry about last night," I begin, not sure how many things I should be sorry about.

"I had fun," she says, still miles away. "But we should never meet on a Friday the thirteenth. That's why it got so...so... messed up."

Still, I feel her lips, which kindles the same sort of interior sparring between pleasure and revulsion that I experienced whenever Dylan finished with me.

"You know that guy we bummed smokes from?"

She laughs and it's as if she's just been flung back to earth. "Pretty hard to forget."

I don't know what that means. Last night's bar is a wash of lime juice and salt. The buzz of a zipper coming down. A faded denim crotch. The heavy smell of malt. A urinal at my left shoulder. *Oh god.*

"Did something happen?"

"I waited a long time for you to come back." She hesitates. "Maybe you just made a mistake, but…you didn't come out of the ladies'." A pause. "You came out of the men's room." If the sound she makes is meant to be a laugh, she has failed. "And Mr. Reeves wasn't far behind."

"Oh, Norah."

When my phone is charged I pick up my message—only one— from the oncologist's office. The date is scheduled whether I like it or not. Merry Christmas.

By the time the sun sets, turning the lake orange, my head is almost back to normal but my gut still refuses to accept anything but toast, and even that is a bit dicey. Cole hasn't returned and his phone goes directly to voicemail. I've walked Beckett four times, partly just to get some cold air in my head, and partly because I don't know what else to do. For half an hour I sit at the desk in the corner with my pen hovering over my open journal. I write the date. I underline the date. I write "Barrie" in capital letters. Letting the nib rest on the page, I watch ink bleed into the paper until it soaks through. It doesn't surprise me when the ink takes on the shape of the stain of the young bear we once found on County Road 26. I shove back from the desk and go to watch out the window where Saturday traffic ribbons out of and into the city as if not one person wants to be where they are.

I fall asleep on the couch with Beckett curled warm into my belly. I will miss his cool wet nose, his perky little ears, his sproingy tail. I will miss him, really miss him, miss him like crazy. When I wake up, I hug him so tight he squirms out of my grasp and does a little hokey pokey round dance that concludes with one sharp yip. There is no seam between falling asleep and waking up, no relief from myself or the fact that Cole still isn't back. At the computer, I click on my favorite Bali site and browse through a few pictures, but even the spectacular shot of an Ubud rice terrace with its undulating greens doesn't unclamp the binding inside.

My bed. *Our* bed. Palace of pleasure turned to bed of nails. When I bought it with its puffy pillow top it was in part to assert my liberation from Mark. My dresser. A cheap four-drawer dark-stained faux-mahogany. Cole's dresser is a stack of plastic bins on a rolling frame. The blurred contents of balled-up blues and browns in one drawer, songbooks in another, and guitar strings, capos, picks, and various and sundry ephemera in the third. I imagine taking one of his broken steel strings and twisting it in my fingers, and wonder if I could do it; use it as a garrote. I'd likely just end up with sliced fingers.

Aside from my little desk—the one piece of furniture I took when I left Mark—there are only Beckett's two rugs, one on either side of the bed, and every other scrap of wall space is occupied with bookshelves, every one heavy with books. The closet is another mass I don't want to look at. I hate closets. I lean my forehead on that door and rock from side to side.

Winter is coming, and I agreed to stay, but maybe now I've set myself free again. Just like that. If I stay, it will be my sixth winter on the roads, my fourth driving the plow alone. I like the height, how I can see ahead and behind, and the cars as they edge behind me, aching to swing out into the narrow space between the plow and the shoulder's ice. I sit high, looking down, but still I am powerless. Powerless to stop them, to keep them safe, powerless to see beyond the drifts, powerless to change anything beyond the next streamer that will fill in what I've cleared away.

I lie down on top of the covers and sleep.

I wake up and take Beckett outside, zipping up my coat against the lake's chill. Beckett gets busy in the hard grasses. And my stomach is still roiling. Am I, among all the other things that I am, also a lesbian? Bisexual? A bisexual murderer? A lying, cheating, selfish, dying person who won't let her lover love her? A self-pitying, lying, cheating, selfish, etc.? My gut pinches with every footfall. The cold air does nothing to assuage the nausea. I crash into the bushes, buckling and retching.

I need to eat.

At the store, I experienced a mixture of panic and relief when I didn't see Cole. All the way home, the smell of roasted meat makes me desperate, almost delirious, to tear into its flesh.

By the time I get home I'm swooning with lust. I pop off the Ready Roast chicken's clear plastic lid, ignoring the green beans with pine nuts I bought for something healthy. The potatoes are slathered in oil and salt, and I anticipate their crispy sweetness on the outside, their creaminess on the inside. I rip off a leg, catch strands of the dangling tawny-colored flesh with my tongue and then wrap my lips around the bone and suck. Oh sweet Jezuz that's good, good, good. Hot fat drips from inside the succulent skin. I gobble all of it up. Skin and all. I want it all in me right now. Snapping open the container of potatoes, I shovel in a handful. The warm meat and salty bliss of potatoes slosh and roll around in my mouth like happy pigs.

I'm only halfway through the beautiful beast when the sound of key in lock alerts me to Cole's return. Before I can stash the evidence, he's here in the kitchen, a shadow against light. With one hand I snap closed the chicken lid; with the back of the other I swipe my greasy face.

His hair is gone. Completely, totally, absolutely gone. All those tight arbutus-colored curls have been shorn, leaving a waxy sheen in their stead. And two fingernail-sized nicks brown with dried blood.

I come at him where he stands stooped as an old man. "What have you done?" I say, guilt for my chicken sins evaporating.

His face buckles. "What have *I* done?"

"Oh, Cole. I'm so sorry." I wrap my arms around his neck. He doesn't move. "Where have you been?"

His laugh is sad and slow. "Playing *Left for Dead* at Matt's."

"Come. I'll make you something to eat. Drink?" With my arms still around his neck, I kind of pull/drag him toward the kitchen.

He stops, removes my arms, and turns his gaze full on me. "Why are you with me anyway? I mean, what is it you want, Brett? Really. Do you actually want something, anything from me? Why don't you just tell me, please, because I'm so done with this bullshit."

"I just want to be happy," I say, but instantly regret the naïveté of this statement, and I'm not even sure it's true. I try again. "I want us to be happy."

For a second he looks as disappointed by this answer as I am, but then his face blooms a righteous red. "And that's how you do it? Awesome." His body rigid as stone, the ceiling lamp haloing his burnished head. "Right. Sure. Of course. Everyone wants to be happy, Brett. But everyone doesn't go sucking off strange guys in public toilets."

"Norah told you?" I breathe.

"That's the worst of your worries? That Norah betrayed *you*? That's good. Really good." Stretching his neck up, he tilts his head back and takes in a long breath. "And no." His eyes on me again. "It wasn't Norah who told me about your so-called 'kiss.' It was Josh, who didn't seem to know that you'd also kissed his wife." His mouth twists on the word *wife*.

My own mouth has filled with small sharp stones.

"I thought we were going to be okay," Cole says, turning away from me, his smooth head like a moon.

"You shaved your head," I say.

We were okay. Now we are not. If I had a reason or an explanation, a justification, an excuse, or any way to present what happened at the bar, I would say it now.

"You loved me," I say.

Cole pauses but doesn't turn, so I continue, a frantic itch scrabbling at my throat. "Why?"

He shoots a fiery glance toward the dark window where there is no view except our shadowy selves coming back at us. "I don't know, Brett. I don't fucking know. You used to be smart and sexy and fun." Closing his eyes, he shakes his head. Then his eyes pop open and he looks me full in the face. "Shit, Brett, we used to have fun. It wasn't just the sex. We had fun. Remember the night we raided the strawberry patch in Horseshoe Valley? Down between the rows, you all smeared red, the mosquitoes eating our asses off. You were so fucking beautiful I thought I was the luckiest guy in the world. And the time we went bare-assed into the bay and I froze my nuts off and the moon was just bright enough to light up your face. Those were the corny-assed moments when I loved you so much I thought I'd split right open. But now..." He rubbed his knuckles against the shiny side of his head. "Now you're just...mean."

Mean. I try that on and it fits. "You're right."

"Oh fuck. Fuck. Fuck. 'You're right'? That's what I get?" Cole's hands clutch at his head as if desperate for hair to pull. The sound he makes is awful—like he's pinioned on rock. "Where are you, Brett? Where the fuck are you? Here? Bali? In some burned-down cabin in the mountains? This is home. Right here. Right now. You need me. You need me and I'm here, and instead of letting me in you kick me in the fucking nuts." His hands drop. "I'm dying, Brett. I needed *you*..." His voice trails into silence and he stands by the closed door still in his coat, looking not at me, but right through to the other side.

I'm underwater and having trouble hearing. The words arrive at my ears, but that's as far as they get. All I can say in response is, "No, you don't," which part of me knows that even though it's true, it's also a cop-out. Also, he said, "needed." Past tense.

Beckett stands with his tail erect, all four legs slightly splayed in that ready stance, staring hard at Cole. The air goes out of Cole and he drops into a squat, taking Beckett's head in his beautiful, smooth hands, his hands that sort eggplants and bananas, that check for bruises and rot, his hands that knead the sponge of doughs, tap sifters that rain sugar, his hands that find melodies and rhythms in the strings of his guitar, his hands that spread speckled almond butter on coconut oil-softened toast, his hands that cup my breasts as if they are rare birds. He buries his face in Beckett's neck where black meets white. "I'm going to miss you, boy," he murmurs.

Miss him? "What do you mean, 'miss him'?"

As Cole stands, his head moves from side to side as though scanning the room for some misplaced item. "He's your dog, Brett."

"He's *our* dog," I protest.

"I need to get some stuff," he says, putting a hand to his abdomen, a pained look crossing his face. "Matt's building doesn't allow pets." He moves toward the bedroom, toward his guitar, his sports bag, his boxers with the little red devils, his white cotton button-down shirt, his flannel sleep pants that sometimes open at the front and his low-slung jeans that fit the way they're meant to.

My voice sounds false and weak. "You can't leave."

But he doesn't respond, just keeps moving toward those things that will take him away from me, toward a life where he doesn't have to clean up the mess I make.

I wonder if the caterpillars are feeling the cold.

I'm running, my braid slapping against the light padding of my jacket. Beckett keeps a precise distance from my calf, his sturdy legs made for this steady pace, his gaze fixed straight ahead.

Blue like Daddy's eyes, like Goldie's eyes—that clear, perfect blue of their eyes—that's the color of the sky today. A late fall sky with no clouds and no wind. But snow is on its way. Snow will come and snow will stay, the caterpillars know. I am running, my arms pumping, my breath strong. I taste copper in my throat. My feet hit the path like a heartbeat, *thumpthump, thumpthump,* and I will not stop. I can't slow down because if I do my stomach will turn over and punch its way out. Along the path the grasses are stiff and brown, all color bled from them—the pretty yellow and orange flowers that line the summer shore all dried and dead. My heart pumps high in my chest. I am running, running. Beckett's mouth is open, his long pink tongue working, and we run and run and run.

Maybe it was that one decision to buy a dog that tilted things for Cole and me. When he moved in it made sense—he was sleeping over all the time, and his place was just a room in a house full of smelly old men where I would never stay. I don't even remember that there was a decision, just one day all his stuff was at my apartment and none of it was at his anymore.

In my runs along the waterfront, I'd see them: masters and canines, throwing and fetching, yellow dogs with loppy ears and downy coats, small wiry dogs that spin in circles, great black and brown beasts bounding into the lake after a goose or a stick. In the mountains we had rabbits and chickens and goats, but no dog, ever. It would be safe to have a dog, I remember thinking that: a dog would be safe.

Cole and I sat on the ottoman, the one he'd chosen, the one that signaled the beginning of "us," clicking through doggy pictures until we both snapped upright, a soft *ooh* sifting out of both our mouths when we stopped at the wire-haired terriers, our heads bobbing in agreement.

Maybe it was the long drive down to Missouri, a oneness of purpose, that sealed us somehow. This wasn't browsing through the 400 Market for a desk or a lamp. This was a living breathing being, a companion; this was Beckett with his black ears and tail and delicate black saddle over his little wiggly rump.

Near Indianapolis, we stopped at a Super 8. Beckett whined his way out of his fleece-cushioned cage and into our bed. We didn't make love, an unthinkable omission on any other night.

Beckett changed the weather in our world. It seemed all for the good. We were, all three of us, for a long time, and in our own ways, happy.

Now I am running. Beckett runs beside me. And I have chased sweet Cole away. He's running now, too, although he would have stayed. Staying is his nature while mine is to run. I want to run around the lake, a hundred kilometers or more, and then around again, but after ten kilometers, I've lost steam. The insides of my stomach have lodged themselves in my throat. I called in sick because I can't tolerate the faces of the men I work with—their jolly slap-you-on-the-back insults and sideways looks, their fat bellies and sex talk they pretend they don't want me to hear. And now that the plows are about to be launched, the boys on the yard will pull out their favorite story. The way they tell it is as though it's hilarious as well as a perfect example of why women shouldn't drive snowplows. The way I remember it is as the most terrifying moment of my life.

The auger squealed against nothing. Whatever sand was left had frozen in the hopper. Not the sound I wanted to hear, not when I topped the hill and below me the dip of Horseshoe Valley Road shone black. No sand left for the wheel tracks, no traction, and the township's sand camp was at least a kilometer away. Brakes weren't an option, only an easing from the accelerator, a prayer, and my sweating hand lifting the wing. I should have loaded brine, but the forecast said clear—a precautionary sweep with sand was all that was required, but a bitch wind had sheered across the county and turned all the roads to glass. And I was careening down into the valley.

Banging the control, I cursed, "Come on, you prick; pick up that sand. Give it to me, give it, give it." I was going to die, but I wasn't going without a fight. I jerked the lever again.

Then some strange angel of calm descended; some lover or kind father who stroked my head and made me caress it instead and say, "Okay now, baby, that's it, just let it go, let that sand flow like you know how. Open your sweet mouth and drop that load in front of the tires. Yes, baby, yes." And hallelujah, the auger jumped, caught a batch of that frozen sand, and ground it out into a sweet spiraling under the wheels—and I was still alive.

Then, like a bright blue top, a car came spinning out from the south side of Line 7, the woman's face like an Edvard Munch drawing, flickering in horror at each revolution. I checked the ditch. If I bore left I'd hit the bank and topple the entire rig. She spun once more, her hands rigid on the steering wheel. As her car spun in slow motion I could see every line on her face, hear her final plea full of regret for the things she hadn't done—kissed her son before he left, forgiven her mother, learned to tango, or called that old lover from Naxos.

I hit her. There was no way around it. Her car, anyway. It spun and spun until finally thumping to a stop sideways in the ditch. She was a bit banged up, but nothing broken. The county's insurance paid, but I've never let a box get below half since then. And I've never lived it down. As if I were the only one who'd ever clipped a car.

I want to treat my death like a lover. Try explaining that to the boys in the yard.

If I could ride with Mel, I'd have gone in. I long for his not-talking, not-questioning presence; his profile steady on the road—on the shovels of cold mix, on the asphalt, on the *shaagi* he once pointed to in its smooth trajectory overhead, saying it reminded him of me. That sleek determined blue heron, steady and patient, didn't seem at all like me. Not one little bit.

I bend to rest my hands on the tops of my knees, panting, sweat cold between my back and T-shirt. Beckett sprawls belly flat to the ground, his jaw resting between his paws, his eyes never leaving me. "Just you and me now, little buddy," I say, which makes him perk up and tilt his head.

Wheeling around, I push off running, not quite so hard, along the crushed stone path to Barrie, to "home."

Thumpthump, my heartbeat and feet slow to stop. Unzipping my jacket pocket, I dig out my cell phone, tap in the passcode, and swipe my thumb upward on the screen until Mark's name rolls into view. It isn't even a button anymore, just an image of one. I don't have to actually push anything. I barely even touch it and it clicks and then begins to ring. I'm still staring at the stupid little screen with all its circles and dots when I hear his voice, his familiar rocky voice sounding as if he just woke up.

"Brett?"

I run my thumb over the red circle and his voice stops asking. Beckett gives a sharp little bark and dashes toward the lake and zips back to me, although some of his exuberance seems to have diminished.

My hand vibrates and the screen lights up, *Didur, Mark*.

"You realize that I can see who calls. It's a little thing called caller ID," Mark says when I tap the green circle and bring the phone to my ear. "What's going on?"

"Mistake," I say, but I'm having trouble breathing so it sounds like, "Miss." The "take" part is just a suck of breath inward.

"What? Where are you?"

"Sorry," I say and hold down the button at the top of the phone to put it to sleep.

Beckett barks again, rushing in a tight circle around me. "Let's go," I say. Seagulls scream above us. My legs pump hard, picking up speed as I round the lake's curve, my braid slapping my back.

11

I'm in India although the crowded street looks more like Bangkok with its statues of the Buddha in every window. Goldie is there with a different face. Her skin is brown, her eyes an eerie black, but she has her own soft yellow hair. She is in a doorway of an open-air market of painted dolls, fruit, spices, and lengths of azure and magenta silks. Seeing her there halts my frantic wending through sharp indifferent shoulders. I squat in her doorway. "Goldie?"

But she opens her palm. "*Paese?*" she says. Her eyes are empty sockets.

"Goldie. It's me, Brett." I grab her outstretched hand and pull. "Let's get you home." Her arm lengthens but her body is rooted. "Come on," I say. But then I see. She's been nailed to a board. I push the board, rolling it out into the street, bumping into people, pushing toward my hotel, but I can't remember where it is. The airport, then. They're after us—dark men with knives and guns. I push and I push, but they're upon us. Sirens cut into the clatter of wheels and the cacophony of shrill voices. A single siren repeats its warning. We come upon a membrane, like a gelatinous skin, preventing our progress.

The street, Goldie, and India vaporize as I wake to the alarm clock's bleating. It is three p.m. and I have to get to work.

Goldie in trouble. Goldie trapped. I've read that everything in a dream represents some aspect of the self, which would mean that I am nailed to a board and that I am the board, both slave and master of a malevolent force. As I push off the bed, I feel the prick of nails catch my nightshirt. Goldie was begging, but not for herself. Even if I'd put some thin coins into the cup of her palm they would not have fed her. She'd been blinded. She couldn't see me. You don't have to be Carl Jung to figure that one out.

Life is divided as if by a fallen tree in the forest. On the far side, before the fire, the woods surge with vitality and light—creatures and flora, buds and tendrils, Spanish moss, golden larch, clusters of purple and white, orange and yellow squeeze-headed flowers, porcupines with quiet quills and bark-filled teeth, weasels and ferrets, sleek auburn foxes and singing coyotes, pussycat-faced cougars, and bears too. On the near side, where Mama has lived forever after, the earth itself is scorched, bereft, smelling of singed hair and pungent salves that don't soothe. On this side of that dividing log, for twenty-seven years, Mama's feet haven't danced, her hips haven't swayed, and her eyes don't focus on anything I can see.

I've managed, though. Pretty well up until now. Never smoked, though except in rare states of blind drunkenness. I didn't partake when all my high school friends were shoving them in my face to prove how tough and how free they were. I believed I was proving something more lofty, that even with the rebels I didn't need to fit in.

A new tree has soundlessly fallen. Small animals scurry out of the forest.

In the solitude and intensity of working the plow alone, I find a heavy sort of freedom. From high up in my seat I can see the reddened faces of men and women up early to shovel out, only to have me heap the ends of their driveways. Gurdjieff used to instruct his disciples to dig vast trenches that would take an entire day to complete. When done they would come to him expecting praise and reward, only to be instructed to fill in those same holes. This was one of his many devices to stop the ego in its tracks, a shock intended to still the mind. I guess that makes me a kind of spiritual guru.

I'm on nights now, those endless twelve hours alone with the plow on deserted back roads, my eyes bugged from constant surveillance of computer readings, mirrors—upper and those at road level—headlights, spray levels, precise turns. I wanted to be gone by the first snowfall, but I'm still here, grounded like those stupid geese that will be frozen right into the lake if they don't fly away soon.

At home, the apartment hums as it waits for the light. Out of habit, I go first to the kitchen. In the fridge, each sealed container might as well be stamped with a word I can't wipe off: *Expired.* Lentil salad with flecks of peppers and purple onion, a drawer filled with gray-green kale and rhubarb-like chard, their browning leaves spotted with holes. Ingredients for the breakfast I won't make. The nausea hasn't abated. I run my left palm along the counter's smooth, cool edge, past the Vitamix, the slanted block of knives with handles aimed at my throat, the ceramic pot Aunt June sent one Christmas, decorated with a black and white dog, filled with a jumble of steel tools for making things to eat. Every item on the counter is clean and quiet, the way they've been all week. At the window I can see the lake where those stubborn geese refuse to leave the rapidly shrinking open water.

I've called Norah. Only twice, though. It could be the night shift/day shift difference between us, but she hasn't returned my calls. It's still dark, but sleep doesn't like me anymore, so I clip on Beckett's leash and out we go, keeping to the well-lit pathways, my hand clenched around the mace spray in my pocket. After a brisk twenty-minute jog, I'm still far from the respite of sleep and dreams.

I should start drinking. Drink hard liquor and watch movies like *Bridesmaids* or *Anger Management,* or if I were one of those real women I'd be watching *Serendipity* or *Before Sunrise;* something to make me spit my drink laughing or spill it crying. Because I am numb and cold inside and out, I do neither of these things and not only on account of the nausea. I am honestly trying to feel some emotion. I mean, shouldn't one be able to push up feelings as simply as women push up their breasts?

The doctors called what I had a "therapeutic" abortion. Norah considers it murder. What if I had canceled that ap-

pointment? If. If. If. Only. Norah had carried that second one
to term. If she had just held on. If it had just sent out stronger tendrils to root itself in the tender wall of her womb. We
wouldn't have snakes in our bellies, their scales catching on
every kind word we've tried to utter. I could be the auntie, the
godmother, the good friend. Perhaps then I wouldn't have to
turn so quickly from the mirror.

I avoid the bedroom where the comma of Cole's body is
printed in indelible script on the left side of the bed, no matter
how much I smooth the duvet over that cooled place. Instead,
I sit on the ottoman to text Norah the surgery date. The eastern sky is a dull orange-brown all the way down to the water.
I count three cars on Blake Street as they inch along in the
newness of ice.

I will never be a mother. I was correct: I can't bear children.

The closet was Goldie's place. The hinges didn't squeak, and
she fit in between the wall and the trunk stuffed with our winter
things—heavy red blankets with a wide black stripe at each end,
thick oily mittens, mothballs, and cedar. She'd run there, try to
slam the closet door when I'd pulled her hair or told her to bug
off with her crazy face, but she was little and it usually didn't
properly close. But sometimes it did.

It wasn't that she couldn't get out. She could reach the inside latch, but there were times when I'd find her much later,
squeezed into the narrow space, bits of carob nibs and almond
slivers nestled in the bowl of her skirt. Once I found her, eyes
closed, the petals of her mouth open, and some sweet she'd
secreted away like a sticky jewel in her palm. "Come on, sleepy-
head." I prodded her with the toe of my gum boot. "It's raining.
Let's go catch frogs."

She started up, all moist and pink from sleep, smelling of
butter and vanilla, her voice much bigger than her small body.
"Puddles!"

Three-year-olds don't hold grudges.

We should have worn black, but we had no clothes. All I had was my smoke-drenched nightgown and some patched jeans and T-shirts from Tree Telfer's parents. Marion wore a lacy black shawl over a pale blue blouse and a long black silky skirt. The river wasn't as wild in the fall, but Daddy and Goldie's ashes got pulled downriver real fast. I kept looking at Marion's pretty shawl and wishing I had a thing like that. Mama's crocheted shawls were all ash just like the beds and the table and the cradle Daddy had carved for Goldie. And my Cindy doll whose eyes didn't close. I couldn't look at the river. Couldn't get the taste of ash out of my mouth. I just wanted to pull Marion's shawl from her shoulders and wrap it around myself.

Afterward, alone in my cousin's bed, before he came to stay and made things all right, I managed to stop breathing for a long time, but some force in my chest punched its way out and a great suck of air forced its way in. I pulled a pillow over my face and pressed with both my forearms. Too soon, I lost strength and let go.

When I was with Mark, I often held my breath. It didn't work then either. The sex was good—scaldingly good—and Aunt June had assured me that good sex was the most important aspect of a healthy relationship. She never mentioned anything as pedestrian as respect or kindness. I stayed close to the burn of him, clung to his meanness, fed on his rage. After all, the sex was good.

Then sex did what sex is designed to do.

It's been over a week since Cole left with his glossy head and his stuffed Maple Leafs sports bag. Today is Saturday. Beckett has abandoned his cushion on the floor and has taken to sleeping on Cole's side of the bed, a place forbidden until now. We had a good run this morning, and now he twitches in his sleep, his head on Cole's pillow.

The blank pages of my open journal glare at me. I sit and pick up the pen, the one Cole gave me with its sprinkle of gems along the side. It's pretty, but the jewels dig into my fingers when I write. Cole asked me what I wanted, and I gave him a platitude. *Happy.* Happy? What would happy look like if there were such a thing? In a perfect world, Goldie would be thirty years old, Mama and Daddy would be putting on their fine things—Mama's beaded earrings with the peacock feathers, a silk flower behind her ear, a touch of lipstick; Daddy in his good blue jeans, a shirt that isn't flannel—in preparation for a dance at the community center. I'd be braiding Goldie's hair, and her little daughter's too. Her daughter would look just like her. Mama and Daddy would be a little creaky, but they'd step out like true back-to-the-landers, ready to stomp and swing all Sunday afternoon. That would make me happy.

Squeezing the pen until the bite of the gems registers, I rein in my focus. What might my perfect life look like? A happy life. At the notion of me being happy, my gut does a little back-flip. Still, I peer into a hazy future where I am smiling under a bright sun and there are no dead animals to be scraped from the pavement. I have a villa or a palapa or whatever they call a beach house in Bali. I have lovers, of course, from Australia, Africa, Italy, and Peru. They bring me bottles of honey and wine, and flowers—fat fragrant ones—for my hair and to put in slender vases. I sit at a small table under green leaves the size of umbrellas with swooping rice terraces at my back, the turquoise and white sea before me, and I am writing. Poems mostly, which some of my lovers put to music. At night there's guitar music, or flutes and the soft bonging of drums, cicadas and tree creatures. Under the swirl of mosquito netting and warm breezes, I fall asleep listening to these songs. Maybe I don't even need a mosquito net. Norah visits. She stays for a week, possibly two. She brings her children.

Releasing the pen from my grip, I stretch to standing and return to the glare through the window. I am Virginia Woolf, Anaïs Nin, Iris Murdoch. I am not any of those brave women. Will I ever have the courage to tell my story? My journal pages are blotched or scribbled on. My poems come out sour as cherries that should have been sweet.

The date for surgery is set, but beyond the swinging doors of the operating theater I see only blackness and silence. I know this is wrong—that what's supposed to be saving me looks like its own ass-end.

I should call my mother. I miss her. Not the one with the faraway eyes of the last twenty-six years, but the one before that, the one whose warm hands braided my hair and fastened it with ribbons, the one who sang "Gypsy Rover," "Love is a Rose," and "Early One Morning." The one who danced. That one. I need her.

I go back to the window overlooking the street and the lake beyond. The lake is clenched under the weight of ice. Not even a fringe of water remains at the shoreline. The geese have fled at last. On the sidewalk below, a woman wrapped in an endlessly long scarf clutches a hump swaddled in the blankets of a baby carrier, one gloved hand pressing the pink-capped head against her chest. Delicate clouds puff from her mouth. She is singing. Her walk is more bounce than walk—a one-two step in rhythm with the song's steamy billows. Checking the sidewalk for reassurance that the Bobcat has done its job, I also check her feet for proper footwear. She wears sturdy hiking boots, the kind Mama wore. Across her back, the carrier strap's X makes her coat swell into four Vs. She wears a long denim skirt with flowered gores at the bottom, like the kind Mama made from old jeans patched with leftover fabric, but this one looks store-bought. The sole of her boot is the last I see of her. It has a good tread.

When I press my palms into my eyes, stars burst into the darkness. The image of that one wool-covered hand cradling her pink-capped head shimmers in negative relief behind all the stars. Her hand. What hands do. My hand pushing Goldie out of bed.

Turning from the window, the blank living room stares back at me. I have enough money. I could go. I could call Norah and tell her to tell Josh to tell Cole to come get Beckett, and fly out by Friday. I could keep my womb and die in peace in a beautiful place. At the bathroom mirror, I brace myself on the counter's cool edge, and find Cole's eyes reflected there. Not his lips or his nose, or his head with or without those tight red-brown curls. Only his eyes. When I peer into the depths of my own eyes, I find they are sunk deep into the image of his, so deep I can't find my own white-blue ones; only his warm caramel ones flecked with bits of dark chocolate and rimmed with a fine black line. They watch, steady and keen like an owl's that won't blink or look away. It occurs to me, my belly pressed into the counter, my nose almost touching the glass, that I might truly love Cole. The thought sets a fist to squeezing whatever organs live under the ribcage. I swallow hard. I will not vomit. The thought creates a sudden shift in the mirror, and my own naked face comes into focus, my eyes as bald as Cole's head.

I'll walk. I'll run. Maybe all the way around the lake as far as Sutton. A hundred K. I could do it.

In the front hall I squat to tie my laces, but suddenly I'm lost. I can't remember how to tie a shoe, don't know which bunny ear hides inside the other or when it's supposed to dive down a hole. I crumple to the floor, one foot lolling like a drunk, and gape at those inscrutable strands trailing along the floor. I pick up one plastic-tubed end, then the other, and stretch them high and wide. How do you tie a shoe? Which half begins? I could pull the entire blue strip right out through each and every eye-hole. But then they would all be staring at me; all ten of them.

12

I'm back on days, which is merciful because at night sleep is elusive, but during the day non-existent. Mel is doing the cold mix. He prefers it to driving. I'd like to tell him how much I miss driving with him, his brown hand loose on the wheel, his deep unhurried quiet. But you don't say stuff like that on the yard.

I love the deliberateness of the plow. Although everything is happening at once—the computer telling us how much salt and sand to put down, how icy, how cold, and having to watch the low mirrors to make sure everything's coming out right, there's a slow-motion sense to it all, and a welcome distance from everything else. Like distant friends. Angry boyfriends. Cancer.

When I sit down to open my lunch, Mel is in the doorway looking directly at me. All the other guys are out in the garage or on the roads. In the room there are stacks of files, the smeared window, dirty sunlight, and Mel's eyes.

"What?" I say, more than a little startled by his direct attention.

His shoulders lift just a little and his head tilts slightly, but his eyes stay fixed on me like sun through a magnifying glass, until I begin to sweat.

Pushing back the brim of his hard hat, Mel says, "You'll be going soon, eh?"

The food I haven't eaten yet sticks in my throat. "Going?"

From his jacket pocket, he extracts a small brown paper bag. Placing it on the table in front of me, he says. "From my Franny. Raspberry leaves. Make a tea."

Before I'm able to form a question, he's gone through the door and out into the yard. I unroll the top of the bag and peer in as if the contents will give me an answer, but it's just a bag of dried green leaves not smelling at all of raspberry.

By two the snow has completely melted, so the plows get parked and we're back in the truck on garbage and ditch duty, which suits me fine. I need the air and the movement. I also need Mel.

After loading up the shovels, trimmer, and pitchforks, I climb into the driver's seat. I need to drive, need to feel the resistance of the road, need the rhythm of the brake and gas pedal under my feet. I need to be in control. Mel's lined face appears at the driver's side window. For a moment he stands there, his face unreadable, his body still, before moving away and around the truck to get in the passenger side. The door closes soundlessly as I put the truck into reverse.

It happens so suddenly that for a second I believe it's just a pothole I've hit, or a piece of scrap blown off the back of a truck.

"*Nimoosh*." Mel says it as quietly as a prayer.

"A dog?" I veer to the right, bringing the truck to a jolting stop on the shoulder. "I hit a dog?"

I'm out of the cab and running toward the black shape on the road. I drop to my knees, rip off my heavy glove, and press my fingers lightly to the dog's black nose, my other hand on its side. It whimpers.

"It's alive."

"Hush now, you'll scare him." Mel puts a blanket beside the animal and begins to search through its fur.

The dog's eyes are open. His body rises and falls with his breath. The quiet whimpering has become a throaty whine.

"You're going to be fine, boy," I say stroking his head while searching his collar for tags.

"Leg's broke," says Mel. "I think that's all."

"How did it happen? Why didn't I see him?" I want to say, Why didn't *you?*

"He come out of nowhere. Like a *jiibay*." I've never seen Mel look mystified. He sweeps his gaze into the still trees on the far side of the ditch and back out toward the road. The closest house is a red brick farmhouse set at the end of a long

willow-lined driveway, too far to carry a dog with a broken leg.
He's some kind of cross—maybe lab and border collie. His
rumpled fur is silky, and he has a white patch on his chest in the
shape of an inverted heart.

After we shift him onto the blanket, Mel lifts him into my
arms, and we walk back to the truck in silence. When Mel grabs
the handle to crank down the side of the truck bed, I shake my
head.

"You drive," I say. "I'll keep him in my lap."

The dog rallies as we drive and struggles to stand, its nose
twitching toward the open window. There's no vehicle in the
driveway, no answer to our knock at the front door, and no
response at the side door either. I write a note explaining that I
hit a black dog, that he's alive and awake, and that I'm taking it
to the nearest vet. I include my cell number and stick it in the
crevice between door and frame.

"What does it mean, Mel?" I say once we've turned on to
Bayfield. "Why did I hit a dog?" The dog is panting now, its
constant whine blending into the engine's hum. "It's okay, boy,"
I soothe, stroking his soft ears. "You're going to be fine."

Mel doesn't answer.

"Mel?"

His hands are still, both wrapped around the steering wheel,
not draped or drumming. He brings the left one to the place
under his chest where his belly bulges. "In here," he says. "Answer's in here."

I mimic his gesture, but all I feel is sick. I say so.

Mel nods as if I have answered the question.

Beckett is at the door, prancing in tight circles, ready to run.
But he stops his dance short and begins to sniff me up and
down—my boots, hands, and pants—while emitting staccato
woofs. Even after I drop my work clothes to the floor, he continues to examine my smells. It's only when I've put on my
running clothes and grabbed his leash that he seems to relax,
bounding to the door to show me the way out.

There's no joy in the running. I keep seeing that dog on the road, broken by me. The vet said he wasn't chipped, and his collar had no tags. Mel promised not to document the accident because I begged him and promised to take full responsibility.

When we return, there's a message on my cell. "We don't own a dog. Sorry."

I put a notice on Kijiji with the picture I took on my phone. Then I call Norah.

"I'm just in the middle of making dinner. Can I call you back?" she says with what sounds to me like manufactured breathlessness.

"I'm coming over," I say. "I'll help you cook. I'll watch you eat. It doesn't matter. I need to talk to you."

Beckett paces by the front door, periodically dropping his head to sniff along the crack. The living room is dark except for the streetlights' orange glow. I should shut the curtains.

"I have people coming over," Norah says at last.

"No, you don't."

"Yes, I do. What makes you think I don't?" There's no mistaking the hostility in her tone.

"It's the thirteenth. You'd never have anyone over on the thirteenth." I hesitate. "Are you mad at me because I kissed you?" I say, and the rest comes out in an unbroken stream. "Why aren't you talking to me? Why won't you answer my calls? I was drunk, I'm sorry. You're my best friend. My only friend and I don't want to screw it up again. Please, Norah. I need you and I'm sorry." My hands are curled in chilled balls.

"No. I'm not mad at you for kissing me." Her voice has gone tender and sad. "I kissed back, remember?"

"I do remember. But we were drunk and—"

"Shut up, will you? I'm not mad because of that. I'm not even mad."

"Oh, good, that's good."

She sighs. "Cole is coming for dinner."

Any heat my body held drains all the way to my feet and departs through the floor. "What can I do, Norah?" I hate the pleading in my voice, but I can't control it. "How can I fix this?"

A pause full of deliberation before she answers. "I wish I knew. I really do, Brett. But you've shoveled yourself in pretty deep."

"Norah, I hit a dog today and I don't know if I can have this operation and I want to leave for good and I don't know what to do about Beckett and I called Mark and I'm scared really, really scared, Norah, I—"

"Hey. You need to calm down," Norah says in her take-charge voice. "One thing at a time." She sighs. "The truth is I'm torn, Brett. Cole is our friend too."

"But I'm dying."

Before the last piteous syllable leaves my lips, Norah snaps, "Oh, for heaven's sake. You're going to be fine. Just have the operation. When is it, by the way?"

"By the way?" I am eleven years old and *by the way*, your sister and daddy aren't coming back. *By the way*, your mother doesn't want a fuss about it. *By the way*, you're on your own now.

"I texted you," I say.

"Oh, right. December, right? Before Christmas though. That's okay then. Everything will be fine, you'll see."

When I google uses for raspberry leaf tea, I find, aside from all sorts of references and guides on its use in pregnancy and labor, that it's used for gastrointestinal disorders, diarrhea, respiratory issues, flu and heart problems, fever, diabetes, and vitamin deficiency. It also promotes sweating, urination, and bile production. One site says that some women use raspberry leaf for painful or heavy periods, morning sickness, preventing miscarriage, and easing labor. I don't have any of these problems. So what does he think it will help? Heartache? Guilt? There's no mention of cancer in any of the references to what raspberry leaf can heal.

Among the books Cole brought me was one by a doctor about how people cured themselves of terminal illnesses by being happy and positive. One guy was seriously messed up by the doctors. First they gave him some drug that was supposed to cure him, and straight away his tumors shrank to zero. Then he read that that particular drug was ineffective and his tumors popped back. So they gave him blank injections, telling him they'd perfected the drug and it was sure to work. His tumors shrank to nothing. Then the fools told him they'd injected him with a placebo. So he died. I wanted to throw that stupid book against the wall. If I believe, I will get well. I summon all my will to believe that I'll get well, to continue to believe in raw food, juicing, supplements, enemas, cannabis oil, parasite cleanses, etcetera, etcetera… Google tells me that raspberry leaf strengthens the womb but do I need it strengthened before removing it? Or perhaps, if I believe fervently enough, when I arrive in December for the surgery, they will exclaim in wonder, *It's a miracle*. And Cole will see that I want to live and he will come back.

When I plow, I sometimes imagine the blades scraping my cells clean, revealing soft pink flesh shimmering with health underneath. Norah told me she read that the will to live grows stronger the closer terminal patients are to their own death. She certainly hasn't given up trying to make more living things despite the odds. But I push constantly against the sweet suction of death, the end that would finally scour me clean. I resist the drag of longing for that calm, quiet place where I might meet my sister and my father, where I could tell them how much I have missed them, where I could tell them how sorry I am.

My mother answers the phone on the seventh ring. Norah would say that's lucky. I can tell the phone is the same one she's had for twenty years by the static on the line. I sent her a cell phone and added her to my plan, but she's never activated it. I even chose one of those simple child phones with no bells and whistles so she wouldn't balk at the technology. But, no, here is her voice all crackly and broken up by mouse-chewed wires.

"What happened?" That's the first thing she always says: "What happened?"

"Nothing *happened*, Mama. But I've been thinking about you

and I just wanted to hear your…" Something sharp snags my throat. I cough. "I wanted to hear your voi…" It catches again, like a piece of straw in the windpipe. "Sorry," I say. "How are you, Mama?"

"Oh, you know." The sound of her is as distant as the moon.

"Mama?"

"Yes?"

I see it. The thing that will save us both. "Let's go on a trip."

"Oh, a trip is it?"

"Yes, a trip. Why not? Someplace nice and warm."

"It's still pretty warm here. No snow yet."

"No, I mean nice and warm. Where we can float in salt water."

"Why don't you just come for a visit?"

"I'm going to send you a ticket so you can come here and we'll take a trip together, okay?"

"I don't like to leave the land. Don't like to fly. Too far from the ground, you know." Her thin laugh drifts away.

"Mama, please listen. I need you to come. Please."

"What happened? Why don't you come here? It hasn't snowed yet, you can probably fly into Castlegar. Not a lot of work around here, though, unless you want to grow pot. Or garlic. But there are a lot of people doing that already. Or something to do with computers. Do you work with computers? Maybe you could do that." The distinct *click click* of knitting needles starts up as her voice grows even more distant.

"Are you knitting, Mama? I thought you hated knitting." She didn't always hate knitting. But the unknit sweaters had melted in her coiled basket along with everything else.

"Oh no, I love knitting. Everyone's getting a nice long scarf this year. I've been busy." She says this as though confessing a secret.

"Look, Mama, I'm going to get Auntie June to pick up a ticket and get you on a plane, okay? I need you to come."

"You mustn't do that, Brett." Her voice has grown stern. She sounds all at once like a mother. "I'm not leaving the land."

The land. After I left the valley, Dylan enlisted the community to build her a small log cabin at the edge of the meadow,
and planted two pear trees in commemoration. It took six years
and Aunt June's desperation to get Mama out of her house, to
get the project rolling. When I visited her just before moving
to Barrie, I found that it was just one room with a sleeping loft,
meant to be more of a cottage than a home. The place where
our house stood is thick with twitch grass, fireweed, and the
pretty orange and noxious hawkweed. Not a smudge on the
ground or a plaque to say that a golden-haired girl who loved
the squish of warm tomatoes in her mouth and the slip of
frogs in her hands, and a kind, lean man who left peace signs
on the houses and barns he painted, once lived and died there.

I'm driving with Tom today. He's a big guy with a small vocab-
ulary. We don't talk much, which I'm certain is on account of
my being female. He can't actually say anything of the sort, of
course, but I'm not stupid. When I got hired, it was just supposed to be seasonal, to meet some kind of unspoken quota or
equal-opportunity mandate, I'm sure. But I showed them how
tough people with vaginas can be.

When we come back to the yard for break, I take my cell
phone out to the far side of the storage dome to call the vet.
They've called the dog Lucky Catlin. This makes me smile. No
internal damage, a clean break, bruising, and I can come pick
him up anytime. Along the edge of the yard, the yellow trucks
are lined up facing out with their black arms open for the addi-
tion of plows. Behind the trucks, trees' cold branches stripped
of leaves shuffle like boys at high school dances. The sky is bare
too. No snow yet this morning, but it's coming.

Through the mouth of the dome I notice a figure moving
and recognize Mel's stoop and paunch, the faint glow of a cigarette tip.

"Hey," I call into the semi-dark. "How come you gave me
that tea?"

The shovel pauses and Mel straightens. He rests one forearm on its handle. I can't see his face, but I feel his eyes. He's never quick to answer, but this silence makes me itch, like in school when poems bled all over the equations in my head and a teacher waited for an answer.

Stepping into the gloom, I ask again, "Do you think I'm sick, Mel? Is that why you gave me that tea?" The damp smell of sand and salt ignites a memory of a West Coast vacation before Goldie was born, of whales and eagles and pulling mussels off rocks at Fletchers Beach. Daddy and Mama and me rolled in red wool blankets, Daddy naming the stars, Mama singing "Twinkle Twinkle."

Mel says, "How's the dog?"

"He's fine. They want me to come get him. I can't have two dogs, Mel. It took a lot of convincing and signing of things to get my landlords to allow Beckett to stay. They'll never let me have two." I hesitate. "What about you? Can you take him?" I force a little laugh. "Imagine, the vet's assistant named him Lucky."

Mel gives his head a woeful shake. "Wife's in a wheelchair."

"I'm sorry," I say, shocked. He's never mentioned this fact, not once. I know they have children, two boys, and three grandchildren, two girls and a boy, all living on the reserve.

Shrugging, Mel returns to his shoveling, and I see him as not the fifty-something he is now, but seven years old and crowded in with his siblings in an uninsulated shack, scrabbling for a bite of something, a scrap of affection, someone to notice. He told me once that one of the strongest smells from his childhood wasn't the scent of cedar or Balm of Gilead or even the clean smell of a freshly gutted perch from the lake, but rather the smell of his own piss drying on his pants in front of the wood stove before school.

The dog isn't his problem. He doesn't remind me that I promised to care for him, or that we could have just dropped him off at the Humane Society, or that it was my idea to take him to my vet. The yard is wide and empty except for the line of trucks waiting for winter to begin in earnest; our cars, on the other side facing the trucks, are also ready for winter, with their deep-treaded snow tires and fresh oil changes. Mel drives his Pony with its rust flakes at the wheel wells. I always park my little red Yaris next to his truck, like a little sister.

The cold has found its way inside my jacket, so I get in my car and start it. My bare hand closes around the vibrating phone in my pocket.

"Why did you call and then just hang up?" Mark demands. The bass-line thump of his voice is as familiar now as the turn of his back was then.

"Oh," I say, glancing over to the dark triangle of the storage dome's doorway where Mel's dependable shape bends, straightens, bends and straightens. "I hit your number by accident."

"Could have said so."

"I did." My voice is sharper than I intended, but its harshness creates a surge of pleasure. "I did, Mark. I said it was a mistake. Because it was. A big fat mistake."

"What? What the hell does that mean?" An exasperated sigh follows. "There you go—full of double meanings and...*meaning*. Everything with two meanings or more and fuck me if I don't get it. Why did you call, really? I mean really?"

"Shit's going down, if you must know."

He laughs, a smoker's laugh, even though he quit after we returned from India. I think the *beedees* did him in. "Isn't shit always going down with you?"

"You're a mean son of a bitch, you know that?" I'm warm now. Hot, actually. "*You* were the shit going down with me."

"Ha!" Mark never backed away. He was always there with his fists up. "You liked it when I went down, if memory serves."

"Fuck you, asshole. You're still a mean-ass son of a bitch." Steam clouds the inside of the windshield.

"*I'm* the mean one? That's a joke. You're the prize junkyard dog."

Sometimes, we had some good hot sex after we were finished hurling insults and accusations.

"So, who're you fucking now?" I say, unable to keep the twist out of my voice. "Some Rosedale lawyer? Forest Hill doctor?"

"I never—"

"Oh, bullshit. Bullshit! You and I both know what a piece of shit you were. Are. Don't think I didn't know. Going back to check the paint, check the beams, check how she looks with your cock in her mouth."

"You better watch your mouth."

"I'll bet you'd like to watch my mouth." My hand flies up to cover it. What the hell am I doing?

From the garage, Tom waves me in.

I don't hear Mark's response.

"What did you say?"

"I said there's one thing I'd like to watch your mouth doing." His voice is like warm whisky. "You can bring that sweet mouth of yours down here anytime."

The suck of my breath makes me choke.

His triumphant laugh lands like a volley of punches. "You know you want it."

"You can't call me," I say.

"All right, then," he says cheerfully. "Your loss, baby."

Me standing in the doorway with my two suitcases. "Guess I won't know what I had till it's gone." He shrugged, as if it was all such a great unfathomable mystery, before opening the fridge.

I slide the bar across the top of the screen to shut it down. But my chest is pounding as if I've been running hard, and the sweat is cold inside my jacket. That's enough of that crap.

I know what happens when you play with fire.

When I open the apartment door I expect the scrabble of nails on parquet and the swoosh of Beckett's solid little body leaping up to greet me. Instead, he's belly down, all fours splayed, beside Cole, who's on the ottoman tuning his guitar.

For a moment I stand in the hallway, my keys quiet and my breath forgotten.

Into the stillness rushes the swoop of heat coming on, the drapes lifting a little over the register. Beckett's chin settles between his paws, his eyebrows take turns lifting. My jacket has been halted halfway down my arms, my fingers on both sides of the zipper.

Cole begins to sing.

I know this song.

It's "Tonight Will Be Fine," the Leonard Cohen song about a lost love returning for just one night. It's not jaunty the way Cohen sings it, but measured and wrenching like Teddy Thompson's version.

He comes to the part where the woman's love is too vast. But it's Cole's love that's too vast.

My jacket continues its trajectory to the floor. I observe its orange and yellow in a puddle on the parquet. Cole's back is to the living room, his frame dark in the big window, singing to his emerging reflection. The sound of his voice keeps me plugged into the floor. It is steady and deep and private, but he must know I'm here listening, hearing him.

When he comes to the line about there being only one bed and one prayer, his voice catches and that snags a matching place in my chest. He's gone hoarse, but manages to get through the part about listening for her each night.

For nearly six years he's been listening, my step growing fainter instead of nearer.

"...tonight will be fine..."

Maybe it will be. I do want it to be fine. I do. Perhaps we'll be able to touch each other again. Like before. Hot and slow as if none of this shit ever happened. As if I didn't have cancer. As if I hadn't messed with a stranger.

At the chorus, the part about her eyes and her smile, I realize that it's not my eyes or my smile that reassure him, no, it's *his* eyes and *his* smile that have always done the job of reassuring.

The final "for a while" is so soft he almost doesn't sing it.

In the silence that follows, I tiptoe across to him.

"Are you home now?" I whisper.

Below us the gray Barrie waterfront is a road-colored blur with no distinction between water and sky.

Cole stands, placing his guitar gently behind him on the ottoman. "I don't want you to be alone when you have your operation."

"Oh."

For a moment my "oh" hangs in the air like a flag with no wind.

I squat, slapping my thighs for Beckett to come. "You want another dog?"

"Brett." Cole never yells, ever. "Look at me."

I do. I look up at him. His face has lost its youth. Lines around his mouth. My hands ache for the softness of his head.

"You need me now. When you're better, I'll go."

Beckett and Cole stand in solidarity facing me.

"I hit a dog yesterday. I should have taken it to the pound, but I didn't. He's all right, but no one's claimed him. I have to go get him, but I can't. I can't have him here."

Cole's eyes close. "The kindness you show to animals." His eyes flip open. "Does it occur to you that I don't have a place to keep a dog?"

"I don't know that. You won't answer my messages. I figured you were living with the band guys."

"Oh, Brett," is all he says before grabbing Beckett's leash. "Come on, boy, let's go chase some rabbits."

After they leave, I consider cooking something nice for us. Something we'll both like, but I can't imagine what that might be.

The fridge opens with the suck of rubber and it occurs to me I haven't opened the thing for a few days. I shut the door quickly against the smell. Stuck with a magnet advertising the therapeutic benefits of cleanses and colonics is the calendar, a dark red circle around the pre-op appointment date, and a red circle drawn with a lighter hand around the actual date. Beside the faint circle, a tiny question mark.

The beaches in Bali will make the Goa beach where Mark and I walked seem like a swamp and that colossal moon a fac-

simile of itself. I'll take down my hair and wade into the biolu-
minescence, swim until my arms give out, and then lift up and
float back to shore by morning, a healed and radiant goddess.
Or a bloated version of my former self.

Cole can stay here. He might have to eventually find a cheaper apartment where he can have the dogs, but I'll leave him
some cash, and prepay Lucky's board at the vet until he's re-
habilitated. Even as snappy-smart as that sounds in my head, I
know this is magical thinking. When I look into the weeks ahead
I see nothing. Blank. An operating table and then blackness.

Maybe that blackness is just some game I'm playing in my
head, another ploy to avoid the inevitable. The truth is, I'm
saturated and sick to death of my games.

Norah answers on the seventh ring. This time, she's not breathless. "Sorry I brushed you off last time," she says and then
waits for me to speak.

"I want to make things right," I tell her.

Her laugh isn't unkind. "How do you propose to do that?"

"I kind of hit a dog yesterday..."

"Yeah, I think I heard that in your crazy-talk yesterday. What
happened?"

I describe the accident, the dog, and taking him to the vet.

"But this is very good," Norah says, surprising me. "To meet
a black and white dog is auspicious." She pauses. "I'm not so
sure about hitting one, though."

"But it's just a broken leg. Nothing that won't heal."

"I'm sure."

"Dogs are great companions," I say. "This one is very sweet.
Trusting. Really cute."

"I don't want a dog, Brett."

"Oh no, of course." I was sure she'd take him. "I wasn't
suggesting that. Anyway, I'm sure this dog has a family. He's
obviously been well cared for, and for sure they'll be looking for
him. In fact—" I glance at my calendar, which doesn't actually
have anything on it but the surgery date. "I'm going to take a

trip tomorrow after work to where we found him and knock on a few doors." Covering the calendar with the flat of my palm, I add, "Want to come along?"

I steam brown rice and add Nori and sesame seeds to make it palatable. Cole eats this gourmet delight without comment. Beckett wanders away, disheartened by the lack of potential scraps, and whuffs down on his cushion. Cole doesn't argue when I say I'll clean up and goes to the ottoman to play his guitar. He sings softly to himself, maybe working out the lyrics to a new song, while I sit at the kitchen table scrolling through information on the after-effects of hysterectomy.

Later, in bed, he sleeps. I do not.

Norah swings open the car door and peers in, assesses my grimy work jacket and cargo pants, my scummy boots, and says, "Yeah, you're right. Let's take your car."

"You and Cole?" Norah says. "Back together?" This comes before we've even turned onto Bayfield. She rummages in her purse, probably for a Handi Wipe.

Depressing the clutch and shifting into second, I let out a long sigh. "I think I love him."

Norah's purse drops through her legs to the floor with a thump. "And this is a problem?"

My head moves up and down as though weighted by a pulley.

"Let me ask you something," she says. "Have you ever been in love before? I mean crazy, stupid, out of your head in love?"

"Kind of," I answer.

"Kind of? 'Kind of' crazy stupid in love? That's not quite working for me. Are you talking about Mark or Cole here?"

I tuck my chin, take a breath, shift into third. "Dylan."

"What? Dylan? Who the hell is Dylan? Why don't I know about Dylan?"

"He's my cousin."

"That Dylan? Oh, right." She hesitates. "Your cousin?" she repeats carefully. "Oh dear god, Brett."

I gear down, keep my eyes moving from the road to the cars to the rearview mirror. At the red light at Wellington Street, I look down at my right hand kneading the end of the gear shift.

"I was young," I say.

"How young?"

I decide to have out with it. "Eleven. Twelve."

The sound she makes is the sound of a knife piercing a tire.

I roll down the window. Cold air floods in but doesn't cool my skin.

Finally, she says, "Well." After another long pause, she asks, "How old was he?"

"Twenty. He was twenty."

"Dear god. Dear, dear god."

"Please stop saying that, Norah."

"Well," she says again.

I shift into a different gear.

"So. What happened? Tell me nothing *happened*."

There is something blocking my throat.

"What did he do, Brett?"

I cough hard. "Everything. He did everything, dammit. He taught me everything."

Norah grips my arm. "Dear god. Oh, Brett. Dear god. Sorry, I can't help it. But…Brett, did you tell anyone? Was he charged? Oh dear god, you poor little thing!"

I want to stop her talking, stop her saying *dear god*, but my mouth won't move. "Have you reported this?" Norah goes on. "Where is this bastard? You can still have him charged, you know. You know that, don't you?"

"You don't understand," I say. "You asked if I ever loved anyone. I loved Dylan."

"He's a pedophile."

"He was good to me, Norah. Really good." Except when the blood came and he wouldn't touch me anymore. "It's not right," he said. "Too dangerous." Told me not to cry and that he still loved me.

I put the car into first and let the clutch out too fast, jumping us across the intersection.

"This is bad, Brett. Very bad."

She's right. I've always known that, but how do you stop that squelching in the heart? By running headlong into anything that kills it, that's how. Air rushes through the open window, a rhythmic flush of cars passing in the opposite direction, and Norah's sucked-in silence.

Then she says, "Now I understand why you don't want children."

I take a hard left into the vet's driveway. "Really?"

"What 'really'?"

"You understand? You get it?"

She picks up her purse and clutches it against her chest. "I understand why you don't want to have a child. With that kind of abuse in your past. But the rest of it…" She looks off in the direction of the clinic. "Why are we here?"

"I want to take some pictures of Lucky to show people," I answer, cranking up the hand brake. "Let's go."

The black dog with the white patch on his chest struggles to his feet when we enter, greeted by a cacophony of yips and yelps and husky barking. His leg is encased in a white cast, skin showing pink where he's been shaved. He's calm, though, as he pokes his nose through the cage, his eyes half-closing as if to say, *Why did you leave me here?*

"This place stinks," Norah says, shifting from fine leather boot to fine leather boot. "Just hurry up and take those shots and let's get out of here."

I crouch, my hand threaded through the wires to stroke Lucky's neck, my forehead pressed into the cage. His breath smells like wet newspaper. I wonder what they're feeding him. "I'm so sorry," I murmur. "I'm going to find your family so you can go home."

At the first house, about half a kilometer south of where I hit him, a woman not much older than me with an oxygen rope trailing behind her and two prongs up her nose, looks over her reading glasses, then tilts up her head to have a closer look at the phone's small screen. "That might be the Youngs' mutt," she says doubtfully. "They're on the other side about a quarter mile up." She flutters her hand to the north.

Jumping back in the car, I say, "I think we've got it!" I raise a high-five hand to Norah, who taps it back gingerly.

"You need to tell me more about this Dylan creep."

"Norah, he wasn't a creep. It wasn't abuse. He was good to me. He loved me." Loved.

"You were a child."

I nod. "I was." No one knows. No one has ever known except for Dylan and me. It was our sweet secret. He stopped because he wanted to protect me. He stopped because he loved me too much. I want to tell Norah why our loving was good, healthy even, how because I was too young to have his baby, he stopped touching. To be safe. But the membrane between then and now is rupturing. Now I can't open my mouth.

"And there you were, half your family dead, and he comes along and takes advantage of you. He should be tied by his balls and hung upside down!" She thumps on the door handle and stamps both feet.

I balk at the picture this evokes, and my defenses rise. "It wasn't like that. He gave me something. He didn't take anything away. I wanted him. I needed him."

"Oh my god, Brett, you're worse off than I thought. Dear god. Dear, dear god." She's moaning and rocking, her arms wrapped tight around her middle. "You have to know how wrong that is. You just have to."

The problem is that I do know, but knowing doesn't make the feelings go away, doesn't clear them the way vinegar can clear glass.

"This is it," I say, pointing to the fish-shaped mailbox with YOUNG & SONS stickered on its scaly side.

Norah pulls her purse from the floor and sits holding its

handles like an old lady waiting for a bus. "Does Cole know about this?"

This is the question she shouldn't ask.

"You haven't told him?" she presses.

"I can't," I say, my fist on the door.

Twisting the handles of her purse, Norah stares out the windshield. "This is serious, Brett."

"He doesn't need to know everything. He knows about Mark. He knows about us." I turn to her. "That's enough."

"Us? You mean you and me?" She looks exasperated. "You tell him about a drunken kiss but you don't tell him you had an abortion, don't tell him your cousin raped you, don't tell—"

I shove open the car door and heave myself into the sunless driveway, slam the door behind me, and stride to the front door, crunching gravel to sand under my boots.

No one answers the bell at the front door, so I walk around back to a large shed from which the spine-grating sound of metal on metal can be heard. Before I step into the open doorway, I spot a long chain hanging from a wire strung from the back of the house to the shed. At the end of the chain is a dirty red leash, its ragged end on the ground. By the back step, there's a wide plastic bowl that's been tipped, bits of kibble strewn in the dirt, and a steel water bowl floating with dried leaves. While I take in the tethered life Lucky escaped, the grinding within the building goes on, pausing to idle, then starting up full-throttle shrill again. Clouds form and pass. My hair grows an inch. Winter warms to spring, and still I can't move. Can't walk to the door and say, "Hey, I found your dog." Can't turn and walk back to the car, pick up the dog, and take him home, damn the consequences. I wonder how much it would cost to ship a dog out west to Mama. She needs a dog. I've heard that the presence of dogs can heal depression, ease loneliness, that sort of thing. Like Beckett does for me.

"Hey."

I didn't notice that the machine noise stopped, didn't hear the man's approach, or even see his shadow on the ground in front of me. Now I take this all in, along with his bright clean face, not at all the grizzled, straw-sucking hillbilly I imagined.

"Can I help you?" he says, twisting his hands into a stained yellow cloth. The sleeves of his Happy Face T-shirt have been torn off and the knees of his jeans are gone. He might be twenty-five.

"You have a dog?" I jab a finger at the leash's raw edge.

"Dante," he says.

This takes a moment to register. "Your dog's name is Dante?"

"I know, right?" His grin creases into his left cheek. "He's a very cool dog. We thought about Balzac, but..." This is obviously a line that has made people laugh, but when I don't respond his expression shifts. "Why?"

"Where's your dog now?"

He stares wistfully at the broken lead. "He's been gone a couple of days. We've been up and down these roads all— " He stops, gives me a sharp look. "That why you're here? You've seen him?"

"Is he black with a white upside-down heart on his chest?"

His face bursts wide open and then shuts down like a window slamming. "Is he—?"

"He's fine," I answer quickly. "Just a broken leg. One bone. Clean break."

"You found him?"

"I hit him."

"Oh." He's clearly at a loss for how to take this. He takes a couple of quick steps toward me, and I take one back. "Where is he?" He's worried, not angry.

Indicating the leash, I say, "You keep him outside?"

The young man laughs. "Can't keep him in. Something wild in him, you know? I take him for runs twice a day to try to work it out of him; rigged up this mess here so he could run a bit more. Back and forth at least." He sweeps one arm toward the back of the shed, where I see the beginnings of a wire fence. "I was building a big pen for him when he ran off." A wide smile showing a row of even teeth takes over his face. "Where'd you say he was?"

"At the vet's. I can go get him now."

"So?" Norah asks as I close the car door in slow motion. "Is this where he lives?"

"Yes," I say. "This is his home."

"Are you crying? Why are you crying? Brett. Brett honey, why are you crying?"

13

I've stopped writing poetry. Sometimes I still eat the right food. Sometimes I drink the juices and smoothies and not the coffee. My stomach won't calm down. I'm trying, really trying to be good. The blackness beyond the hospital doors is simply fear, I've decided. I just have to get a grip.

After delivering Dante to his owner, I find Cole already awake and on the ottoman, working out the chords to some sad-sounding song. Beckett on his cushion, perked his head up when I came through the door, but didn't rush to greet me.

I come to them, snuggle into the sliver-sized place beside Cole, letting the warmth of him seep in through my heavy pants. With his head tilted toward the guitar's body, Cole continues to work his fingers along the strings.

"Thank you," I venture, not directly into his ear, but close enough for him to hear over the music.

He thumbs all the strings at once, creating a discordant, irritated and irritating twang. "You're welcome." He doesn't look up. "Now can I work on this song?"

"Of course." I struggle to keep the hurt from my tone. "Cole?"

He makes a flat sound through closed lips. Drumming his long fingers on the side of the guitar, his foot keeps time to something I can't hear.

I bring my hand to his cheek and hold it steady even though he flinches at my touch. "I don't want to make any more mistakes. I think I…" I take a hard breath. "I think I love you, Cole."

His response is a reverse response, like spring runoff sucked back up the mountain.

"I've never been so sorry in my life. I have no excuses. None.

Please, Cole, look at me. Remember me." I stroke his head, his soft head, my words blurring in my mouth.

Those long fingers wrap around my hand, pull it off his head, and place it in my own lap. His brow buckles like a belt.

"Why don't we just make love? We can, you know."

He stands in one motion, sending his guitar bonging to the floor. The look he gives me stops my blood, so full of pain and something else that looks too much like hatred to bear. I bend over, pick up the guitar, and set it on its stand. If we just touch each other, seek out those sweet spots we know so well, we have a chance of beginning again. I could make him feel good, erase those lines around his mouth and replace them with kisses, lots of kisses.

He's gone to the kitchen where he opens and closes, opens and closes, the fridge, creating a rhythmic percussion of jars and bottles. I go to the bathroom for a hot shower. Letting the water course down my body, I undo my braid and shake out my hair, and stand under the scalding water until it runs cool. No Cole parting the curtain, no smooth strong hands on my buttocks, their calluses catching just enough to arouse me. Just me with my empty breasts and lonely bum. He's gone by the time I towel off and return to the living room.

He leaves behind Beckett's accusing stare.

I lie on top of the duvet, the damp towel still around me, my hair stuck to the pillow. I drift into a brief sleep where a blond boy plays at the edge of the lake with a small black and white creature. When I come closer, the creature swells into massive proportions, eclipsing the small boy who runs off into the water and vanishes. The creature turns its tail to me and lifts its hind end.

It's dawn when I awake to Cole's face hovering over me, a gentle tug of the towel from my body, and a fleece blanket floats down. Moist lips press my temple. His eyes steady as a cat's but without reproach. He puts a hand to my cheek and lets it rest there.

"Cole," I whisper, but he slides his hand down and across my mouth.

"Shush," he says and brings his face so close I feel the prickle of his night's beard before I drift back to sleep.

Cole is chopping something red—a pepper or a tomato. "Why don't you tell me a happy memory?" he says without looking up.

Goldie, squatting in the garden, her small hands digging, sun in her hair, Daddy there in rolled-up sleeves, patched jeans, one eye tracking her movements, dug-up twitch grass and dandelions dying between the rows. But I don't want to talk about them or that late summer day, because whenever I try, something pricks my windpipe. And if I fast-forward to the temples at Khajuraho with their pink and gray and cream-colored stone sculptures of endless pleasures, even if I don't say Mark's name, he'll be there in the story, and I don't want him in the room with us.

Cole is waiting. The *chop chop* has stopped. Through the window, which is opened just a crack, comes the *swish swish* of cars in the slushy half-winter afternoon.

"I used to have fun with my cousin Dylan," I say. "Aunt June named him after Bob. My other cousin is Donovan, after Leitch."

"I know, Brett. You've told me all about your aunt June and her groupie days. Actually." Cole pauses, looks to the steamed-up window. "I'd like to know about you."

"We went down to the lake to launch some little wooden boats we'd made," I say. "They got pulled away into the lake so fast." Dylan's hand on my back, his smile on my face, the two of us crouched at the shore…

"Do you ever think about going back to the mountains?" He lowers the blade but doesn't start cutting. "I know it must be hard. But you never talk about the good things. There must be something…?"

"I always loved spring when the snow melts and the streams turn wild." The ice on this lake is too thin yet for the fishing huts. They'll be out in January, guys freezing their asses off hoping for fish that probably shouldn't be eaten.

"But what about your mom? Don't you miss your mom?" He says this with a studied casualness, as if I'm to believe there's no weight to the question. As if he'd asked when was the last time Beckett went for a walk. He starts again to chop. Red on the white cutting board.

"I've missed her since I was eleven years old. Can we talk about something else? Like, why don't you tell me a happy memory? What's *your* happiest memory, Cole?" I'm itchy, as if sand is caught between muscle and bone.

Cole begins to talk, something about fishing with his dad in Algonquin Park, or maybe it's the smell of wood smoke or how he balanced a canoe on his head. I'm standing at the window watching two homies swagger by on the sidewalk below. Pot smoke wafts up like skunk tang through the window's open slit.

I will let you love me.

But the itch has turned to a burn and Cole's voice drones on about a pair of loons disappearing and him fearing they'd drowned only to turn up on the other side of the lake what seemed like hours later.

"Brett, are you okay?"

"I'm going to be sick." I lurch past him to the bathroom where I drop to my knees on the cold floor.

Cole comes and gathers my hair, holding it at the back of my neck. My gut cramps again, jerking my whole body, but nothing comes up.

With his palm on my forehead, he pulls me back to rest against his leg. "It doesn't feel as though you have a fever," he says. "What have you eaten?"

Last night I ate a spoonful of the rice, but it tasted like mold. "Not much," I admit. Looking into that white bowl full of chlorine-scented water, I think about goldfish and other small dead animals making their journeys through the labyrinth of pipes out to open sea. "I do want to be happy," I say quietly and this time I'm sure I mean it.

"Have the surgery, then."

I pull away from his leg, but he's still holding my hair and I jerk back. "You know?"

"Know what?"

He lets go of my hair and I wrap it in my hands, sit back on my heels. "That I'm considering not going through with it?"

Cole rubs his own stomach, around and around the way pregnant women caress their swollen bellies, and a slow smile moves his mouth. "You have no idea who you've been living with, do you?" He stands, offering me his hand.

The nausea has passed, leaving in its wake only empty space, as if I have no middle part. I go with Cole, holding his smooth, solid hand, back into the kitchen. His pile of chopped tomatoes has sprung a watery red river from the cutting board, along the counter and onto the floor. While he wipes up the juice, I begin to read from the boxes on the shelf opposite. Organic, pure, wild—ginger, chaparral, red clover, Pau d'Arco. I haven't had a cup of any of these, nor put one vegetable into the Vitamix, and I haven't brewed one pot of coffee, for many days. In fact, the mere thought of coffee makes me want to throw up again.

I put my hand on the small brown paper bag that Mel gave me and roll back the edges. "When you were researching herbs that heal cancer, did you come across raspberry leaf tea?"

"Not that I recall," Cole says, pushing the red mass into a saucepan with the dull side of the big knife. "Why?"

"Mel gave me this tea, and I thought maybe somehow, he knew."

"You haven't told anyone at work? Don't you have to book some time off?"

I drop my face into the bag and inhale. It smells like all the other herbs, like grass after a fire.

"I guess so," I say, my eyes roaming to the calendar. "It's

scheduled for just before Christmas. Wouldn't that make a nice present? I could wrap it up in shiny red paper, with a bow and everything."

"It's not funny, Brett."

But my laugh has sparked his and we are chuckling in earnest. He brings his tomato-red hands to my face and I grab them, rubbing them all over my cheeks and into my hair. When he tries to lick my face, I pull his hands down my front, under my shirt. Tomato juice leaks into my pants and onto the floor. I scoop a handful of tomato mush from the pot and rub it into the soft bristles on his head, both of us laughing from way down deep.

It's good. Really good.

I open my mouth and suck his sweet wet fingers all the way in.

After we've loved each other with careful, tender strokes and kisses, and I'm lying on my belly, hands folded under one cheek, Cole takes a pen and connects the freckles on my back.

"The Big Dipper is easy," he says. "Done."

The pen tip tickles as it searches my back for stars.

"Aha," he says, victorious and proud, the pen skipping across my skin. "I can make all of Ursa Major."

"Get out," I laugh, rolling onto my back.

"Aw, you just squashed the baby bear."

Only that one time have Mel and I had a bear. There was so much blood the entire road was stained red. *Mkwa*, said Mel when we'd turned on to County Road 26, but when we stood over that shimmering black body, he corrected himself: *Mkoons*. The bear wasn't even a year old.

14

I keep thinking about my mother. In the years after the fire, she flickered through Aunt June's rooms like a celluloid home movie. She might have said goodbye from Aunt June's front step. Or maybe I left in the middle of the night and hitchhiked to Castlegar. Maybe I walked most of the way under the inverted bowl of breaking sky. I could have left a note. What is certain is that we didn't have some tearful farewell embrace. She didn't put her hand where my heart should be and say, "I'll always be with you." Maybe Mama was sleeping that morning when I left for good. Maybe I did leave her a note that said, *I'm sorry*. Maybe I even signed it *Love, Brett*. Now, I like to imagine that I kissed her damp forehead and slipped that note under her pillow. I probably just shouldered my bag and closed Aunt June's front door with a quiet click.

The road from Nelson to Castlegar is mostly flat, especially once past Highway 6 where the mountains run north on either side of Slocan Valley. Sunrise is always late, sunset always early. There's more darkness than light, even in summer.

On the way east, I wanted to call. Every phone booth at every stop between Calgary and Toronto looked like a place where I might enter and emerge a superhero who could turn the world around. But I didn't and I wasn't.

Lately, she's with me all the time. She's like a wraith at the roadside on those dark nights when the hum of the plow makes my eyes go dry and long to close. I see her in the white-blue eyes of a sudden deer.

When the call from Aunt June comes, I'm almost relieved. It's a mild stroke, and Mama's able to walk, but she needs help. She's home and June is with her, but she's asked for me.

When I tell the guys at work, the smeared sun through the

office window blotches their faces as they nod and get back to their machines, slapping on their hard hats and heading out to the yard. Mel stays, leaning across the counter, his surprisingly smooth brown hand tapping the county map.

"Take the tea," he says.

This startles me. "For my mother?"

"Best if you drink it every day." He shoves himself away from the counter.

"Why, Mel? Why did you give me that bag?"

His eyes narrow, as though both scrutinizing me and deliberating.

"Just tell me. Please. What do you know?"

This makes him laugh. "Not a whole lot," he says and shuffles out to the yard.

My horoscope this morning says that I should try to be kind and considerate, and that I need to take care of my support system. When I read it, I set down my raspberry leaf tea, and look at my dog. He doesn't have opinions about what I should and shouldn't do. And he'd likely go on loving me even if I withhold his bacon-cheese treats. I'm fun, even if I'm not kind. I can be generous. I'm loyal. At least I used to be loyal. I can be loyal. How does one learn to be considerate? There should be a Kindness 101 continuing-ed course. All I want is to make love, do my job, and travel far. Cole complicates things with his love. He is my support even though he may leave when I'm better. He insists on going west with me. I told him I should go alone but he took my wrists in his hands, pulled them around his back, and held them there so that our bellies touched. "I'm coming with you," he said. So, he's coming with me now, just as a partner would.

Stroking Beckett's smooth white and black head, I say, "I will be kind. I will be better to Cole than I am to you." If I'm kind, he might stay a little longer.

As for my mother and my aunt, I will attempt to think before I speak. I will do my mother's dishes and mop her floor. I will bring her food. I'm ready to tell her that I am sorry. I hope she can understand.

Aunt June was crazy happy when she told me Donovan was coming home with his daughter and Dylan just couldn't wait to see me. I haven't seen either of my cousins for years. That last time it was all about the new cabin, and my rage at Mark was burning so hot that Dylan kept his distance. Everyone kept their distance.

I drink the last of my tea, rinse out my cup, and put on my work jacket, thinking all the while about kindness, how I might practice such a thing, and what might happen if I succeed.

When I bring Beckett to Norah and Josh's, it feels almost like old times. I watch her strain leaves, spices, and chunks of ginger from steaming cups of milky chai tea. It reminds me of the time Aunt June turned over a cup of cold tea she'd made for me. She clasped her hands in glee and told me how wonderful my future would be, how handsome men would be generous, and how I would travel the world gathering stories to tell. "My aunt June used to read tea leaves," I say.

Norah nods absently. "You know how I knew I would marry Josh?" she asks. "The day I met him he was wearing a green shirt." She fixes me with her clear eyes. "That morning, a chestnut blossom fell off a tree and right onto the sidewalk in front of me. A chestnut blossom. And…" She puts up a hand as if she's stopping traffic. "When I walked past the bridal shop in the mall, they were fitting the mannequin with a beautiful pure white gown with seed pearls."

"I think you make this stuff up," I say, not unkindly. "You met him in a bar, remember?"

Norah brushes this away. "I don't make it up. I study it." She regards me, her hands pressed together as if in prayer. A curtain of gray falls over her face, and, crossing her forearms on the table, she leans into them, creating a ledge for her breasts.

"We've been filling out forms," she begins. "Pages and pages of forms. We have to prove that we'd be decent parents. Prove that we have the means, that we are healthy, that we're not axe murderers. We have to provide letters of reference, have home inspections, dental records, have our asses checked…"

"You shouldn't worry. You guys are poster parents." Swinging out my arms, I add, "Look at what you've created. You both have good jobs, a beautiful home…no criminal records."

She slaps the table, making the teacup clatter against the saucer. "That isn't the point."

"But it's true," I insist. "They should give you a baby. You deserve one. After all you've—"

"That's the point. Exactly the point." Metal chair legs screech on the tile as Norah stands, making Beckett's head pop up from between his paws. "Any toothless idiot on welfare can make a baby. Nobody asks them to prove they're worthy."

"It doesn't seem fair," I agree.

"You just need to know how to copulate. Monkeys copulate; hell, worms copulate. But you also have to have a womb strong enough to hold them. To keep them in."

"Norah," I say, standing to reach for her. "You're right—it isn't fair."

The splatter of leaves forgotten, Norah rushes across the kitchen to reach for a drawer under the telephone stand. Her face puckers from an effort not to cry. "I want to show you," she says, yanking open the drawer. "Look." She shakes a folder filled with legal-looking forms. "They might as well ask me how many times a day I take a shit. They've come five times already and will probably come at least three more. I want a baby, Brett. I don't want a five-year-old kid who doesn't speak English. Am I a bad person?" She stuffs the folder back in the drawer and bangs it shut.

"You're not a bad person. Of course you want a baby who's like you. That's just normal."

"I'd be such a good mother."

"You would," I say, staring at the closed drawer. The alcove above the telephone is brilliant with red velvet bows and green cedar fronds. She hasn't overdone it; she never does. Just tasteful sprays of living things and real velvet—not that dollar store garbage. "You'll be an awesome mother." I reach out to hug her and she lets me.

"You'd be a good mother too, Brett." When I begin to pull away, she holds me tight, insisting, "One day."

"Let's not start, Norah," I say, prizing myself free.

From the kitchen I see that the family room is decorated for Christmas with clear glass ornaments and delicate white lights on a silver tree. I'm struck with a terrible urge to go get my boots and put them on the kitchen table. I remind myself of my horoscope. Kindness. I turn toward her silence. Norah lifts my braid and winds it around her wrist. "I haven't been a good friend," she says at last.

"Not always," I say, watching the twist and twirl of my hair in her hands. "But mostly."

"No. I had bad thoughts about you. I thought...things..." Her voice trails back into silence.

"What things?" Her hand is close to my face now. Surely if she is envying this horse's tail of mine, hellfire and damnation will be upon us anytime soon. This could be my final curse—waking up with my hair left on the pillow.

"You should have given me your baby." This is said in a whisper, more to my hair than to my face.

My baby. "Norah, god, I didn't even know you then."

"But I thought it. That's the point."

"Thoughts don't hurt people. Having bad thoughts doesn't make you a bad person." I hesitate. "You were in pain."

"So were you."

Yes, I was. "But it *happened* to you. I *did* it."

"Doesn't matter." Norah's voice is so quiet I have to bend down to hear her. "I should never have those thoughts."

I picture removing my boots from her table, setting them back on the mat by the front door where all the boots and shoes are in precise twos, heels parallel. "You are forgiven, Norah. If I had a baby, I'd give it to you."

Her head jerks up. "No. No, it's not right. You shouldn't

give babies away." Dropping my braid, Norah takes a step back. "Some people do. When they have to." Her rage has softened into sadness. "I just hope they will."

"What kind of information do these bastards need in order to know what kind of person you are?" I slide open the drawer. "I'll write you such a kick-ass reference, they'll give you a basketful of babies."

With a gentle touch, Norah pushes my hand away from the drawer. "We've got that part covered," she says.

Our foreheads bump lightly as she closes the drawer and I turn. She has paused there as if considering, as if waiting. I want to kiss her, deeply, truly, kindly.

She straightens.

"Of course," I say, and Norah shoots me a quick glance.

"I don't need a basketful anyway," she laughs. "Just one." Her gaze drifts past me out to the playground. "Only one."

"I'd like to have a garden," says Cole, as if having a garden in our third-floor apartment is an option.

When I don't respond, he continues. "That guy who runs the Unity Café on Toronto Street wants to create a community garden."

I'm packing warm clothes for the trip west—fleeces, corduroys, gray work socks with the red stripe at the top. I love these socks. They remind me of Daddy.

"What do you think? Wanna get involved?" Cole is supposed to be packing too, but he keeps pausing to look out the window to ask me questions about gardens.

"You should pack your blue sweater."

"You must know a lot about gardens. Didn't your family have a big one?"

"Yes, we had a big garden." I see it now so clearly it spreads out inside my suitcase, and I want to tell Cole all about life on the other side of the fallen tree. "Goldie loved to peel back the leaves from the first bursts of corn and nibble the tiny, pebbled rows inside. Her name was Alex, have I told you that? But we always called her Goldie. Dad and Mama wanted strong names for us, names that could stand by themselves." I see her now, see Daddy, see Mama, see them in the garden, all of them alive, all of them happy. "Goldie liked to split open peas and run her tongue up through the center. And she'd pop cherry tomatoes, letting them squirt out her mouth. She liked to run around naked. I can see that little monkey squatting beside the river waiting for tadpoles to turn into frogs." I feel Cole's listening and it warms me, loosens something tight inside. "The squash survived that year, its long crazy full-leafed paths snaked away from the house and up into the trees. They dangled from the branches like Christmas ornaments. But the corn dried right on its stalks from the heat of the fire. After we moved to June's, our neighbors harvested what they could and brought the vegetables to her place in town."

"Tell me more," says Cole.

"I couldn't eat the vegetables. All of them tasted like fire. I only ate crackers and a little cheese. But the cheese tasted like glue, and not the good kind, either, but the kind that's made from dead horses." I stop. The images in my open suitcase have pixilated into things I don't want to see.

Cole speaks in a whisper. "What about your mom? Did it bring you closer?"

"I never saw her eat a thing," I say. "Mama didn't eat. She walked." I stir the insides of my suitcase, one wide circle to blend them into one pile. "Aunt June says she can still walk, but she's using a cane." I pick up a denim shirt and shake it out. With a short laugh, I say, "That should be interesting—in that small cabin of hers with all of us there." I lay the shirt on the bed and pull out a pair of jeans. Sensing Cole's stillness, I turn to find him staring out the window. "Come on," I say, my horoscope coming to mind. "Toss me some clothes. I'll help you pack."

When his drawer sticks, Cole gives it a sharp yank. His

T-shirts and underwear jump and out pop his boxers with the little red devils. Those devils look like lost children on the floor, faded and forlorn.

"Cole," I say, squatting to retrieve the boxers. "You still have these."

"Of course," he answers absently, but I hear the gap before he says, "You okay?"

"I bought these for you."

"Yes." He's being cautious. I can understand why.

The little devilish faces grin with their pitchforks aimed in every direction, including at me, except on the ass which is so worn the devils are almost blanked out. "You like them?" I ask, giving the boxers a little shake.

"I guess."

"They're stupid, aren't they?"

Cole is silent.

"I mean, really, what was I thinking? Hot Stuff? What a cliché."

"Brett, come on. We were going at it like rabbits then. It was our joke. It made us laugh, remember?"

"That was five years ago."

"Six this spring," he says. "June twenty-second."

"You remember the date we met?"

"A week before my birthday. You had on that black blouse with the lacy cuffs. No makeup." He points to my left breast. "And your braid hung down there. I kept thinking how good you'd look with your hair all messed up."

Burying my face in his underwear, I breathe in the faint smell of chocolate-scented body wash mingled with laundry-soap lemon.

"You remember what *I* was wearing?" His question has a laugh in it which I don't echo.

"Your green work shirt. Green apron. Your underwear elastic showed above your jeans."

"Could be. I haven't a clue what I was wearing. Pretty sure we both had other things besides clothes on our minds."

"Yeah, getting them off."

That sound like pebbles rolling in honey, that's the sound of his laugh.

"Throw them over here." Cole opens his hands. "We might need them."

We. We've been laughing again. We've been making love, tender as spring grass, as if either of us might be crushed under too heavy a hand. We've been saying *we.* As if we are a couple again. As if we have a chance. As if that Bali calendar isn't still pinned above my desk.

I fold the faded devil underwear and nestle them in beside my own underthings.

"Have you moved the date?" he asks.

I nod, considering the path his thoughts must have just taken—following the images from boxers on the floor, my heels in the backs of his knees, to my vagina and then to its disease, and that dark unseen place that's about to be removed. He's witnessed my flip-flop from resistance to acquiescence and back again too many times to not know how relieved I am to have to postpone the operation.

"They gave me till the end of January." It feels like a gift. I told that woman who thought I didn't want to have surgery because my husband wouldn't like it that I didn't know when I'd be back from caring for my mother, even though I have a return ticket. She said, "This can't wait forever," as if I thought it could. As if she could read my mind with its notion that if I could postpone my trial date, the cop wouldn't show up and the cancer would get bored or tired of waiting and just vaporize. It'd get thrown out. I'd be acquitted.

She booked a date, and said, "Don't play with fire."

15

Mama's hair has blossomed silver-white. Dust and ash halo her head in the afternoon sun. The right side of her face sags slightly and her mouth droops but not as drastically as I'd feared. She didn't come to the door. It was Aunt June, full of old-lady bustle, who took our coats and bags. In Mama's small cabin, vanilla-cinnamon baking overlays the smells of cedar and wood stove fire.

The four-footed chrome cane with a curved handle beside Mama's chair captures my attention. My heel bumps the door. My hands ache for the warmth of Cole's hand or the handle of my suitcase, but they hang by my sides, hurting like frostbite.

"Mama," I say, shoving myself into the room.

She nods, one half of her mouth lifting into a smile. She says, "My world traveler." She sounds drunk.

Cole steps forward, leans in to hug her. "So good to finally meet you," he says, and June says, "Aren't you a fine-looking young man?"

Mama pats him on the back as he begins to straighten, but then her hand stops moving and she holds it there, firm on his shoulder, peering into his face. Cole is used to women staring at him, but something in my mother's gaze seems to unsettle him. He offers a wary smile, hovering half-bent at the waist. Patient as always.

"You," she says, squinting. "You," she says again, less sure, still holding him captive in that awkward stance.

I step in beside Cole. "Mama," I say. "This is Cole, Mama. He's my—"

"Friend," Cole finishes.

"Cole?" Mama asks, confused. "But—"

"It's okay, Mama," I say quickly. "You've never met him before."

She releases him and sinks back into her chair, turns to June. "Is there tea?" she asks as if she hadn't just lost her bearings.

We sit in a kind of rectangle, half in the kitchen, partly in the living room, and the conversation moves from snow to the effectiveness of plows in the mountains and how with all the rapid melting whole roads get buried in an instant, to how there are no jobs and how all the young people coming through the valley look just like the ones avoiding the draft fifty years ago. "Like your daddy." Mama sighed. "All that hair."

Again, she fixes a glassy gaze on Cole, who runs a hand over his new crop of short curls.

Aunt June puts Mama's pipe in her right hand and Mama lifts it with effort, clamps it unlit between her teeth, takes a couple of fake puffs, and then sets it down. "You look like someone," she says, which makes Cole chuckle. "Do you smoke?" she asks him.

"No, ma'am," Cole says with a warm smile. He wants her to like him. She seems confused, as if trying to place him.

Tipping her head to the good side, Mama says, "I went to a fortune teller on Baker Street. Before this." As she turns her palm face-up, her laugh is loose in her mouth. "She said my hands were like wood and fire." Fixing me with her left eye, she continues, "I don't know what the hell that means."

"What else did she say?" Cole asks this from where he perches on the edge of the kitchen counter, his hands braced behind.

"Oh, I don't remember," Mama says, shifting in the chair's deep cushion. "It's just a crazy web. Who could read this anyway?" With her left hand, she picks up her other one and turns it over. She's right—her palms are laced with crisscrossed roads; anyone would get lost.

The rasp of Aunt June clearing her throat brings our attention to her. With her back to the sink, her hennaed hair blazes in the late sun. "Dania is very good. She *sees*. Tell them what she saw, April. Go on, tell them."

Mama's body sighs deeper into the cushions, the right side listing. "She said something about me being grounded."

"Grounded?" My mother is anything but grounded. Whatever may have tethered her to earth snapped the day of the fire.

"Not like that," Aunt June barks. "She meant stuck, held.
Unable to move. Not grounded as in rooted."

"No, no," says Mama. "She meant rooted." The *r* sounds like
w, which might have been comical, but it isn't. "I'm bound to
the earth. I have deep roots."

The spring Mama was pregnant with Goldie, I went up the
mountain behind the cabin in search of some sort of gift for
the baby. I'd been up the mountain with Daddy in search of
wild berries, morels, and puffballs, and to hunt grouse for
dinner, but never by myself. I was seven. I traveled the path I
knew along the ridge until it grew so steep, I could touch the
ground with my hands as I climbed. The world was elegant
larch with its bright green drape of moss, spindly pine, and
poplars clattering their new yellow-green leaves. I was searching
for a chunk of soft moss or a fossiled rock to put in the cradle
Daddy had built. Instead, when I stepped off the ridge and into
the dark cool under the pines, what I found was the bleached
skeleton of a small bird.

June told us that Mama naps a lot since the stroke. One of
the boys' beds has been brought from town and set up in the
south-facing window for Mama so she doesn't have to climb
the ladder to the loft, which is where we'll sleep while we're
here.

She sleeps now, one eye open a slit, the side of her mouth
gaping. The cool sun blanches the pale skin of her face.

"Lots of vitamin C and D should bring her back faster,"
Aunt June whispers at the sink while we prepare tea. "The
moon's in Sagittarius, which is good for her rehab."

My look must be blank because she flashes me an indulgent
smile and continues. "It's all about activity, variety, and mobility.
Isn't that the best? And you're a Taurus so you've got the tenacity to drag her along."

"That's a good thing?" Cole has joined us. He puts a hand between my shoulder blades, which settles some ragged feeling I haven't been aware of until this moment.

Aunt June laughs in a way that makes me start, all throaty and girlish. "Oh, you know Brett. She's like a dog with a bone."

She's flirting with my man. I step back from the sink, slopping boiling hot tea onto the floor planks. Neither of them seems to notice.

Mama sleeps in the bed with its carved wooden headboard that I crawled into, smudged, dazed, and suddenly an only child, twenty-six years ago. The same bed where, a few months later, I became something else: a lover, a beloved, a nymph; Dylan's Lolita.

Setting the cup on the tiny table at her bedside, I touch her shoulder. She wakes with a spastic jerk. "It's okay, Mama. It's me. I brought your tea."

Only one eye opens. I consider pressing her other eyelid up but am suddenly oarless. Mama has been damaged for almost three decades, but now she is debilitated. I owe her and I don't know how to pay.

"Can I help you sit up so I can plump up your pillows?"

"Don't talk like that," she says, slightly slurred.

"Like what?"

"Like I'm stupid or old." She struggles to sit up, waving me away as if I were a bug or a bad smell.

I drag a chair from the kitchen table, pull it up to her bedside, and wait for her to reach for the tea I've prepared just the way she likes—heated pot, milk in the cup first.

Life has death at its tail. Not one of us gets out alive, so why do we mourn when a death simply means that they got to go home first?

It's because of this.

If it weren't for my hand, my meanness, which still lives sharp and insistent in me, and my self-centeredness, a trait for which I am often proud, my sister would be almost thirty years old. We would be scouring thrift stores for castaway gems to wear to parties where people drink homemade wine and play jazz as if they liked it. She would flop on my couch and bitch about her patients—how one collected toenail clippings, and another who obsessed over the exact number of times anyone used the word "essentially."

Mama regards the cooling cup. "Did you put in the milk first?"

"Of course. That was one thing you did teach me." I feel my shoulders sag. "I mean, it's one thing that *I* remember—how you take your tea."

Both her eyes narrow. She turns to the window, hoping, perhaps, for someone to arrive. Someone who doesn't remind her of everything she's lost.

"You'd better drink it while it's still warm. The milk is really cold."

She frowns at this but doesn't face me. "You didn't want to come, did you?"

"I'm here," I say, some ancient heat rising in my chest.

"Please don't be like that," she says, turning to fix an eye on me. "You're all I have."

Now she realizes it. "What about June and Dylan? They're here." This feels like spitting, and I want to clamp my hand over my mouth to keep it from landing. Instead, I lift the cup and offer it to her.

"But you're my family," she says, taking the tea and setting it down with a shaking hand.

"So are they," I say, and follow her gaze back out the empty white window where the two stripped pear trees bend under the weight of snow.

"It's different," she says. But her attention is on something outside. A branch. The driveway. Anything but me.

"Here comes…" She hesitates. "Ed?"

"Cole, April," June says from the kitchen. "His name is Cole."

Mama's face screws up into a frown as Cole comes in the door with an armload of firewood, shaking off snow and stamping his boots.

"Ed?" Mama asks.

"No, April. Cole," repeats Aunt June. "His name is Cole."

Morning has slid down the mountain and arrived white and eager at the cabin. June went home last night after supper, temporarily relieved from her duties.

"It's Christmas Eve, Mama," I say when she asks me what day it is.

"I was making a sweater for each of you," she says.

"Each of who?" I ask. In a basket beside her is a coil of pale yellow, blue, and pink knitting. "I thought you said you were knitting scarfs."

"Goldie's was finished. Yours was half done. I spun the wool with Marion. It was so oily my hands stank of mutton."

The basket is a mess of hazy color, the fine wool hairs catching the morning light.

"It was blue, to match her eyes. With snowflakes. She loved that snowman Ed made. She wanted to make a snow baby."

I don't remember the snowman. "That was a long time ago, Mama."

She lifts out a ball of pale blue wool. "Feels like a week."

"I know," I say, reaching out to touch the soft wool fibers.

Mama speaks in a low monotone, as if reading. "In some South American country men make flutes out of the leg bone of their wives." She squeezes the ball, one hand barely making an impression. "After they're dead."

I know this story. "A *quena*. It's folklore, Mama."

"No, it's true. I should have asked for his, what's it called? Femur? Humerus?" She snorts softly. "No, not humorous."

"Tibia. The story says it was from her tibia. But real *quenas* are made from clay or wood, sometimes bone, a bird's bone, though. Like a condor."

"I should have kept a piece."

It hurts to watch Mama struggle to straighten in her chair, but I have to resist the urge to adjust her cushion.

"Two. One from each of them."

She drops the wool into her lap.

"Mama."

With her left hand she pushes a lock of fallen hair across the right side of her forehead. "I should have learned to play the flute." Her hand floats down to rest on the difficult one. "But now it's too late."

"Aunt June told me the doctor says if you do your exercises you could regain full use of everything."

"I always wanted to be musical."

"I remember you singing. You sang all the time. I loved your singing."

"Cole plays guitar?"

I nod. "He writes beautiful songs. He's in a band."

"Ed played in a band. He played at Multifusion with Ross."

"I know, Mama. I was there." Daddy was so handsome with his long coppery hair, his crazy big smile, and Mama swaying in front of the stage holding Goldie wrapped up in her shawl.

The cabin darkens like rain coming, but outside Cole is bent to the snow shovel, puffs of steam sparkling around his face.

When my mother fixes her good eye on me, I have to again hold myself back from lifting that right eyelid.

"It was my pipe."

"You want your pipe?" I glance around the crowded room.

She makes a gesture as if brushing away a wasp. "The fire," she says, and the stuffing goes out of her. She deflates into the cushions—her cheekbones, collarbones, even the bones in her fingers poke through the skin. The fuzz of her white hair against the chair back gives her a Renaissance-like halo.

"You think—?"

"My Brett," she says. This is the first time she's spoken my name and it sounds like "bread."

"Mama, no, it's not your fault."

Only one eye leaks tears. "You knew, didn't you? You hated me."

"*Hated* you?" I drop to my knees and put my head in her lap. The hardness of bone against my cheek registers through the cloth of her denim skirt. "Your pipe didn't start the fire, Mama. It wasn't you." The room itself seems to hold its breath while I wait for her response to my head being on her legs. She shifts. And then the weight of her palm registers, her fingers in my hair.

"Like when you were small," she says, her voice blurred.

Withdrawing from the bony warmth of her lap, I grasp her pale hands. "I missed you." I lift both hands to my mouth. "It felt like I lost you, too, in that fire."

"Everything was lost," she says, her gaze roaming out the window, past Cole in his dark-brown jacket, to the patch where the two bare fruit trees stand.

"Not everything, Mama. I don't believe everything was lost."

"You don't hate me?"

"How could I hate *you*?" I set down her hands into her fragile lap and push back into a squat. "I'm the one to blame."

"You were so little," she says, with that same faraway look. "How could anyone blame you?"

"Because I'm still alive, Mama."

This makes her go still for a long moment. Every fiber of me begins to hum with urgency to name it, to speak, to confess. But how can I tell her without the cabin's beams letting go and cracking down on both our heads?

"I was mean to Goldie."

"Of course." She offers me a sad half-smile. "That's what sisters do. June is still mean to me." She half-laughs and stretches out her good hand to pat my head. "You were ten."

"Eleven. I was eleven. And I pushed her." My arms wrap my knees in a fierce hug. I begin to rock.

"Oh." Mama's hand flips up in the one gesture of dismissal she makes so well. "Children push each other."

"No, you don't understand. She was in the closet because of me." This sounds to me like yelling, but my mouth is buried in the cloth of my pants.

"Brett."

I look up to find her face fixed, no imbalance, clear and direct.

"She loved that closet. It was her place."

In my mother's sleeping loft with its long horizontal window to the meadow, Cole and I make silent precise love so as not to squeal the boards over Mama's bed below. This internal coupling results in an orgasm that pretty much annihilates me. Containing it is like containing a bomb going off in a tank.

The moon is an eyelash in the black mountain sky, the stars so dense they mirror the snow below. Because Cole is nearest the window his profile is softly illuminated. His eyes are open.

"Cole?" I whisper.

His response is more moan than murmur.

I touch my fingers to his lips. "I can't bear it."

"Hm?" The vibration of his "hm" is oddly comforting.

"She thinks she killed them." My fingers ride with his nodding head. "They always thought it was from the stove pipe. Creosote catching fire. But maybe her pipe *did* start the fire."

"Hm."

"But we got out—Mama, Dad. Me."

"Hm."

I remove my fingers from his mouth and curl them into a tight ball which I cover with my other hand. "Goldie didn't."

Cole rolls on his side but doesn't try to touch me. "I know," he whispers.

"Because of me." I just say it. Plain. Out loud. My words hover between us. I can almost see them. For a moment I believe I can snatch them out of the air and stuff them back in my mouth. Instead, I wait for the gavel and the verdict, my eyes open. I won't go to the gallows with a bag over my head.

After a moment's silence his response comes quietly. "I know that's what you believe."

"It's true, Cole." I will have to prove not my innocence, but my guilt. "Please don't make this any harder—"

"Oh, Brett, baby," he says, one hand appearing from beneath the covers and covering both of mine. "My big brother beat the crap out of me regularly. I used to hide in the hay loft. It could have burned. He pushed me out the window into the manure pile and I broke my leg. It could have been my neck."

"But it wasn't. You're here. She's not. She just wanted to be near me, and I... She just wanted to—"

"Come here, baby." Cole pulls me tight to his chest. I let him hold me but the comfort is cold. Both he and his brother are alive. They slap each other on the back and hurl benign insults the way men do, pretending that they're just joking and not locked into a pissing contest.

Mama still loves her porridge. Aunt June calls it gruel. I sprinkle it with toasted almonds, currants, and pumpkin seeds.

"Maple syrup or honey?" I ask my mother, who has risen from the deep cushions of her chair and seated herself with less difficulty than when we arrived, at the kitchen table.

"Maple syrup." She raises her eyebrows as if this would allow her to see up and into the bowl on the counter. "No nuts. Not yet."

Scraping the bits from her cereal to divide them between Cole and me, I resolve to pay attention, just as I do when I'm on the lookout for bent road signs, dead animals, potholes, or the sudden jamming of the sand mix. Like that. With the same alertness and attention to detail—my mother's mouth a new route, full of detours and unexpected turns.

The sound of an engine arrives through the muffle of heavy snow. Mama cranes her head to see. It's a dark green pickup with a dent on the passenger-side fender the size of a young deer.

"Dylan," breathes my mother as if it's the folk singer himself.

My throat closes. My eyes close. No sound aside from the last thud of my heart as it shuts down.

When the heavy wood door swings open, Mama pushes herself to standing and June flies across the room to embrace her son. His coat is open, his jeans tight, and his eyes a creamy brown. His shirt collar pushes up a fringe of his still thick hair. A pair of reading glasses pokes out of his shirt pocket. He's on me fast, both arms lifting me off the floor in a suffocating hug.

"Oh, you are fancy, little cuz," he says as he sets me down, his full-lipped smile wide and warm. "Fancy, fancy."

I'm wearing blue jeans and a turtleneck sweater, no makeup, and a single braid. "You're full of shit," I say, forcing a laugh. "This is Cole," I say, gesturing across the room.

"A merry old soul," says Dylan, and Cole's forehead wrinkles a little as he extends his hand.

"Cole Laird," he says. "Pleased to meet you."

"Laird of the manor! Good Scottish name. Or Nat King..." Dylan gives Cole a once-over and shrugs. "Guess you're too young to know him."

Cole slides his hand out of Dylan's grip. "I know who Nat King Cole is."

"Cole is an old soul," I say.

This creates a flutter in both Mama and June that rises and settles with an air of satisfaction.

Dylan shoves his fingers into his jeans pockets. "So how do you like the cabin we built for our aunt April? Real fancy, eh?"

Reflexively, Cole glances around the small space and nods. "It's very cozy," he says.

Mama presses her hands together as if Gandhi has just arrived. "Care for some tea?" she says, barely slurring, and looking up at him with eyes I've not seen for decades; alive and keen.

"I don't want you to fuss," he says.

"I've missed you," Mama says as Dylan bundles her into his arms as if she's a child. Mama is nearly six feet tall. She bends her neck to put her temple to his cheek.

Looking right at me, Dylan smiles a toothy smile and says, "I missed you too."

June leans close to my ear. "He was here last week."

"You're lookin' real fine, Auntie. Almost good as new already, eh?" But he isn't looking at her; he's looking straight at me, his eyes all jolly. He's forty-six and he kisses my sixty-three-year-old mother not as one would an aunt, but as one might kiss an old lover.

Aunt June is already filling the black iron kettle to put on the woodstove. I join her, turning my back to the miniature melee, and reach for the bag I've tucked into a row of glass jars neatly labeled with the Latin names of local herbs: *Chamomilla, Hyssopus, Rosa canina, Ulmus rubra.*

"What'cha got there?" Aunt June presses her hip to mine, peering into the brown paper bag softened from dozens of rollings and unrollings.

"Just some herbal tea," I say, pinching some out to stuff into the silver tea egg I've brought with me.

"Obviously," she says, leaning over to give the contents a sniff. "But what kind?"

"Raspberry leaf." Swiping a towel from the rack I lift the lid of the kettle.

Aunt June's eyes narrow with eerie scrutiny. Cole insists that I tell them, but I haven't had the guts or the heart. I guess I'm out of internal organs. But June surprises me. She's smiling. "Helps with nausea," she says.

She's right, it has. A wave of understanding passes through me. Mel gave me that stuff when he could see that I wasn't feeling well. I thought he knew that I had cancer; figured his wise old native soul could see right into me. But, no, the puking was just puking. No skunk medicine. Just logic.

June pats my belly. "Good womb strengthener."

The kettle sends out a stream of vapor. I pour boiling water into the cups June has set along the counter. Soon I'll stop drinking the tasteless stuff. Soon I won't even have a womb. I'll be able to quaff a good glass of merlot once in a while. I miss drinking. The last time I had alcohol it ended up green and frothy in the toilet and I lost my boyfriend.

"Well then," June is saying. "This is the perfect time for a reading. We're all on the tip of the iceberg. Mercury's in retrograde so let's get our communication straight and clear. Big things are on the horizon and we need to be prepared."

"Oh, come on," says Dylan. "Do we have to?" He sounds like a five-year-old.

Aunt June spreads her worn tarot deck across the kitchen table. Her scarlet hair is a fire I could be warmed by. Its flames tip toward me as she bends her head in some silent invocation, her palms pressed together. When she looks up, I see how her pale blue eyes have faded with age.

"Choose a card," she tells Cole. She claims he gets to go first on account of his being the "guest," but I see the way she looks at him. The way I do, that's how, only I'm eleven years older than him, not forty plus. I can't help but wonder if this is who I'll become in thirty years.

As instructed, Cole hovers his left hand over the fan of cards. Abruptly, his hand halts, his middle finger crooks and descends on one card that looks precisely like all the other cards, and he slides it out. "This one," he says, and before June can stop him, flips it over.

"No," says June, snapping out a hand to stop him. But it's too late. The card is exposed. *The Lovers.*

Sighing, Aunt June slumps back in her chair. "All right then. We'll do a one-card reading. It *is* an important card. *The Lovers.* Sixth card of the Major Arcana." Her look is so intense she might as well be grabbing Cole by the crotch. "This card represents your inner lover," she continues. "Your deep soul beloved. Anima and animus together. Your yin and your yang. You understand?"

Cole frowns. "Sort of," he says. "I guess."

"It's about loving your masculine and your feminine sides. Balance. Deep inner bliss without need or greed. Love that comes from your one true heart." Spreading her fingers across her chest, June casts a besotted, beseeching look right at Cole. "This is who you are meant to be, Cole. You are coming home."

My cardboard heart begins to rip. One half, soaked with tenderness for Cole and his one true heart that has never failed me; the other half, blue with astonishment at how my aunt is behaving. She stays in her seat, but she is also crawling across the kitchen table toward him. Cole leans forward, genuinely trying to understand what's coming out of my aunt's mouth.

"You've lost him, Mom," says Dylan, giving her shoulder a hard squeeze. "Just tell him to marry my little cuz and they'll live happily ever after."

June swats at him. "Go on, then," she says. "Go chop some wood for your aunt April."

She doesn't react when Dylan slaps his palm on the table and pushes himself to standing, and doesn't seem to notice that he slams the door on his way out.

"Your turn, dear," Aunt June says to me, gathering the cards into a neat pile.

"I'm good," I say. "No need." I give the table's edge a little push so my chair slides backward. "What about Mama? Do a reading for her."

"She's had many turns." Holding me in place with her gaze, Aunt June shuffles the big cards. "Just choose one card, like Cole did. All's fair in love and war, as they say."

"You sure about that?" I say, but no one laughs.

"Here, just choose one card," she says, sweeping her hand across the table as a perfectly even row of cards fans out underneath.

I pick a card without hesitation, not because I'm sure which is the right card, but because the point is simply to choose a card. So I do. I push it face down toward my aunt.

"Oh," Aunt June says, both hands collecting over her heart. "Of course: *The Sun*."

There's a naked yellow-haired child riding on the back of a white horse, hands spread wide.

"You've both selected cards from the Major Arcana. These are significant times. Do you know what this card means, Brett?" Aunt June asks, her eyebrows lifted with almost comical emphasis.

"I'm going to buy a horse?"

She laughs as if humoring a child. "No, dear. When *The Sun* appears in a reading it's a very positive sign. It means that your plans, goals, and/or desires will come to fruition. Your relationships and self-knowledge are reaching maturity. It's a good time to begin something new. Everything is growing and there are celebrations ahead. You are well blessed. This is a time to be happy and give thanks." She takes a long, calm breath. "Health-wise, *The Sun* indicates good health and bright blessings." Her expression shifts into one of gravity. "*The Sun* can also indicate the birth of a child."

My stomach turns sour. Good health. The stove has suddenly blazed to life and I have to restrain myself from ripping off my clothes and running out into the snow. Cole's eyes burn holes in me. He wants me to tell June, tell my mother, *tell, tell, tell.* But I am good at not telling. If I can do one decent thing in this life, it will be not to burden my family with news of my disease and matrilineal dead end.

Cole puts a hot hand on my shoulder. "That sounds awesome. Good health, new ventures, blessings, happiness, mature relationships. What's not to love about that?" When he squeezes, his middle finger finds a divot between bone and muscle at the edge of my shoulder and begins to massage little circles. "I'm going to meet my inner lover and you're going to be happy. I like the way that sounds."

My cancer is my issue. Not Mama's, not June's, and not Cole's. When I wrote to Mama, I didn't mention it, nor did I speak of it on the phone. I wanted to leave it behind, at least for the time spent with my mother, but here in her home I feel the cramp of it deep in my belly.

I also keep secret this new longing I have to have her sing to me. She can't sing and she needs me. There was a time when she picked bits of glass and stone from a cut in my knee, mixed pungent herbs for poultices to bind my chest, pressed cool cloths to my fiery head, and rocked me back to sleep when my dreams teemed with pale, writhing creatures. Now my own belly teems with forces I can't control, and my mother has neither poultice nor lullaby.

Being confined in this small cabin makes me wish I could teach my heart to be still. At home I can appear as though I know what I'm doing—tough girl slinging dead things, driving big trucks, unassailable, untouchable, safe—but here, without distraction, I feel exposed, like everyone, including Cole, is onto me. I don't even have the distraction Beckett provides with his bright, eager eyes and his staccato yips. He's so easy to please—a ball launcher, bacon-cheese treats, and his rugs at the sides of the bed. I wish I were easy to please. Instead, I find myself longing for euthanasia. If I must stay alive, then I just want to hear my mother sing. It seems I want only what I cannot have.

Aunt June used to tell me, "Be brave, Brett. Your mama needs you strong." At least once a day for at least five years until I got the hell out of there. The thing is, although I did get the hell out, as far away as I could—first Toronto, then Europe, India, and Thailand—I continued to carry a nugget of brave in the hard shell of my heart. Carried it back and forth across the country, from apartment to apartment, and never unpacked it.

But here, I feel undone, cracked open. I don't feel brave and I don't feel strong. Is this what my mother's sudden frailty has done or is it because I am face-to-face with Dylan? I just want to go home. But I don't know where that is.

"Donovan's coming from Kelowna," Aunt June says, her mouth full of cranberry muffin. "He's bringing Amara."

"How old is she now?" I ask. How long ago did I receive that birth announcement? Eight years ago?

Holding a hand over her mouth to keep the crumbs in, she mumbles an age.

Cole laughs. "Eleven?"

Nodding, Aunt June swallows and reaches for a glass to fill with water.

Dylan stands by the front window, one hand resting on the ledge, the other in his jeans pocket, his eyes fixed on the rutted driveway. I want to stop looking at him, want to turn my head, chop wood, sweep the floor clean, plant a garden, bury the dead, but I just go on staring at his profile, the dark stubble, the rise and fall of his chest under the flannel shirt, the cinch of his belt.

When the door opens, a balding paunchy man in a navy-blue parka blusters in, shepherding a fair-haired waif of a girl. The tiny cabin bubbles with sudden activity and chatter. Bouncing in two quick steps toward Dylan, the girl leaps into his arms, and wraps his neck in a tight hug. His forearms form a seat for her, and the hand I can see pats her scrawny butt. I can't take my eyes off his hand, how it cradles her. Her legs are open with her feet knotted behind his back. The cabin floor tilts.

Cole has his hand out. "Cole. You must be Donovan."

"Call me Don," says my cousin, accepting the handshake. "This is Amara." He indicates the girl whose face is buried in Dylan's collar, his face obscured by her fine hair.

"Look, Uncle Dylan," says Amara, uncurling her freckled hand to reveal the browned husk of a milkweed pod, its white spider-silk blossoms clinging to its long split. "I saved this for you." She nestles her mouth behind his ear and whispers, "There's treasures inside."

Drawing his head back to look, Dylan removes one hand from her bottom to take it, and in doing so, shifts her a little to the side. Her pelvis tilts up, tucks into his side. Maybe she's unaware that she's just adjusted her sweet bits to keep contact. This isn't a new intimacy. When did it start with her? They hold on, each with one arm as if clutched in a tango, the sexiest dance on earth. Every Thanksgiving, Easter, and Christmas he gets a go at her, and she can't wait.

"Look," she says, squeezing the pod so its contents ooze out. "It's full of fairies."

Everything is shaking. The floor. The table. The chairs. All the glass jars on the open shelves, clattering against each other as the ground trembles and everything that isn't nailed down crashes to the floor. *No.* I put out a hand to steady myself on a chair back and clear my eyes. They talk and laugh, get "caught up," kissing Mama, hugging Aunt June, the prepubescent girl bouncing in Dylan's arms, her crotch against his belly.

From deep in my bowels, I dredge up my voice. "Why don't you put the girl down, Dylan?"

He swings around so that her back is to me, his expression a mixture of amusement and astonishment.

"I've never met her," I say by way of explanation. "I'm Brett. Your dad's cousin," I say to Amara as Dylan sets her down as gently as glass.

"So you're like a cousin's cousin?" she asks.

"No, get this," I said, dropping to one knee thereby putting myself between her and Dylan. "I'm your first cousin once removed."

"Removed?"

"Yeah," I say, taking both her hands. "But don't worry about it. We'll just be cousins."

For a moment she studies my face. "Okay," she says. "Or friends?" A flicker of a smile darts back to safety. Dropping her gaze to my hands, she says, "Your freckles are pretty."

"So are yours," I say.

With a delicate touch, Amara runs a finger along my arm, tracing an imaginary line between spots. She stops just above the elbow at the half-moon scar there. "What happened?" she asks, tapping it lightly.

"I got burned," I say. "When I was your age."

"Does it hurt?"

Stretching up and away from her inquisitive touch, I say, "Only when I press it."

Aunt June has conceded to Christmas enough to order an organic turkey from the farmers' market and do up a dinner with cranberries and sweet potatoes and parsnips. Since we missed her Solstice meditation, she's allowed a certain air of festivity on this day, contenting herself with its pagan proximity. Seven of us are crammed around a table meant for four, platters of turkey and vegetables set behind us along the counter and window ledge. The air is thick and wet from snow and woodstove and breathing.

I've managed to arrange the seating so Amara is between me and her father. Dylan coos to Mama, who is in the seat

closest to her bed. When I wiggle out of my fleece vest, Amara
reaches back to help me. Her smile seems to wish it weren't shy.
Asymmetrical freckles spread like the speckles of a sparrow's
egg across her nose and cheeks.

At the table, I think about the medicine wheel Mel gave me,
how he called it the "Indian Bible," and how each of its four
colors hold all the teachings one could ever need. Mama, with
her freshly fallen-snow hair, is in her rightful place at the north,
and June with her hair-on-fire is perfect in the south. But this
little girl shouldn't be sitting in the west, the direction of wis-
dom, fruition, and harvest.

I feel as if I am hiding. Maybe these people believe they are
seeing me, but while they converse with my relatively sane face,
I am deep in the forest chewing on my memories. Memories of
Dylan, who was the only one who saw me, who saw a beauty
in me, and who cared enough to touch me so that the pain
released, however briefly. I see his tenderness, his gentle hands
on Amara's shoulders. I see, too, how the pain of her mother's
leaving is diminished in his glow. I am sorry for hiding. I would
drop my mask if I could, to watch it shatter on the wood planks
of this cabin and skitter to the corners. But it is cemented to
my face.

After the meal, Amara sits on the blond plank floor, ar-
ticulating the arms and legs of a heavily made-up doll with a
pinched waist and sparkly purple bits around her meager hips
and pointy plastic boobs. On Amara's chest, thumb-sized
bumps show through her jersey. I might be the only one who
notices this, but I feel the strain and ache of them. There's no
stopping them and I want to lean into her ear to say that they
won't always hurt, but that the eyes of men will always land first
on them before they swivel to her face. And I want to tell her
also that they will be a great source of pleasure. My own breasts
burn a little.

She walks the doll toward me, her loose cross-legged posture
unbuckling and rising with the doll's movements. All my dolls
were burned. Even my Cindy doll who gave me the creeps with

her ever-open eyes. I wish my eyes were closed right now, because I notice that Dylan is watching not the progress of Amara's doll, and not even at the bulbs of her nipples, but at that open place between her legs. I can't really tell if it's happened yet. I can't know if Amara's loss has been deep and accessible enough for Dylan to have come to the rescue.

The doll spins in some hip-hop dance. Amara's freckled face is absorbed, oblivious to the attention of the adults who track her every fiber. Strands of hair hang like a wet mop over her forehead. In this cramped little cabin, everyone is sweating from the woodstove's heat.

I miss Mel. Everything with him seems so simple and quiet. I want to be driving trucks and sweating over asphalt and praying for creatures whose only crimes were to listen to the call of their own nature. I want to put my feet on the dashboard and ride deep into Indian country to eat dried moose with blueberries pounded in. I want to take Franny, Mel's wife, with us because she knows about plants. I want to be anywhere but here.

I watch this young girl with her pimped-up doll and think about the one I had. By the time I was ten, Goldie had taken over Cindy and I was glad of it. Cindy didn't seem to give my sister bad dreams. Goldie was a fearless, wild thing. Most of the time she ran around half-naked. But sometimes in the night, also like a young wild thing, she needed the warmth and safety of her big sister's body.

"Hey, Amara," I say, squatting down beside the girl. "Does your dad ever take you up the mountain?"

She shrugs one shoulder. "Sure."

"Does he tell you about trees and plants?"

She seems to be vaguely interested in this question. "Some," she says, looking up at me. "We live in Kelowna."

"I know. But all around are mountains," I say, making a wide sweep with one arm. "I work with an Ojibwe man who tells me legends about nature. I was just thinking about larch trees. Do you know about them?"

"They the ones that lose their needles?"

I shuffle closer. "That's right," I say. "Would you like me to tell you the legend?"

"Sure," she says, glancing around the stuffy room and stopping at Dylan. They exchange a private smile that snakes a current up my spine.

Mama, June, Donovan, and Cole lean in toward me like small children. I clear my throat and move closer to Amara, resisting the powerful urge to snatch away her doll and push it into the firebox.

"Many years ago," I begin, and Amara rests a light freckled hand on my thigh, her focus fixed on my mouth. "A big winter storm was on the way. A flock of birds were flying south for the winter. They asked the larch if they could shelter in its branches during the storm. The larch is a majestic tree and liked to admire its own reflection in the clear water of the lake." I pause to look out the window where the naked branches of a larch stand out dark against the snowy rise. Amara follows my gaze. I turn back to her. "It didn't want the birds to mess up its beauty, so it said *no* to the tired flock. It wanted to sleep for the winter and the birds would be too noisy. So the birds had to fly on to find another place to shelter from the storm." I stop for a moment to let the impact of this sink in. Amara's mouth hangs open in horror, her pale eyes threatening tears. "Creator saw this," I continue. "And because the larch refused to protect those in need, Creator made it lose its winter coat so that it would know how hard winters are."

Everyone is looking out the window at the bare tree, seeing it perhaps as vain and selfish, but also as a victim of disproportionate punishment. I draw in my breath. "And that is why, according to legend, every autumn the larch trees lose their needles."

"Couldn't that tree just say *sorry*?" Amara asks, her thin voice rising.

Dylan barks a laugh. "Guess not."

"It's a legend, dear," says Aunt June. "It's meant to teach you something."

"Creator sounds so mean."

"Life is mean," says Dylan. "Shit happens."

"Dylan," says Aunt June. "There are better ways to say that. Life moves in circles and waves. Life isn't mean, it just is. There is a gift in everything, even the bad things."

Donovan pushes himself from his perch on the counter and moves to the door. "I should go chop some wood," he says.

Amara's lost interest in her slutty little doll. Cindy did not have a stripper's costume over big tits and narrow hips or a gem-pierced belly button. Her eyes were scary, but they weren't half the size of her head and painted black and purple like bruises. I pick up the doll. One of her tiny stilettos slips off and lands in the gap between two floorboards.

"Uncle Dylan," says Amara, unfolding her legs to drop forward onto her hands. "Get Sabrina's shoe for me?" The change in her tone shocks me into letting go of the sexpot doll. She sounds like a simpering starlet.

Aunt June laughs her smoky laugh and Mama watches Dylan as if he's the prince who will make everything golden. Dylan drops to his hands and knees, grinning like a little kid, and begins to pick at the shoe wedged into the crack.

Retrieving the fallen hussy, I shake it at Donovan. "Why do you let her have a doll like this?" I demand of him who is pulling on his parka. "This isn't right."

"Of course it isn't," laughs Dylan, slick like oil. "Not for a truck driver like you."

They're preparing to leave, Dylan behind Amara, his fingers curled into the collar of her coat as he slips it up her arms, her leaning back so her head touches his belly. Donovan is kissing his mother, then Mama, then shaking Cole's hand.

"I'll go warm up the cars," Donovan says, jingling the keys off the hook.

"Let Dylan do it," I say, making both Dylan and Donovan turn. "I've hardly had time to talk to you," I say. "Let him."

"We can come back," says Donovan. "We're going to hang out with Dylan for a couple of days. We'll come up before we head home?"

The cabin air cramps around me. It tightens my face and shoulders. Now everyone's attention is on me. I could say it now, that I want to separate Dylan from the girl so I can whisper to her—what? That he'll drop you when you menstruate? That all this yumminess you feel "down there" is wrong? That sleeping with your uncle is bad? Tell her what? How? She's looking at me too, daring me, maybe. She'll say, "Uncle Dylan makes me feel good." Or whatever the hell I thought back then.

Grabbing my coat off the hook, I stuff my feet into my boots. "I'll come with you," I say. "I'll help you scrape."

As we head out, I shoot Dylan a hard glance.

"So what's up? Something's eating you, I can tell. I read people, you know. It's a gift." Donovan tosses the keys between his gloved palms.

"Really?" I say. Everyone, it seems, has the inside scoop—from Norah who sees signs in every loose thread and grain of salt, to Aunt June who insists all my woes are due to my Taurean bullishness, to Mel who hands me mysterious bags of dead plants, to Cole, who rubs his belly every month before my blood flows, to this asinine statement of my dear naïve cousin.

"You can read Dylan?" My hand grips the handle of the car door. Snow still falls sticky and weighted, coating his nut-brown hair until it appears gray in the half-light.

"Of course. He's my brother."

"Does he have girlfriends?" I ask too loudly. It's as if I have two sets of eyelids, like an alligator or a lizard, and the inside membrane closes when convenient. That inner membrane is a luxury I can't afford to use anymore.

Donovan opens the driver's door with a sharp crack of ice. "Why?" He laughs, but there's no humor in that laugh. "You think he's gay or something?"

It's my turn for a humorless laugh. "I don't know about

that," I say. "He's forty-six, surely he's had a girlfriend or two?"

Dropping hard into the front seat, Donovan jabs the key into the ignition. "Yeah, I guess. A couple."

"How old were they?" I expect he'll snap an accusing look at me, yell or at least protest my insinuation, but he keeps his eyes fixed on the steering wheel. I lean in, one arm across the car's roof, the other holding open the door. "*His* age?"

"She told him she was eighteen."

I smack the roof. "Fuck, Donovan! And he was what? Forty? Forty-five? How old *was* she anyway? Eleven?"

"Eleven?" Now he swings in his seat to stare at me. "No! She was fifteen." He propels himself up out of the car, knocking against me as he rises. His voice drops low, as if someone in this yard deep with wet snow and naked trees could hear him. "Mom spoke to her parents. The girl said he was just a friend."

The bones in my legs that I rely on to keep me upright are rebelling. My hand grips the zipper of Donovan's jacket. "You have to keep him away from your daughter."

"Oh." He looks relieved, happy almost. He's got this, apparently. "He'd never hurt Amara. She's his niece."

"You have to listen. Listen to me." With both hands I pull him close, smell burned coffee, eggnog, rum on his breath. "Don't ever, ever let them be alone together."

He covers my hands with his gloved ones. "Oh, they aren't. We're always all together when we visit." He's so sure.

"What about when you're asleep? Donovan, you have to hear me."

His eyes narrow. He can read people. "Something bad happened to you, didn't it? That's why you're acting this way." The seams of his gloves dig into the backs of my hands.

A fire springs to life in my head, so hot and bright I want to drop and roll in the snow. I snap away from him and his gloved reassurance. "That's what you think?" I stop, kick at the tire. A curved clump of gray snow releases from the wheel well. "Actually," I begin, gathering myself. "It didn't feel bad." I kick the tire again, but I got it all with the first kick. "But it was."

"What are you two on about?" Dylan is fast-tracking it from the cabin, his coat sleeves flapping like broken wings as he pulls it on.

The moon is cresting over the eastern range, a cup, a vessel, the edge of an ear. The snow has paused in its falling. Amara in her white fake fur coat with its pink-lined hood bounds like a young rabbit beside him.

"What has my big bro' done now?" Dylan asks.

He must have seen me grabbing at Donovan's jacket.

Dylan draws up beside us, stamping and huffing like an ungelded horse, his gaze flicking back and forth between Donovan and me. Amara yanks open the car door to extract the scraper and begins to push off the snow.

"Just giving him some sisterly advice," I say, but my voice is as frail as an old woman's.

"Oh yeah?" Dylan stares at his brother, his pupils contracting and expanding then contracting again. His irises have dark splotches like splattered paint. Beside the paunchy Donovan, Dylan could be his son. Even in his bulky coat, Dylan appears sleek and young.

Slinging an arm around my shoulders, he pulls me close. He smells of cloves and ginger. "You listen to Brett. She's always been the smart one in the family. The prettiest too," he adds, catching my neck in the crook of his elbow. "Fancy."

I duck out and away from his grasp.

"Come on, Uncle." Amara has tossed the scraper back into the car. She drags on Dylan's arm. "Let's go."

Amara isn't pretty. Perhaps she will be one day when her face has grown to accommodate her teeth and she acquires a bit of meat. Maybe she will blossom into beautiful and Dylan will be sixty or seventy and she will avert her gaze from his hungry eyes. But now her hollow-boned body bends to him like a stem to sun. Aunt June told me Amara lost her mother a different way—coming home from her first day of fourth grade, she found the house empty and a note in cursive. Becky needed time. She was sorry, but she couldn't be a good mother yet. Hoped they understood. She was in Peru. Medicine men. Healers. Shaman to call back her spirit. Two years have passed, and the jungle seems to have swallowed her whole.

Donovan opens the door to his car, but Amara says, "I wanna go with Uncle Dylan."

Donovan hesitates, glancing at me and then quickly away.

Swinging open his truck door, Dylan sweeps his arm in an inviting arc. "Your chariot awaits."

I watch Donovan watching Amara leap up into the truck. Without looking at me, he slides into his own front seat, slowly shuts the door, and puts the car in gear. Dylan's truck pulls out and the two vehicles bounce off down the lane as if Christmas has been such a grand time, as if Mama isn't half-crippled and alone, as if Aunt June isn't half-mad and alone, as if all of us are healthy and happy and merry, merry to all, as if they aren't leaving me standing ankle deep in an empty field with my cells eating away all the sweet pink bits, as if tonight Dylan isn't going to slip between Amara's unstained sheets and help himself, as if she won't open her legs and whisper, "I love you, Dylan." Maybe I should have screamed, torn open the car door, spilled the truth, and said it plain.

Cole is at the window. So still. We watch each other as the moon slides up the sky, pouring blue light onto the snow.

Feathers fly up behind the retreating car. I pluck a pin feather from my mouth, its fine hairs splitting. I spit, but more rise from the broken nest that is my heart. I want to apologize for everything. Cole waits for me, but I will take three rapid steps and let the swift cold current off the mountain lift me up.

I'm still here, sinking into the snow, waiting to be heard, waiting for my heart's latch to spring open, waiting to die, waiting for my mother to sing. I pull one boot, then the other from the suck of snow and move toward the figure of the man who seems to love me anyway, and who waits for me to come in from the cold.

The moon and stars have been swallowed into the night sky. Snow falls and falls, obliterating the runnels where my cousins' trucks came and went. When I climb the ladder to slide in under the duvet beside Cole, he puts a hand on my belly. I fold both my hands on top of his.

"There'll be a scar," I whisper into the dark.

He nuzzles into my hair. "I don't care."

"*I* do. Remember I told you how that nurse tried to reassure me?"

"That I wouldn't be able to tell?"

I nod. "Nothing about how I'll feel—only what it will or won't do for my 'husband.'"

"Brett," Cole whispers.

"What?" My hands are sweaty, my belly sticky. I lift all four of our hands off me and roll to my side. The snow pauses and the sky splits to reveal a crack of moon just above Cole's shoulder. "You have the moon on your shoulder," I say.

"You could have scars all over your body and you would still be beautiful to me."

Beautiful? "I'm scared," I say.

"I know, baby, I'm just trying to tell you something."

But I'm thinking about the hard knobs of scar in my chest, across the backs of my hands, at the root of my tongue, and other places I can sense but never prove.

My mother's covers rustle as she shifts in her small bed beneath us. The muted crackle of fire in the cookstove's wood box is the cabin's only other sound. *The Lovers. The Sun.* Health. Love. Happiness. Pretty pictures, but no guidebook to get you there. Maturity. My eleven-year-old self is locked inside, beating her fists against my ribs, kicking at my pubic bone.

I have no pain, no physical pain from the cancer, so maybe all those tests were wrong, and when they go in there to take everything out they'll find it's just sad and not diseased at all. I try to stop thinking. It's bad for me.

"Brett?" When I don't respond, he touches my face. "Why'd you act so strange tonight? You seemed all right until your cousins arrived and then you got weird. Kind of like the way you acted when you found out you were sick. Kind of…gone."

I can't see his face. "I feel as if I don't have cancer," I whisper. "Being here, it's all about Mama."

"When are you going to tell her?"

I can feel my bones soften, relieved to have diverted his attention from an unbearable topic to an uncomfortable one. "She doesn't need to know. She has her own worries. I don't want to add this. And anyway, in a couple of months I'll be better and that'll be that."

"She's your mother. I think you should tell her."

None of this is his fault. He is the young hawk pacing the nest, defending his territory, and I should be honoring his grace and his valor. "She doesn't need to know."

"Fine," Cole says too loudly.

The sound of Mama's sheets shuffling below makes us both hold our breath.

When all is still beneath us, Cole says, "So what's with the boy cousins, then? Why do you go all strange when they're around? Did they beat you up or something?"

"No." I need to get him away from this topic. "I hardly knew Donovan. He was at UBC when I moved in with them, and then he moved to Kelowna. I only saw him at Christmas. Winter solstice or whatever."

"What about Dylan? You had this look… I couldn't read you. You couldn't take your eyes off him, but it was like you were looking through him. What's the story? You've hardly ever mentioned this guy."

"I told you—Mama and I lived with them after the fire. But the boys were away at school. We hardly saw them."

"Then why didn't you eat your dinner? I saw how you pushed your food around."

"You have to stop staring at me all the time, Cole."

He clears his throat. "I was sitting across from you." His voice has gone subterranean. "Beside Dylan. At a very squished table. It was hard not to notice. What's the story?"

"There's no story." Rolling onto my back, I fold my hands under my breasts and stare up at the ceiling's wood-beamed apex.

"Oh, there's a story all right."

There's a story all right. "He shouldn't have touched the girl like that," I say.

"Like what? What girl?"

"Amara. He had his hands all over her bum."

"They were just playing. She's just a little girl. You can tell she's crazy about him."

"He's forty-six years old."

"So? He's her uncle and he's allowed to be forty-six."

"She's eleven."

"What are you getting at? I thought you liked him. I remember you telling me about how good he was to you, after the fire."

"He was my cousin."

"I imagine he still is." I hear the impatience in his tone.

"He was my cousin."

It's rare to hear coyotes in the winter. In fact, winters are for the most part silent except for the droning of snow machines and the occasional whump of branches releasing snow. But through the stillness we hear the familiar late summer *yipyipaooo* of a lone coyote.

"Ashawinoodese," I whisper, hoping I have the correct emphasis.

"What?"

"It's coyote in Ojibwe. We've seen a few that've been hit. They're not from our area—mostly west and south. Mel had to ask his wife and she had to ask some elder on the reserve, because he only knew the words for dog and wolf, not coyote."

"Brett."

I pivot my head to face his dark shape against the dark window.

"What happened between you and Dylan?"

"He was my lover."

Mama sits on the side of Dylan or Donovan's old bed installed by the window, her hair soft around her face, which, in the low yellow light from her bedside table, looks young, the way I remember her, but sadder of course. I've been massaging her feet and calves the way Cole used to massage mine after a run. I want Mama to be able to walk properly again. Walking is her medicine.

It's still too mucky and treacherous outside, so I've been goading her into exercising inside the cabin where she careens back and forth—table, chair, chair, counter, stove, chair, chair, table, bed. She goes without her cane, mostly silent, determined as hell. It occurs to me that trait may be bred in the bone.

I'm kneeling on the floor with her feet in my lap. No freckles on these pale, smooth feet. Mama's baby toes are small as peas. "Let's get you changed," I say.

Mama fumbles with her sweater's top button, the fingers of her right hand disobedient, the ones of her left not yet dexterous enough in their new dominant role.

"I'm going to send you a new sweater," I say, slipping a brown plastic button through the slit in her plain brown sweater. "A pretty blue one. Maybe with flowers at the collar. Would you like that, Mama?"

That new boss hand stops the movement of mine. "I wanted to knit *you* a sweater for Christmas."

"Scarves, Mama. You were knitting scarves."

From outside, we can hear the thwack of steel against wood as Cole splits wood. He's been out there all morning. He wanted to borrow Mama's car and go to town, but I pleaded with him to stay with me, promising not to say another word. Not one more word.

One half of my mother's mouth lifts completely, the other half about a quarter. "I was. I tried a sweater, but…" The sound of Mama's chuckle does something crazy in my chest, a synesthetic smell of music or a taste of green. My hands turn at the wrists to hold hers.

She pulls them up against her throat so I can feel the long skein of muscle moving under the skin when she speaks. "I couldn't help you."

"Help me?"

"Grow up. You did it by yourself."

"It's okay, Mama."

"No. It isn't."

"It's okay, Mama."

"You did a good job, Brett."

The sound of my name in her mouth is perfect.

The cabin is too small for a private talk, so after Aunt June arrives and Mama has had her careen back and forth through the cabin, I ask my aunt if we can go for a snowshoe up the mountain. The first bit is slippery with snow-softened earth, but as we crest the first rise a layer of firm snow catches our boots and makes the walking somewhat easier, although the pitch is steep and I haven't run for over a week. I'm grateful when the terrain evens out and we stop to fasten on the snowshoes.

"All right," June says, straightening to her full height, which, haloed by the sun halfway up the eastern sky, impresses me the way a full-grown stag might. "What's on your mind then?"

I'd intended to get right to business. To ask if she could tell me what she knew about the fire, how it really started, what happened to Daddy at the hospital, and ask what she knew about Dylan. And Amara. What she saw. Aunt June knows about so many things—the stars, the planets, fertile growing times. What does she know about her own son? But now my throat is caked with dry mountain air. It occurs to me that I may never see my aunt again, or perhaps just once when I have to come to bury Mama. She is older by five years than her sister, but Mama is the weak one. June is sturdy-boned—too big and vital to die first.

"I just wanted you all to myself," I say.

As we walk, I put a hand to my belly, thinking about the lives that pass through wombs—some who make it, like Amara, me, Norah, Cole, Dylan, and Donovan, and the others who don't, like Norah's babies, mine, and Goldie of course, who only got to ride around the sun three times.

Although she appears to be keeping an eye on the ground before us, I'm aware of June watching me. Our snowshoes grate on the slope's hard snow and my chest squeezes from the effort of climbing. June's breath is steady and deep. As we pass under a fir tree, she reaches up to pull down the drape of brilliant green moss from a protruding branch. "It makes good dye," she says, stuffing it into the bag she wears across her chest. "For wool."

"Mama still knits," I say.

June pulls up, her legs wide to accommodate the shoes' width. "Why don't you come home?"

My balance a bit precarious, I take a step back and tilt my head in search of something to focus on. "I'm here," I say, but my voice is thin.

"Are you really?"

"It's not—" I begin, but I don't want to say this isn't my home, because I'm afraid that will offend my dear aunt. She tried. She bought Cinderella sheets to replace the boys' Maple Leafs ones, took me down to Baker Street to buy clothes that fit when Mama couldn't even manage to buy bread or milk. It was June who walked me to school that first day, she who signed forms, dispensed cod liver oil, and put a cool cloth to the back of my neck.

"Not what? Home, is that what you were going to say?" Her mottled face has gone the color of beetroot. "It's not about the house, Brett. She's your mother. *She* is your home."

Under us, under the snow, are tough mountain grasses, dirt and mineral bits, the crust of stone that is this mountain, veins of water, and the creatures. I hear them now right through the bent wood and gut of my snowshoes, through the hard rubber of my boot soles, and through the wool of my socks. I hear them digging, scratching, having sex, nursing their young, squirming, crawling, and dying. Beneath all the layers of life, death, and decay, there is water as clean and pure as light. Beyond that, at the core, is a living liquid fire. Under my skin I move through the layers just like that—through the dividing, multiplying cells of cancer, past the wreck of my womb into the fire at my core where I am truly alive.

She stomps one foot then the other, testing her bindings. "What is it, Brett? You're the color of the road."

"The fire," I begin.

Aunt June nods as if she's been expecting this.

"Goldie." I stomp my own feet. The left binding is loose. With the wide sinewed shoe dangling from my foot, I say, "Mama thinks the fire was her fault."

"I know," June says quickly. "It doesn't matter how many times she's been told."

"But what did start it? No one ever told me anything. No one ever talked about the fire. Ever."

"We tried to make things normal." Her mouth is a dark line in her pale face. "Stupid idea." She shrugs and it takes a second for the heavy canvas man's coat to settle onto her wide shoulders. "The investigator said he figured it was from the chimney pipe—a spark out the top that landed back onto the roof. But your mama never bought that." June's gaze scans me up and down as if she were appraising me at auction. "But that's not the real question, is it?"

Aunt June's cheeks are mottled like the inside flesh of an exposed apple. She smells like apples too, ones with cinnamon from the oven. Up here on the mountain, my feet trapped in woven rackets, I don't smell the evergreen; I smell warm apples in my aunt's hair. She's waiting for me to say more, to tell her the burden of my sins. But now I only want to pull off my glove and touch the bruised-looking skin on her cheek. To warm it. To make it the way it was when I was ten and we were all happy and had no reason to believe it could be any other way.

She hasn't taken her eyes from me. Light puffs of steam cloud under her nostrils. A chill has slid down from the peak and swirls at our feet. Swiping off her knit hat, she shakes out her brilliant hair.

"How can I, how do I, is it possible…?" I stammer, feeling more like eleven than thirty-seven, but I'm determined to push through. I've been a coward far too long. "How can I atone, Auntie?" My voice catches.

"For what, child? What do you imagine *you've* done?"

As she stretches on her cap, a gray-white line is exposed along the hairline. She'd look pretty if she let it grow in; a cap of silver would suit her so well. I'm doing it again—I'm so good at leaving. Terrible at staying.

Her nostrils flare. The snow all around is unblemished old snow. The sun on it makes my eyes sting. I fix my gaze on my wise, wild aunt. Behind her the mountain muscles into the sky, thick with spruce, pine, and fir—greens against the hard white.

"Atone, is it?" Aunt June squats again to untie her bindings, then pulls them off one after the other, to jab their narrow heels into the snow. They stand like two webbed portals. "What you're trying to tell me is that you, too, think you started that damn fire. That it? That why we're up here?"

I've turned my head away, talking now to the bare branches of a tall larch. "No, I don't think that I caused the fire. But…"

"Go on. Better said than not said. Otherwise, it just festers underneath and poisons everything." She doesn't say *as you can see*.

She is so right. Still, it doesn't ease the passage of words through my mouth. "Goldie was in the closet. Daddy had to go back…" My feet sink into the warming snow.

June is nodding again, a bit impatiently it seems, which only serves to make my throat tighten even more. The silence between us swells like a puffer fish.

"They both died," I say and take a breath. "Because of me."

June swipes off her hat and throws it into the snow. "How the hell do you get that?" she demands.

I squat, pulling at the long leather thong of my binding. "I don't know how to…" I pause. What is it exactly that I want or need to do? "To let them go."

"Forgive yourself, you mean."

"Yes," I say. "That. Forgive myself..." But forgiving myself feels like fresh betrayal, as though they had never lived or died or that none of it matters.

June waggles the two upright snowshoes but makes no move to put them back on. "What if..." she says. "What if there's nothing to forgive?"

She's wrong, but I say nothing and begin swinging my legs away from her in long wide arcs, snow chunking through the webbing and skittering along the snow's crust.

Birds spring from branches overhead and make sounds as if they are happy. I just need to get far, to get higher, and away. June knows her way back, and she's got too much insider goods to take my departure personally. I trudge uphill, the snow growing heavier as it melts, my breath loud enough to drown out June's approach from behind. Not until she's right behind me do I realize she's never been far.

"You think you're the only one drags guilt around like a sack of stones?" There's a faint strain in her breathing. She's so tough, so rugged, so sure, that it's a bit unnerving to hear the rasp from her lungs. Her hat sags over one eye.

"No," I answer simply. I don't think I'm the only one, but mine is the only sack I'm familiar with. For a fleeting moment I envision a rope or chain, thick and ancient, uncoiling and snapping away as my hands open and the weight of its load releases. In that brief second I experience a strange lightness that makes my head swirl.

My aunt eyes me, waiting for more than a plain "no" perhaps. But that's all I have. With a start I realize that my mouth is hanging open. One of those birds, high in the branches, lets out a shrill two-note song before flying off, and snow like a handful of salt filters down.

"Maybe what you need to feel is a different thing," she says.

"Something else?" I close my mouth, then open it again. "Like what?"

"Sadness, for instance."

I scour my insides for sadness and find it right there where I left it.

"You know why my boys don't have a father?" she asks, her eyes hard.

I shake my head. "Not really." Something about Vietnam and booze and him going back to the States.

"I should have thrown him out sooner," she says, glancing up the path unmarked by boot or snowshoe. "But I thought the boys needed a father. Even if he was a drunk." She pauses, taking in a breath and holding it. "And a…" Her breath comes out in a gush. "A mean son-of-a-bitch."

When she doesn't continue, I say, "How? What kind of mean?"

Off comes the hat again. She swirls it on a gloved finger, deliberating. "Okay, Brett," she says, her ruddy cheeks rumpling. "I will tell you…"

Her statement sounds conditional. "If?" I ask. If I promise not to tell? If I let her finish without interrupting?

She shakes her head, drops to her haunches, and begins. "Everyone thinks it was because he was a drunk. Everyone knew he drank too much. But he was the life of the party, you know." On goes the hat, looking momentarily like one of those Islamic *kufi* caps. June's mouth stretches into a stiff smile. "That's what got me—he made me laugh, loved to dance, howled at the moon. He could get those coyotes howling like the devil." Her chuckle sounds like stones in her throat. "And he was a sexy bugger. Liked to experiment, you know." Her eyes hold a question, but I'm not sure if she's asking permission to elaborate or whether I do, in fact, know what she's pointing at. Both options leave me a bit cold, so I meet her gaze as expressionless as I can manage. Her head drops. She picks at the binding, tugs the end, and then lets it sag into the snow. "A little light bondage," she says.

Do I want to know this? I do not. Auntie with her hair the color of poppies, a strip of tired gray at the hairline, soft apple cheeks and skin loose on the bone squatting in front of me is not the auntie I want to see manacled to the bedpost. I squeeze shut my eyes, but here she is splayed like a deer hide, a flaming triangle of hair. No. My eyes pop open and there she is staring up at me, her mouth hanging a little, a ball of steam clouded in front of her.

"In the beginning, it made me feel good," she says. "I liked it, really. Lots of teasing, gentle at first until I was ready, then a bit rough. It was exciting."

Oh god, no. Please, no details.

"But after the boys were born, he started to stay out longer, come home raucous and crude, and that's when he started to… to, well, experiment more."

"Auntie, you don't have to tell me. It's private."

"No," Aunt June says. "I don't want it to be anymore."

A second bird splits the blue above us to settle into the heavy spruce branches, sending a cascade of sparkling white down around us. Its song is villainous like Vincent Price's laugh. Aunt June looks up. "I didn't mind," she says with a small laugh. "Actually, it was kind of thrilling." Springing to her feet nimble as a deer, she kicks at the snow.

The rapid fire *ratatat* of a woodpecker loosens another branch of snow. Stepping away from the falling white, I hope June will notice my discomfort and stop talking. But she doesn't. Those unfocused blue-white eyes are fixed on me.

"It was Easter. How fair is that?" She stomps one, two, sending up snow foam through the webbed gut of the snowshoes. "The boys were wired, but they were happy. They'd gotten fighter-man dolls—you know the kind—real macho-like, and heaps of foil-wrapped eggs they'd spent the morning hunting and the afternoon eating." Off goes the hat, this time to be flexed and released like a muscle between her hands. "But they weren't fighting. They were good boys, you know."

It's a struggle to nod, but I do.

"There was a power outage so the house was dead quiet. He came in from drinking his face off, stinking of beer and stale smoke, and ordered the boys to bed." June's eyes have turned milky.

The woodpecker pauses its relentless battering. I look up to see the red tip of its crown tilted as if listening for Aunt June's next words. But then he's back at it, a blur of red and white and black. The woods vibrate with his hammering.

I'm hooked now. It seems as if I know this story, if I push into whatever details she's about to reveal, it will give me an answer that the entrails of all the broken creatures I've touched have not imparted.

"Tell me," I say quietly. "I'm listening."

"You're a good girl, Brett," Aunt June says, squashing the blaze of her hair into the lacy white cap. "The boys didn't want to go to bed; they wanted to have a war with their fighting guys. They wanted to play outside. It wasn't cold and there was still light. But he told me to wait for him in the bedroom and he'd put the boys to bed."

Despite the chill in my legs, I don't move. June rubs her flushed face with both hands, then leaves them there, flat against her cheeks, her fingers covering her eyes. "Bastard," she mutters. "But I did what I was told. I went. I waited."

"What did he do, Auntie?" The sound of my voice disintegrates in the white air.

It's as if she stops. Stops talking. Stops breathing. Stops standing here on the mountainside with me. Whatever she remembers of that night has rendered her tinier than the space between the woodpecker's blows. If she were fidgeting with her hat or kicking snowshoes or talking about rough sex from forty years ago, I would hear her, see her, smell the warm apple smell of her. But I don't.

Into that empty space her voice suddenly booms and echoes. "It was one hell of a night," she says. "When he finally came to the bedroom, he smacked me across the mouth when I asked if the boys were asleep and told me to shut up. I could say that he was different that night, that he acted different, but when I look back I see that it was like a progression…inevitable, you know? The gag he put on my mouth didn't surprise me. The rest did, though." She pauses, and when she speaks again her voice doesn't boom or echo. It's gone quiet as the grass under the snow. "I should have gone to check. Taken off the gag. I should never have…well, never have *obeyed* him."

"It's okay," I say, holding out a hand as if to stroke her, but she's too far away. My hand in its leather glove hovers in midair.

"It's not okay. Not at all. But here's what happened." Seeing my look, she adds, "Don't worry, I'll spare you the gory details of what he did to me and had me do for him. It was after what he did to me that ended everything. It was the boys. I found them also gagged—with duct tape—and wrists and ankles bound with rope to their beds, face down." She's speaking fast now without pause between words or sentences. "Naked. He'd stripped them and spread-eagled them on their beds, their sweet little bums purple with handprints. He'd passed out after he was done with me and when I went to check on the boys that's what I found, both of them wide-eyed and rigid on their beds, their faces turned toward each other. They didn't even scream when I pulled off the tape. I couldn't untie the ropes. I had to cut them off. I gathered them both into my arms and they didn't say a word, didn't cry or nothing. I didn't know what to do so I poured them a bath and made them both get in and then I called the police. It was Sunday night I remember because we'd had an egg hunt that morning and the boys still had chocolate on their breath. I think he must have heard me on the phone because right then when I was telling the dispatcher what had happened or as best I could I heard the front door slam." Aunt June stops, blinks, then takes a very deep breath, holds it a moment, then lets it out in a swoop. "That's it, Brett. Never saw that bastard again."

The mountain falls into cavernous silence. The trees withhold their snow. In a small voice, I say, "I had no idea."

Her head bobs as her eyes return to focus. "What I'm trying to tell you is this: that underneath the fire is a sadness that's so much harder to bear than the rage."

"Yes," I say.

What has happened up here on the mountain is not what I'd

intended. My questions, at least the ones I thought I had, have not been answered. But something more fundamental, something underneath, has been unearthed. I will tuck this story into a safe place for a time when I can let its full impact register.

We spend another hour winding our way down the slope. Aunt June's hat stays in place, our snowshoes keep us from sinking, and we turn our conversation to plans on how to care for Mama.

Mama's going to be fine. She's already walking without that ugly cane and tea barely trickles from the side of her mouth. June and I persuaded her to let us arrange a local woman to help her—an hour or so each morning to get the fire going, make her breakfast, and set up the rest of her meals. June will keep tabs on her and come up from Nelson every few days.

Still, as Cole and I wait outside I feel her eyes on our backs through the window. I'm achingly aware of the dark empty places in her I never considered until this trip. Pieces of snow have been filling the air with their watery white for days. My feet slide in their dark sogginess as Cole and I stand at the top of the hill waiting for June, who will drive us to the airport. Despite Cole's heroic efforts, the relentless fall of snow covered and recovered the dark runnels of Mama's driveway. My coat is too heavy for this rain-snow, my back is slick with sweat, and my breath is a fog. We haven't been speaking. Or touching. Cole stands two arms' lengths from me, gripping the handle of his sports bag with both hands.

"I'm going to need new boots," I say. "These are done."

Cole extracts his phone and slides it on. "It's almost ten. June should be here soon."

A chickadee bounces onto a fallen tree, twitches its little black-capped head, and trills its five-note song.

"Don't chickadees fly south?" I ask.

Cole's temples bead with sweat. He shrugs, shoving his phone back into a pocket, and turns his head away from me to stare down the empty driveway.

16

I *am the one who stays above it all. I stay safe by not letting anyone all the way in. I'm too cool to care, but I'm smokin' hot. You can come close, but not too close. I'm dangerous. You'll get burned or frozen out.* I should have warned Cole.

I put down the pen and listen for his song coming from the living room, but the apartment has fallen quiet.

Then I hear him. He's standing in the bedroom doorway. "Who are you, anyway?" He shifts his weight. "I mean, who the fuck are you?" These words could be spoken in fury, but they are not. They are weary and flat.

We're home now, but the apartment is cold. Beckett is still at Norah's. We are alone and I'm tired. June drove us to Castlegar Airport. We stopped over for two hours in Calgary and then once we landed in Toronto, had to pick up the car and drive to Barrie. It's late and I'm tired and I don't want to even try to answer him. The trip was subdued. Cole read or dozed or paced the airport, flipped through magazines and novels, touched the cool faces of watches at a kiosk, and drank five Americanos. He mumbled answers to my rare questions, avoided eye contact, and feigned sleep. Now we're home and I can't sleep and he can't sing and he has a question I can't answer.

"You slept with your cousin." Dark pockets have settled under his eyes. "Who does that?"

I try to stand but both my calves cramp. "I need a glass of water," I say and hobble by him to the kitchen. *Who does that?* Me. I did that. I can formulate nothing for my mouth to say that will explain, defend, or, god forbid, describe how or why that happened, nor why it gave me solace, tenderness, and absolution. Instead, I put water in my mouth and wait for the inevitable closing of the door. My breasts hurt. I feel like throwing up. My hips ache. Cole won't leave tonight, but soon he will. Again. If I'm lucky, it will be after the surgery. If he's smart, it will be before that.

He turns around, goes to the bed, and lies down with his back to the door. I close the door and go to the couch where I lie on my side. I just want to close my eyes but they refuse to close.

The next day, after I drag myself home from work and before Cole has to go in to work, I sit as I have done for nearly six years, with my side leaning into the curve of his spine. It isn't liquid the way I'm accustomed to feeling him, but I stay in hopes that continuing the ritual will bring him back. I feel the weight of his heart's *thudthump* right through his back's long strong muscles, the labor of it. We are both unbearably tired. Weariness may be the only thing we share right now.

When the hall phone rings, Cole and I glance at each other. No one calls us anymore on that line except people who want money. "I'll get it," I say, pushing up off the ottoman.

He says nothing, picks up the Leonard Cohen song he'd been singing when I came in. "The Sisters of Mercy."

It's Donovan on the phone, his voice shrill and breathless. "I had to call you. I don't know what to do." Gone is the slap-you-on-the-back jolliness of when I'd tried to warn him. *Oh, he'd never hurt her. She's crazy about him. See?* Amara bounding through the snow, her pink satin-lined fur hood slapping her narrow shoulders.

Now Donovan's wheezy voice is demanding, "What do I do now, Brett? I can't call the cops on my own brother."

Cole hasn't even turned to see how I respond to this call, doesn't see me in the dark front hall, the hot receiver slipping in my hand, how it dents the side of my head. Cole doesn't turn. He keeps singing that song about them not being lovers like that. *Like what?*

"Brett? I'm asking you. You saw something. You know. What should I do?"

"What happened, exactly?"

"I mean, he was just saying goodnight. That's what he told

me. But you don't get into bed to say goodnight, do you? That's not right, is it? I mean, you got me spooked there. Maybe I'm overreacting. Am I overreacting? I mean, Amara's fine. She's mad at me for telling Dylan to get out of her room. I mean she knows about private places, the red zones, so she wouldn't let him do something, would she?"

"Donovan."

"It's because of Becky. Damn Becky. If Amara had a mother this wouldn't happen. Fucking Becky. I oughta go right down to that fucking jungle where she's probably fucking some goddamn medicine man and wring her goddamn neck."

"Donovan."

"This is my fault, isn't it? Isn't it? I should have listened to you. What—"

"Donovan!"

"What? What?"

"Take a breath." *I* take a breath, a sharp one, hold it for a moment then let it out in a rush.

On the other end of the receiver, Donovan is panting.

"Talk to her." As if I know what he should say.

"What do I say?"

"And get out of that house. Go back to Kelowna or to your mom's but keep him away from her."

"She's mad at me, Brett."

Whatever was left of me then would have shriveled and faded to zero had Dylan been taken from me, had someone found us sticky and flushed under the hockey player bedspread and chased him out.

"I know," I say.

Cole has stopped singing and rests his guitar on his lap. He sits very still, listening still.

"He won't hurt her," I say, the words plain in my mouth. "Not physically."

"What the fuck is that supposed to mean?"

I can't answer because my throat has closed. And the swirl in my belly has become a toxic soup. Bile fills my mouth.

"Brett! What do you mean, 'not physically'?"

I cough. Cole turns on the ottoman to face me.

"Just get her out of there." I try to clear the phlegm that has lodged thick in my throat. "I have to go, Donovan. I'll call you, okay?"

Beckett looks from me to his empty dish. His empty dish in the streetlight's half-light. No dirty dishes. No food left on the counter. Just the dirge of the refrigerator, the faithful fridge keeping cool remnants of food that I will throw out—yellowed broccoli, wilted lettuce, yellow-haired carrots soft as neglected penises, and splotched black kale. I will take them one by one and then in bunches and place them in the plastic-lined bin, the one other people put cat shit and dirty diapers into. Some other truck crew will take it all away. To become food for mealy white creatures to swarm through.

When I hang up, Cole stands and studies me for several long moments. Once again, I'm being judged and I have no alibi. "You really think he's messing with Amara?" he asks.

"I don't know, Cole. How can I know?" I try to hold his gaze but my eyes keep skittering away. "I'm so tired," I say. "I'm just going to lie down for a bit."

Cole is pulling me to shore, but my boots are filled with lake water and I'm dragging him down. We're on a riverbank, my lungs filled with green water. He's pumping my chest. My ribs crack.

"Brett, wake up."

It's just sleeping, that's all. Sleeping underwater.

"The power's out," he says. Sweet Cole, his wintergreen breath on my face.

"I love you, Cole," I murmur.

Whatever he was going to say gets extinguished in a sharp suck of breath. Then he says, "I love you too."

After those words there are no sounds beyond his breathing, no refrigerator hum, no whuff of furnace, no tick of bedside clock.

"Are there candles?" Cole asks.

"In the bathroom," I say, but then I'm not sure. "Are we home?"

"Yes, we're home." There's a hesitation as if he's waiting for me to say something, and a rope-like gnarl uncoils in my gut. I should apologize, atone, explain, but I can't think what I've done wrong, only that I have.

"I'll get them," I say, rolling to the side, fluffing off the duvet.

"Yeah, you go," Cole says in a tone I've never heard him use. Bitter, that's what it is: *bitterness.*

I yank at the twist inside, yank until the source of my guilt, my wrongness, is exposed. *Dylan.* With a sick lurch, I remember. I told Cole about Dylan. In a rush, I start across the room, cracking my shin against the bottom corner of the bedframe.

Cole does not come to my aid. He doesn't ask if I'm okay. Not a peep, not a word in this milky dark where I am blind.

"What time is it, anyway?"

"My phone says it's 3:46."

"I'm supposed to be in at four. Give me your phone. I'll call in."

"You'd better just go." He sounds bored.

"Go? How can I go? Is there water?"

"Better hurry if you want a shower. The hot water won't last."

When I get to work Mitch is in a snarl. Some of the boys from night shift had to keep working because three of us were late. Mel is already out when I get there, and Mitch just points to my plow. I back it into the dome and get loaded with brine. Outside, everything is coated in ice.

All through the morning I move along empty dark roads. My chant continues until dawn: *stay home, stay home, stay safe.* No crazy spinning women, please. I am full to the brim with my own spinning-ness.

By the time I get home it's almost dark again. The air in the streets is warm and wet like spring. Like everything else, it is a kind of trick. So I zip up my coat and take Beckett for a run. When he skitters out onto the ice, I call him back. I have to protect him.

The power has been restored, so after our run I pour myself a hot bath and think about my little sister. Not the way I have been thinking about her, through the lens of guilt, but with tenderness. And I even try a new sort of kindness—directed toward myself.

Goldie liked the squish of mud through bare toes in the garden, the hard surprise of crushed rock in the driveway, even the shock of snow when she flung open the front door that morning when winter had just arrived, pajamas half undone, and skipped barefoot out into the yard.

I remember once when Mama tried to explain using her serious voice that in town they wouldn't let us into stores or restaurants without shoes. Goldie kicked her toughened two-year-old heels against the hall seat as Mama knelt, doing her best to coax on one pale blue sneaker. "They're hardly even there. Look, so light," Mama said, turning one shoe over to show Goldie its thin sole.

"No laces?" Goldie asked, her seed teeth couldn't yet catch the S sounds. *Lathes.*

Goldie worked hard at her sounds, her words, so that by summer, the summer before the fire, she could say laces and slices and silly and even sandalwood, Mama's favorite incense.

But saying words right won't save you. Even doing things right won't help most of the time. There's a fire waiting for each one of us. Sitting here on the edge of the tub, my warm, clean feet on the cool white floor, I feel the tip of my own flame, the smoke sifting under the bathroom door. The bristles bend under my thumb—rubbery, malleable, unlike the sharp, uneven jags where the handle has been snapped. Strands of my fading yellow hair twist through the brush's maze of bristles, not at all like the white-yellow of my sister's dandelion-puff hair. Her face at the window on night shift. Her face in the chrome surface of the January lake. Goldie. Who will always be three. I stoop to retrieve the broken handle from the bathroom floor and decide to leave my hair loose today.

Cole still isn't home. I tried to write in my journal, but I couldn't stop thinking about Donovan's phone call, about Amara and about Dylan. Would Donovan call the police? Would they even charge Dylan if he did? If Amara won't tell, then what does he have? If he isn't hurting her…but my head is crazy. He *is* hurting her. She's a child. And he will break her heart.

The key in the lock is quiet as a stone sinking in water. Beckett scrambles to his feet to stand alert by the front door as it slowly opens.

"Hey," I say.

"Hey," says Cole, stepping inside and closing the door behind him.

Reaching for his coat, I ask, "You okay?"

Cole jerks away from my touch, grips both sides of his coat. "Why didn't you tell me how old you were?" His voice cracks.

"I didn't lie," I say. "I've never lied about that."

"You didn't tell me," he insists.

"What are you talking about, Cole? I'm thirty-seven years old. You know that."

"No." When he shakes his head, a wave of beer smell hits me. Unzipping his coat, he shrugs it off and hangs it carefully on a hook.

"You've been drinking?" I watch as he sways into the living room. Beckett looks up at me. His tail has stopped wagging.

"Why wouldn't you tell me?"

"What haven't I told you?" But I know what I haven't told him. "I couldn't. It was hard enough."

His laugh is wet and not amused.

The membrane over my eyes has slipped back inside the sockets and I am left seeing everything. A twelve-year-old in love with a twenty-year-old, her cousin—the great love of her life.

Beckett follows Cole into the living room. When Cole sits

to stare out over the winter rooftops, Beckett pushes his skull against his master's limp hand.

"You're a puzzle, Brett. A great big thousand-piece jigsaw puzzle. You know that? You're a thousand-piece puzzle."

"I am sorry, Cole."

"Sorry? You're *sorry*?" His speech is mushy like Mama's.

"Yes." I come to stand behind him, aching to touch the soft new growth on his beautiful head.

"I'm going to kill that fucker."

"He didn't hurt me, Cole."

"The hell he didn't." Cole lurches to his feet, his hand clenched as if around a knife. "Don't you defend that…that… that cocksucker!"

Beckett yelps and I take a step back. "How did you find out?"

He swings to face me but his eyes are unfocused. "I had to talk to someone."

"Norah?"

Cole slumps back down to the ottoman. "You know, I've never been lonely, not really. I'm not a lonely guy. But then I met you, and now I'm so goddamn lonely I can't stand it." A sob bubbles through his words. "Is love supposed to make you lonely? Is it? Because I love you so fucking much and I'm the loneliest guy in the whole fucking world."

"Cole." I squeeze in beside him and take his head in my arms, pulling him to me. "I don't want you to be lonely," I murmur, stroking his hair's velvety new growth. He lets me touch him.

"I just want—" he begins, but then sits up straight. "No. You know what I want? I want to kill him. Hang him by his balls. I'm going to kill him. And there we were all buddy-buddy howdy fucking do. I should have known, shoulda seen. I'm the one who should be sorry. I'm the one who's sorry. You were trying to protect that little girl, that's what you were doing, and I'm out there shoveling snow with that asshole. You shoulda told me. Shoulda told me then so I could have killed him right then and there—just cracked a shovel right over his sick fucking head. You shoulda told me, that's all." Cole goes on, snot and tears smearing his face, my shirt, and hands as I try to brush it all away.

"It's okay, Cole. It's all right. Donovan will make sure Amara's safe. Don't—"

"Don't what? Worry? What about other girls? Will he make sure all the girls are safe? How will he do that, Brett? How?"

I fall silent. Beckett pushes his taut body into the ottoman, offering his head to Cole's dangling fingers which set to moving through his fur as if in search of something.

Then he's crying again, an ugly crease dissecting his forehead. He turns on me. "Have you ever wondered what *I* want? What *I'm* doing? You've never even asked." He gulps his words.

I put my ear to his mouth. "What do you want, Cole?" I say, my right hand reaching to cradle his head. "Tell me now."

The muscles in his back stiffen. "I don't know what I want." His voice is suddenly clear and sharp. "That's the fucking problem. I thought I wanted you. I had some stupid idea about kids and a house. Thought the band would do something, that we'd be discovered or some stupid naïve shit, like CBC would have us on and we'd get picked up, that—" He sits straight up, stares hard out the window. "But you know what? I'm a stock boy in a grocery store, playing mediocre music in a garage like a goddamn teenager."

"Cole," I say, trying to pull him back. He's stopped crying, but he's rigid as stone. He shrugs off my hand. "And now. This." Dropping his head, he closes his eyes. "Fuck it."

Beckett twitches his attention from Cole to me and back to Cole.

I stroke the hard plank of Cole's back. "You mean Dylan?" I ask.

Touching his lower belly, Cole says, "I don't feel good," and lurches off the ottoman.

The sounds of retching and cursing through the closed bathroom door turn my own stomach, but I force myself to stand outside the door. "Your band is good. No one sounds like you."

His breathing is hard and I can feel him convulse. Heavy liquid gurgles into the toilet bowl, followed by coughing and the toilet's flush. "I'm sick," he says.

Trying the door handle, I find it open. I run a washcloth under cold water. Cole is kneeling, his eyes clenched, his arms hugging the toilet rim. Squatting, I put one cooled hand on his forehead, the chilled washcloth on the back of his neck.

"That's good," he whispers.

"You're good, Cole. You're a good man," I say, pressing my palm into one temple then the other, and then letting the washcloth hold itself, I take both his hot cheeks in my hands. When I turn his face to me I feel the light growth of the night there. Even his stubble has no barbs. "It's going to be okay."

His eyes search mine. "How can you know that?"

"It's going to be okay," I insist. "I'll get you some water."

"Water's good," he says and jerks away to hang his head over the bowl as another spasm takes him.

Beckett stands at attention in the bathroom doorway, a question in his bright dark eyes. "Let's get Cole a glass of water," I say, and our little dog does a half-circle dance as if that's the right answer.

When Cole stops retching, he goes to the bedroom, and after a short silence I hear his ragged snoring through the closed door.

That time Cole asked me what I wanted, I said to be happy. Even then I wasn't certain if that was true. Or if I even knew what happiness was. The idea of happiness seems like being on an escalator that only goes up, or wearing prescription glasses that you don't need, or winning a prize for a contest you cheated in. I've done things that might have made me happy, such as traveling, driving big trucks, buying Beckett, taking beautiful Cole as a lover, but I come home stinking of intestines and sweat, kill babies, lie, and tell my friend that the only man I ever loved was my cousin.

Cole has spent years fitting every key he could find into my lock, and now he is weary from the effort. He brings me tea but doesn't speak. He sleeps beside me, but his hands stay closed. When I come home from work he is dressed and gone. He could be working overtime, walking the waterfront, or listening to his mother tell him *I told you so*. He doesn't say and I don't ask. We are planets circling different suns.

For what feels like hours, I've been sitting on the ottoman, watching the street below through my watery reflection, broken brush still in my hands, when Cole emerges. His face crushed and sleep-lined.

"You're here," he says in a thick voice. It sounds to me like an accusation, but his eyes are flat and distant. "Has Norah called?" he asks.

"No. I'm sure she will when a dog barks three times or she catches her nail on something. You know, some logical reason to call." I intend this to be amusing, but I hear the blade in my tone. So does Cole.

"Norah's a good friend," he says. "You know they're trying to adopt."

It's not safe, I almost say. "I know," I say. "They'd be such good parents." Having nothing more I can say, I rise, go into the bathroom, and begin braiding my hair. Coarse silvery strands weave through the winter blond. The dry air has frizzed the ends and most of my head is framed in a cacophony of fuzz. I have a sudden urge to cut it short. Really short. Buzz cut.

Cole leans in the doorway, watching me with a mix of curiosity and something gray and smoldering behind those caramel eyes.

"It was a long time ago," I say.

"I know, Brett. Doesn't make it right."

"It has to stop," I say. "I have to call Aunt June. I have to tell her."

"Good," Cole says.

"After," I say. "After the operation. When I'm strong."

The word "strong" laughs out of his mouth.

When it is time to go to the hospital, Cole insists on driving me. I have a small bag packed with the things I'll need for a two-day stay. Cole has me put it in the back seat and tells me to close my eyes.

"This will help," he says, unbuckling the seatbelt I've just cinched. "You have to breathe. My mom gave me this exercise to give you."

"Great," I say, squeezing shut my eyes. "What's it supposed to do to me? Make me vaporize?"

He doesn't laugh. "Imagine you can see your breath coming in through your nostrils and follow it down into your lungs and chest. Good. Now on your next breath, imagine it going all the way into your hips. Inside. Now imagine that you are breathing blue light into your uterus. Calm and blue." He pauses. I can feel him watching me breathe. "Don't blow out. Open your mouth and let the breath kind of fall out. Right. That's good."

"I'm dizzy."

"Just try to let as much air out as you can. Yeah, that's good."

"Why are you being so nice to me?" I ask when we're walking up to the admissions desk.

Cole puts a light hand between my shoulder blades. "Have you got your health card?"

The nurse is pretty, with black eyebrows and hair dyed the color of apricots pulled into a tight ponytail. "When was the date of your last period?" she asks, her stony little eyes focused on her clipboard.

The blue cotton gown is rough against my nipples. "Period?"

"Yes, what was the start date of your last menses?"

"I don't remember." Which is true and strange. Cole might know but he is in some other room, possibly worrying about me or taking some deep breaths of his own. Taking the pills has kept me from having to think about the dates. The problem is, I've forgotten to take a few of the pills, doubling up and then forgetting again. "Maybe the cancer has stopped my cycle?"

Her head jerks, chin tucking tight to her throat, and she looks at me as if I had just told her I thought babies grew under cabbage leaves. "I'll be right back."

After I hand in the bottle of my pee, a nurse comes in to fill vials with my blood. I sit twitching on the gurney in a cold open room with lots of other gurneys, some closed in by curtains.

A doctor I've never met arrives and draws the curtain closed so we are in a rectangular enclave, just the two of us. And then he tells me what I do not want to hear.

When I don't respond to the revelation found in my urine, he says, "I suppose you'll want to nip this in the bud, then?"

Cool air moves around inside my mouth. A window must be open. This doctor who doesn't wear glasses or a white coat seems to be waiting for my response.

"'Nip it in the bud'?" The words stick like taffy to the roof of my mouth.

"We should get this moving. It looks like you're close to the second trimester, so it could be hard on you." He studies me for a moment. "I suppose you could say we're in luck."

"Luck?" I can't feel my body. It might be cold. It might have dissolved.

"Well." His face rearranges itself into something like sympathy which is belied by a twisted little smile. "We could kill two birds with one stone, so to speak."

"'So to speak'?" My hands press into my belly. I imagine fluffy fledglings, eyes sealed with membrane, tiny translucent beaks wide. Only one stone to kill them both.

"Well?" He ruffles papers at me. "We can nip this in the bud right now. Up to you."

There are too many metaphors in this room.

The distant sound of Highway 400 wafts on the cold air. Cars. Trucks. Plows. Moving north and south as if they know where they're going, where they're headed, who they will be when they get there. Some of them have children. Some of them may have cancer. Each one of them has lost someone they loved. Maybe one of them has broken someone's heart.

And didn't know. All of them will die. Not one will get out alive.

"I'll give you a few minutes," he says and squeals open the curtain.

"A few minutes," I repeat. As if there's a choice. As if I could be a mother. As if there were a way to "nip this in the bud."

Cole's head is thrown back to rest against the wall, his jaw slack and legs splayed. Held loosely in his hands are an open notebook and pen. He's waiting for me. It could have been hours. Across from him, a woman bends over her phone, tapping with both thumbs while a thin-haired blond girl of about six leans against her thigh and stares at the sleeping Cole.

When I get close, I see lines of verse scratched and written over, noted with keys, on the open page. The words "lonely" and "together" are clear.

I touch his knee. "Cole," I say as gently as I can.

He jumps. The notebook slips to the floor. How he stares at me with such trust.

"Let's go."

"But…" His eyebrows pinch in confusion.

Reaching for his hand, I tell him, "It's been postponed."

"Postponed?" He stands and then stoops to retrieve the notebook. "I was writing a song," he says. Then, "Why is it postponed?"

Waving an arm toward the swinging doors from which I've just emerged, I say, "Emergency. There's been an emergency."

"I was waiting for them to tell me which room…" With one hand Cole turns my head until our eyes meet. "Are you all right?"

"Sure," I say. "A bit shocked is all."

"Shocked?"

It's hard to keep my gaze steady. Hard to think. To imagine. To speak. "Well, you know, I finally get there…" I swallow hard. "Get to the place, the place where I'm ready to actually, uh, let go…You know?" Cole nods. "And then, uh…it doesn't happen."

Dipping his head to maintain eye contact, he says, "But it will? They rescheduled, right?"

I step back away from his touch and from his scrutiny. "Not yet."

"They'll call?"

"Let's go."

As we go back out into the dark morning, I say, "You were going to wait there the whole time?"

He doesn't answer, just wraps an arm tight around me and squeezes; he holds on like that until we get to my car. He opens the passenger door and waits until I am buckled in before clicking it shut and moving around to the driver's side.

Putting the car into reverse, he says, "I was writing a song."

"You said," I say, watching a strip of cars go by and wondering how they all seem to know where they're going. "About being lonely?"

"Wait till you hear it," he says, leaning forward to shift into first. "It's more of an acknowledgment than a complaint. And the tune I've been working on is light…sweet, I guess you'd say. You'll like it, I think. At least…" He shoots me a quick glance before shifting into second. "I hope you do. It's for you."

"Still? Even after all I've put you through?" We're heading toward the lake. It looks so pretty, so placid, so uncomplicated.

"Sure," he says, brightening. "Why not? I've put you through some stuff myself, right?"

While I was on a gurney having my life flipped inside out, Cole seems to have undergone a change of heart. From his jolly demeanor it would seem that he believes we've regained whatever equilibrium we once had. Gripping the door handle, I shift in my seat and stare hard out the windshield. "Like what?" I say, but I've gone flat. No warmth in my voice. I'm in my belly, deep in my belly, turning over that little bird with its mouth full of worms.

"Well, come on. It's got to be tough having a boyfriend who's a grocery boy who stays out late and…you know, stuff like that. I'm not exactly your model husband."

"There's nothing wrong with you, Cole."

He laughs, relieved. "Right. Right. I'm perfect." He laughs again. "Perfection personified."

I hear him, but there's a swelling in my belly—inflating like a party balloon ready to pop. From within that helium-filled space I hear him say something about getting back on the diet, about cervical tumors being slow growing, and not to worry, not to worry, not to worry.

The early snow has completely melted, so I get to ride with Mel again, patching up the messes the first snows have made.

"Thanks for the tea," I say.

Although he looks puzzled, he doesn't remind me that he gave me the tea a long time ago and that I already thanked him. His brown fingers hang loose over the steering wheel.

"It's helping," I add, watching his face for some sign that he knows.

Mel simply nods that slow deep nod and I fall silent again.

At the Tenth Line we turn east and head toward the lake. A porcupine lured out of hibernation by the false spring lies as if sleeping in the middle of the road.

"You want to keep this one?" I ask as we examine the creature.

The quills of some porcupines are too damaged to bother harvesting for his wife's craft work, but this one appears to be intact.

Mel chuckles as he reaches into the truck's bed. "We've got more roadkill than food in our freezer."

The ground is still workable. Mel stamps a foot on the shovel blade and turns over a clod of dark earth beyond the ditch. I work the flat shovel under the heavy body and lift. Its small head drops away, its black nut eyes open to the sky. The quills are splayed as if they could have saved it from the brutality of moving steel. A splatter of them remains on the road.

By the time I reach the hole, Mel has dug out his tobacco and is murmuring a prayer. I try not to drop the animal but rather slide it into its small grave. Of all the creatures we have buried, this well-defended one brings an extra hard lump to my throat.

"Mel?" We are walking together back to the truck. "Did you know that I have cancer?"

After a moment, he says, "*Kaa.*"

At the top of the culvert we stop.

"Really? You didn't know?"

He shakes his head.

"But did you know I was pregnant?"

He points his grizzly gray chin skyward.

"Mel, why did you give me that tea?" I want to tug his sleeve, but he seems to be involved in some interaction I can't access, so I don't touch him.

He lowers his gaze. "Wife gave you the tea."

"She knew? But I've never even met her."

He smiles, showing that bit of gold in the left side of his mouth. "She's a wise woman, my Franny."

I stamp my boot on the hard ground. "Mel," I say, trying to keep my voice conversational, rational, calm. "Why don't you ask questions? You never ask questions. I know you told me people say what they want to say but couldn't you once ask me how I feel or what I think or what I did on my day off or tell me why your wife gave me that stuff?" The words keep pouring out. "Maybe sometimes people can't say what they need to say. Maybe they need to be asked because they don't know if it's okay to tell, or if the other person even wants to know." My voice has gone high and wild. I stamp one foot and then the other and look away from Mel, because I've blown it. Whatever bond we shared has been ruptured by my outburst.

After three cars and two trucks pass, Mel speaks. "*Mshki-ki Kwe,*" he says quietly. "I learned real young not to ask." He chuckles without humor and adds, "The hard way."

I'm not certain I heard right. I know that *kwe* means woman, but *Mshkiki* is Mel's name: *Mshkiki Nini*. Strong Earth Man. In the too-warm dull January morning, I turn back to Mel to study his face, its lines and scars, the eyes gentle as a deer. "I'm sorry, Mel. Really, I am. I just found out I'm pregnant and I don't know what to do because I also have cancer. And I haven't told anybody, and I guess I somehow thought you must know...."

His head jerks back, startled. "Me? How would *I* know?"

"You know things. You always seem to sense things, to know what's happening or what's going to happen."

His startled look transforms into pure astonishment. His eyes grow wide and his mouth opens in a perfect O. Then one side of his lips lifts, showing a glint of gold, into an almost playful smile, and he looks over his shoulder, scans the road, the ditch, and the row of bare trees. "Don't know who you're talking to," Mel says, giving his head a quick shake as he starts walking again.

At the truck he reaches to take the shovel from me. "My Franny, she's the smart one. Me, I'm a truck driver, Brett. That's all. I do my work and when I go home I take care of Franny best I can." He slides the shovel into the truck bed and opens his gloved hands. "But if I tell the truth, she's the one doing the caretaking." He purses his lips at the gray sky and says, "That's it. That's what I know."

January moves toward February with certainty. A patchwork of snow covers the playground, white blotches on the swing seats. The gray sky outside Norah's kitchen window is pockmarked with clouds.

"I know you think abortions are wrong, but don't you think there could be circumstances where it would be acceptable?"

Norah fixes me with that look, that icy eye that says she knows what I will never understand. "I could never have an abortion."

"What about if you had cancer? What about if you might die?" I scan her white and pale gray living room in search of an object on which to focus.

"Brett?" Norah's cool hand slides my sleeve up my arm and closes around my wrist. "Are you...Are you...? Hallelujah, yes. I knew it." She pauses. "You are, aren't you?"

I nod.

"But how? How did it happen?"

"You want the details? I'll give them to you. How do you want them—with or without foreplay?"

She waves away my attempt at levity. "But you were on the pill."

"I guess I missed one or two."

"Oh," Norah says. "But after what happened...it's not like you don't know the consequences..."

"We weren't having sex."

"A miracle?" She sounds doubtful, which I find oddly reassuring.

"But then we did. It had to be the night you and I chased the skunk."

"Oh." She's quiet for a moment. "Oh. You were a bit drunk..."

I laugh, pushing down the sickness of remembering *how* drunk.

She squeezes my arm. "But what are you going to do?"

"I could have everything taken out all at once. Or, I could have the bab—"

"Have the baby? Have the baby. Yes, you could have the baby." Norah's face lights up like a Christmas tree.

"What if the cancer spreads? And do I want a baby? I'm a mess. You're the one who wants a baby." I look away.

"Stop it." Her grip tightens.

I need to turn the conversation. There's that other thing still drifting between us. "About what happened...? Between us, I mean. You know, that kiss...?"

Norah releases my arm and holds her hand flat toward me.

I stumble on. "I love men, you know."

"Love? Really? You love 'men'? Are you sure about that?"

"What do you mean? Of course I love men."

She slaps her hand on the counter. "Cole? Do you love Cole?"

"Cole is…" I say, pressing the sides of the teacup until I feel the hardness of my finger bones. "Young."

"You haven't told him, have you? Again. Again, you haven't told him. For heaven's sake, Brett, is that loving men? Is that how it's done in your world?"

"I want to spare him."

The sweetness between us has soured and now we're shouting, squared off with the kitchen island between us.

"Spare him? Spare him? It's not your call, Brett. It's his baby. His." Abruptly, she swallows her hiss. "It *is* his, right? Not that slime bag at the bar? Tell me it's Cole's baby, please tell me that."

"It's Cole's," I say. "I didn't have sex with that guy."

"Oh Jezuz, Brett, next I was afraid you were going to tell me it's your cousin's."

I am a fool, a monster, and a lonely child in an empty bed. What if, at thirteen or fourteen, I had produced my cousin's offspring? What if I hadn't proudly informed him that I was now a woman? What if the world had tipped on its axis and at thirteen I bore my mother a grandchild? My skin is hot and barbed. I have to pee.

"How am I supposed to protect a child, Norah? How could I keep it safe?"

A sliver of sun slices through the gray sky. Norah turns to regard the place where a shaft of it comes through the window. "You will. You can. You'll see."

"Do you…" I can't find the right words. "Would you…" I try again but fail again to complete the question. "I mean, before, I said, you know, before, if I…I mean, you said…would you…?"

She frowns, January light pale on her pale face. She is patient.

I can't ask. Looking away, I see that I have left my car keys on the kitchen table. She follows my gaze, starts a little, but then shakes her head. "It doesn't matter, Brett. They're just keys."

"But…"

"Never mind." With one hand Norah seems to brush away the possibility of disaster. "I'm trying to be a normal person. I was driving myself mad. I couldn't even brush my hair for fear I wasn't doing it right. I surrender." She gives me a sheepish smile. "So, what are you trying to say, Brett? Just tell me."

"The baby—"

Comprehension dawns on her face. "No." Norah cuts me off. "No, I won't. I couldn't. It's not right." Her shoulders slide down. "I told you before that I should never have said what I said. This is your baby. *Your* baby, Brett. Yours and Cole's."

"But how will I ever...?"

"Trust me," she says. "These things take care of themselves."

I do trust her. Some lost part of me rises to the surface to meet the certainty of her words, and I come around the island to hold my friend in my arms, to hold her close and tight. I hold her for much longer than I ever have, because in truth, I never want to let her go.

For five trips around the sun Cole has whispered, cajoled, and done tricks with his hands to entice my heart to swell back to normal size and pump like a normal heart.

Love is acid rain, an antechamber, a turnstile, a cesspool, or a chain-link fence. Love is an outhouse, a tuning fork, a birdbath, or smog. Love is a shovel, a weather station, a museum, or a cemetery.

I stop writing to listen to Cole singing in the living room. The bedroom door is shut so the tune is muffled, but I recognize the sad melody of "As Tears Go By." Aunt June agreed he was an old soul, and from his choice of music, I'd say he definitely had a life just before this one. Maybe he knew my father in California. Maybe they sang war protest songs together.

I put the tip of my pen on top of the fine line. *Love is a trash bin, a samovar, a meteor shower, or ravioli.* This last bit makes me laugh, but I still can't find a metaphor to take forward. I scan my lists. Lots of containers, most of them poisonous, hurtful, or confining. But Cole's love is not these things. What burdensome thing has he demanded that I refuse to or cannot give? Love is a museum. Full of dead things. A cemetery. Full of dead things. A trash bin. Ditto. What about fireworks, rose petals, chocolate? No, I'm the one who writes *outhouse*.

Cole makes me the raspberry leaf tea and brings it in both hands to set it on my desk. Beckett lies with his head between his paws, only his dark kernel eyes shifting.

Inside, cells divide and multiply, the mathematics of gestation and cancer, while Cole and I watch each other without appearing to. I've never been good at math. I'm good at measuring sand and salt, good at mixing paint, cutting in the edges. I'm good at keeping a steady hand while the ground slips beneath me. But at this. This. Him and me and some decision I'm expected to make, I fail. I need to nip it in the bud, kill two birds with one stone, or simply do nothing until some squalling needy creature pushes its way through without me dying in the process.

After the taillights faded out of the blazing night, the house continued to burn, buckets sloshed from hand to hand, and figures moved against the flames. Marion let go of my hand, said, "You stay here." And then she was swallowed by smoke too. Flames shot high into the sky. It was hot and it was beautiful. I looked for someone to take me to my family but there was no one to ask. They were all so busy with the fire eating up my house. I didn't have words, really, not like now when they trip out of my mouth and razor into everything. That was the night my home vanished in a magnificent show of fire, and whatever I thought my life was or was going to be, vanished with it.

But my home isn't burning now. No one has stuffed Cole into a car and driven him away to die, but he is so quiet it seems he is gone from me nonetheless. When he sits with his guitar by the window, I watch his back as I watched those taillights, and I wish for him to come home intact.

If I don't put on the paper gown and plastic cap and offer myself to anesthesia's oblivion, if I ride out these days and nights without interference or resistance, will any of us survive?

Cole deserves to know. But I wonder if it would be less

burdensome if all he had to do was bring me tea to heal my womb-less body, and not have to hold his breath for the next six months waiting to find out if the bearing of his child will kill the woman he once loved. The oncologist's assistant has been calling and calling. But when I see Royal Victoria Hospital across my screen, I shut off the ringer. They're waiting with the scalpel, likely regretting that they even told me.

Because there's no snow, the contract drivers are suffering, and I'm sorry for them, but for us there's always work. Icy culverts, frost heaves, garbage in the ditches, shot-at road signs to replace, and all the rest of the outdoor maintenance. Our hours are set by the Ministry, so we work no matter what.

I find Mel with his head tucked under the white hood of a service truck, one booted foot dangling off the ladder.

"We're taking this truck?" I ask.

"Riding with Bob."

I think that's what he says, but maybe it's "Get the propane ready." Or "You want to drive?"

"What?" I call up to him, stamping my feet against the cold. No snow, but no sun either.

Mel ducks out from under the hood. "Me and Bob are on culverts."

"No," I say. Stomping my feet again makes my toes hurt. "I'll ask Mitch if I can run the jenny."

"All set here," he says and disappears back under the hood. I hear him clearly when he says, "Think you're greasing."

"I don't want to grease," I insist. "I want to ride with you, Mel." I know I sound like a stupid kid, but I need to be on the road, not stuck in the garage gooping goddamn gears. I need to be with Mel. I can't stay in the yard. I can't stay here.

Raising his arms, Mel unhitches the hood and lets it drop with a metallic *chunk*. As he steps down, he glances at me and lifts one shoulder as if to say *What can I do?*

When Bob says, "I'm getting a coffee. Want one?" I have to bite my tongue not to tell him what he can do with his stupid coffee. When Mitch asks after my mother, the bitch in me snarls but manages to say, "Much better, thanks."

I asked Norah to come with me to the library. I need to research this. The internet is full of awful pictures and information on how to negotiate breast cancer and pregnancy but nothing about what to do with what I have. I've stopped the parasite cleanse I was doing for the cancer. It's the least I can do for this new little parasite.

Norah heads straight for the fiction section and I head to the health section. This library is light and space. People talk here, quiet, relatively subdued, but they're conversing, so it has the feel of a community gathering place. A woman in a pink kitty-cat sweatshirt and clipped gray hair sitting at a computer table is laughing softly. The woman beside her holds a bent-fingered hand to her own mouth.

Women's Health. Christiane Northrup. Menopause. Menarche.

No more long narrow drawers to pull out filled with finger-softened cards. Now we click keys and ask a screen directly. We don't even have to know how to spell—the computer figures it out.

I find Norah with a slim volume of poetry open in her palms. It isn't until I'm close enough to smell her sandalwood scent that I realize she's crying.

"What are you reading?" I ask, peering over the book's edge.

Norah presses the open volume to her chest and bows her head over it. "The first one was too young to know," she says. Her eyes close. "I'm sure it was a girl."

We used to have so much fun. Before Cole, before Josh, before babies screwed everything up. I'd tell her about the rednecks I work with, and she'd tell me stories about the tightasses she works with, mimicking their jerks and twitches until we spilled our cocktails and peed ourselves laughing. Now she is sober, the single rivulets on her pretty face making her look old under the unforgiving skylight.

"The second one was a boy."

"I know," I say, dipping my head just a little to read the book's cover. All I can make out is the author: *Silkin*. It's that poem about the dead son that's brought this on. I read that poem on the train from Toronto to Montreal when I was nineteen years old and I wanted to throw the book out the window and have its pages split and fly like seagulls to sink into the St. Lawrence. I refused to cry then over a one-year-old who died in a mental hospital. And I don't want Norah to cry now over a baby who never lived at all.

"If I'd just been given a year with him," she says.

I want to tell her to snap out of it, that she doesn't know what she's talking about, that it hurts less if you never knew their sound or their smell. But I keep my mouth shut. She wouldn't believe me, the murderer, to know such things. And what I know for sure is that words, no matter how correct, how helpful, or how well meaning, do not help.

"If I'd just been able to hold him," she says, squeezing the unhelpful book even tighter to her chest.

Not long ago she was bouncing out of her seat at my news. Now she's lost in her own grief. I prize the book from her and replace it with my own body, holding her there between the fiction and the poetry, until she sniffs, lifts her head, and says, "So, have you found anything helpful?"

"You are helpful," I whisper into her hair.

It's no longer a question of whether I will let myself die. I don't want to die. For some reason, only now beginning to come into focus, I want to live. I want to do what the living do. It's a strange stirring that makes me feel like dancing with my mother in her funky little cabin. Or running into Cole's arms like in a sappy movie. Right now. Or better yet, walking right into Zehrs and untying his sash and having him right there in front of the grapefruits. I mean really having him.

As we separate and straighten our coats, I say, "If I have this baby—"

Norah's eyes wing open, her head snaps sideways. "When, Brett. *When* you do."

"If, Norah. *If* I do, I want you to be there."

"I want that too," she says and slides the book of poems back onto the shelf.

I'm out of the library ahead of Norah. When I turn to see if she's behind me, a group in the glass-walled conference room catches my attention. Women sit in a loose circle, some with their babies in their laps, some rocking as they doze in strollers, two with infants at their breasts—one on her right, the other on her left. I don't see the mouth or the scalp of the child; all I see is the breast with its blue vein, and imagine its pulse, turning blood to milk.

I can swing a shovel, drag a pregnant coon across two lanes, heave thirty kilos of cold mix at a time, pound steel rods into hard earth, but I don't carry a purse. I have money and I have keys, a cell phone, and a driver's license. You don't need a purse for that. These women all have suitcase-sized bags overflowing with diapers and wipes and bright orange and blue stuffed things. All of them seem to be lit up from the inside like paper lanterns. Some mouths are moving, open in laughter or conversation, while others are curled over small warm bodies. Lively colored books in cardboard and fabric are scattered on tables. They are young. Young, radiant, and happy.

Norah emerges through the heavy glass doors. She has been to the ladies' room to "fix her face," eyes freshly lined with dark blue and lips glossy. Her book bag drags down her left shoulder. On her right shoulder, the ever-present mega-purse—this one in blue to match the sweater she wears underneath her white down coat. In it she will have the severed foot of a rabbit—for fertility as well as for luck. I envision the hares we've dropped into holes, their long muscular legs catching on the way in, imagine how cutting one of their fine slender feet could help Norah conceive again, help her carry the child she aches for. What monster decided such a barbarous thing? I will never cut off an animal's foot. Ever.

"Let's go," she says and turns to regard the maternal scene that has captured my attention.

Her polished face goes gray. "Oh," she says. And then again, but so low it is a moan. "Oh."

In the car, Norah jams the gear into reverse. I've worn away the fleece on the inside of my gloves. I can feel the stiff nubs of leather at the ends. The book *Cancer in Pregnancy*, published in 1996, a hardcover half the size of Norah's car, weighs on my lap. Its cover is Mediterranean blue with gold letters, as if it's filled with stories of sea adventures instead of how much radiation or chemical poison a fetus can tolerate. I open the book to chapter 11, page 120: *Maternal and fetal outcome following invasive cervical cancer in pregnancy.*

Pregnancy may accelerate cancer growth.

Norah straightens in her seat and begins to talk fast, as if a flurry of words will wipe out what she's feeling. She gripes about that stupid book with the sadist who grooms a virgin to be his sex slave, and how badly it's written, but how everyone is gobbling it up, as it were. "You know me, I'd rather read about happy things, like women who overcome trauma—like that one about bees, or the one with the hot Scottish guy," she says. "You know the one about the woman who time travels and hooks up with a Highlander? The one where—"

"Yes," I interrupt. "I did. I have. You lent it to me, remember?" Biting into the fingertips of my gloves, I pull them off and rub my fingers on the warm pages of this book that is already scaring me.

"You have told Cole, right?" Norah says, taking one quick glance in the rearview mirror, one to the outside mirror on her side, and one to the passenger-side mirror. She looks at me. "He knows, right?" After a minute of strained silence, she says, "Jezuz."

Still, I have nothing much to say. I haven't told Cole. I haven't told my mother. I've told Mel but not June. I can barely tell myself that I have death cells and life cells duking it out inside. I just go on scraping roads and try to act normal, although I have no clue what normal actually looks like.

"Well," says Norah as if I'd answered. "Now." She turns to me with a bright smile and shifts into second. "Now you can have a fresh start."

"Fresh? How is this starting fresh?" My fingers are so cold they blend into the blue of the book on my lap.

"Well, you know, you have a second chance now. You can do it right this time." Norah clicks on the turn signal and steers into the passing lane.

Inside my boots, my feet are gummy with sweat and I want to rip off my jacket, but my fingers are paralyzed. "Norah," I say, keeping my chin tucked and my gaze fixed on my steel-toed boots. "I have cancer."

"Oh, I know," she says, making a gesture like brushing crumbs from a table. "But you can take care of that after the baby comes." She shakes her head. "You're having a baby, Brett. That's all that matters now."

I pry open the heavy blue cover of *Pregnancy and Cancer*, right to page 120. This is where it says that the rapid growth of cells in pregnancy can accelerate the growth of cancer cells. How fast? How much time? How much of my uterus will the cancer have eaten away in six months? Turning to the statistics page, I run my stiff finger down the columns. Maybe/maybe not. I might die/I might not just yet. Percentages.

"What did you take out, anyway?" Norah asks, her face bright from the sun reflected in the rearview mirror.

I almost answer "nothing yet," but I'm not in the mood for bad jokes. "A book," I say.

She flashes me a hard look. I twist around to set the book on the back seat, then stick my fingers into the hot air vent. "I need to know what kind of danger we're in."

"Oh, Brett," she breathes, all wistful. "That's the first time I've heard you say 'we.'"

When the car stops in front of my building, I get out, but

Norah puts her hand out across the console to keep the passenger door from closing. "Wait," she says, reaching into the back seat, scrabbling into her bulging book bag.

She hands me a heavy softbound book: *What to Expect When You're Expecting.* The woman on the cover of this book looks so pleased, as if she's done something magical. Not as though she has cancer and can't decide what to do. The cover's colors are muted blues and purples and yellows like sun through blinds on a late summer afternoon. It slips between my hands but I catch it before it lands in the gutter. "But I haven't—" I start.

"It's a good book to have," she says. "It will help."

"But," I start again, my mouth stuck open but no more words come out.

Norah grabs the door handle and pulls it closed. I watch her signal, put the car into first, and swing out into Collier Street, my big blue book on pregnancy and cancer still in her back seat.

The shrill repeat of a car alarm cuts through the sharp January air. Its obnoxious bleating doesn't cease because there is no one in the street to stop it. Parked between a green Ford pickup and a beige Corolla, the saltless black BMW's lights flash and no one runs, no one to push a silencing button. I'm too far away to have set it off but still my belly flips with guilt. Then I see it—black with two broad white stripes, its hind end raised as it balances on its front paws.

"Hey," I call over the beeping. "*Boozhoo,* my *zhgaag* sister, *Aaniin.*"

Spray glistens on the car's black body and drips down the shiny tire rims. I drop to my knees and breathe deep. My eyes stream as I wave the liquid smell toward me like sacred smoke. The skunk waddles up on the sidewalk, crosses the lawn, and makes its unsteady way between the houses. I breathe, bathing myself in its healing juice. *I will be healed. I will heal. I am healing.* I rub its essence over my face and dive my fingers under my collar and down my neck. I unzip my jacket and lift my shirt, waving, scooping, smearing my skin with medicine. Just as I squeeze my hand though my waistband, the car's alarm goes silent. The *taptaptap* of rushing boot soles comes from the direction of Dunlop Street. A woman in shiny buckled boots steers her gaze away from me and slips in between the cars, opens the BMW's door, drops in, fires it up, and swerves off down the street.

"What are you doing?" Cole sounds as alarmed as the BMW did moments ago.

Pulling down my shirt, I hoist myself to standing and meet his worried expression.

"Did you fall?" he asks doubtfully.

I shake my head.

He sniffs the air, as if that's necessary, his nose wrinkling. "Skunk? What is it with you and skunks?"

I leap up and hug him, hold on tight even when he tries to pull me off.

17

At home I want to cook something for Cole even though I'm not hungry, something tasty to make him smile. Flipping through one of the shiny magazines from the checkout at his store, I select a recipe from last summer—spicy grilled shrimp. The illustration is of golden red shrimp piled on a plate garnished with cilantro and lemon wedges. But as I gaze at the glossy photograph, the shrimp become fetuses with arm and leg buds. I close the cover. Not shrimp. Chicken, then? The idea of meat of any sort churns my stomach. Even imagining the smell of cooking meat is more than I can bear.

I ask him what he wants but he asks me what I want. What he actually says is, "Why don't you just make what you want?" And he doesn't simply say it—he flaps his arms, smacking his thighs with the flat of his hands and makes a twisted yowling sound as if the entire world was a mystery he was supposed to solve. He's been sweet to me since the hospital visit, but the strain of the last months is evidenced by his impatience and an uncharacteristic annoyance with small things.

What I want is to want a family, a home in the country, maybe. I want my mother to be well, Amara to be safe, Norah to have a gaggle of children, Mel's wife to walk again; and part of me still wants to lie on a beach as far away as I can get.

"I want to be healthy and I want to let you love me." This is how I answer him, just like that.

He stops his flapping to lower his gaze and fix it on me. "What did you say?"

"I want to let you love me," I repeat. "And I want to be healthy."

Cole takes a step back out of the kitchen, the catch in his throat audible as he swallows. Beckett's nose pokes into the crease behind my knee, so I step aside to let him pass. He stops at Cole, turning his head to the side as if listening for a cue.

"Let me love you." Cole's voice is thin. "Let me love you?" He snorts and gives his head a sharp shake. "What have I been doing for the last five—almost six—years?"

"Cole."

"How about *me* letting *you* love me? Sounds pretty lame, doesn't it?"

"What I mean is—"

"I think I know what you mean. You got anything else up that merino sleeve of yours? Any other revelations?"

I close my eyes and shake my head.

I hear the long sigh. Then, "Make whatever you like, Brett. I'm not that hungry."

I'm giving birth outside Mama's cabin. It's dusk and the scent of balsam poplar thickens the air. As I push, squatting between freshly mounded rows of Daddy's garden, a mosquito lands on my arm. When I swat it, my baby pops out into the dirt. It's a puppy, a baby Beckett. Then more come. Five or six. They aren't helpless or blind, but open-eyed, tumbling and chewing on each other in the garden. I'm bursting with relief and happiness. Mama is calling me from the cabin. But it isn't her cabin; it's our cabin, my first home. The one I thought was gone. I shout to her that I've had a litter, joyous that our home has been restored, as I scoop up my babies. Mama is singing a pretty tune without words. But her voice becomes mechanical. Digital. Insistent. An awful abrasive noise.

Alarm. Alarm clock. Morning. Dark January night. Two thirty a.m. Shit. Twelve hours on the roads wait for me. I had puppies. A bunch of little Becketts. What the hell does that mean? That I love my dog? That I'm a bitch? I run my hand over the spot where Cole should be. I'll be gone before he's home from work. Beckett jumps up as I shuffle off the bed, ready to run, ready for breakfast, ready to begin.

What if I ask Mel to have his wife make me up a different

cup of tea? There must be herbs for that. Is it too late? What
if I "kill two birds with one stone," as that doctor so compas-
sionately suggested. Then the emptiness will be real and not
just imagined. What if I have the baby and give it to Norah?
The eyes in the bathroom mirror are the color of whisky or
wet sand. My hair in the light from the hallway is dull as straw.
I'm leaning on the counter, hands braced on the sink edge. As
I stare into those strange eyes I feel a pulsebeat where my belly
presses against the cool stone. It could be my own heart, the
pulse of its blood through my veins, but I don't believe that.
I rock back, both hands lifting to land on the stretch of skin
above my pubic bone. It's too early to feel movement, I'm sure
of it, but there it is, under my hands, two heartbeats so close
together it might be one.

In the mirror, the black holes in the center of the eyes contract, then spring open into deep wells, almost eclipsing the
colored edges. Does she have eyes yet? I haven't been able to
look it up. I bypassed the maternity section at the library, and I
haven't opened the book Norah took out for me, believing that
if I don't pay attention to it, it won't be so. But it is so. It is.

Many times I've spoken it out loud—in the car, in the plow,
on the running path with Beckett scrambling along: *I'm pregnant.
I have cancer.* But each time the words freeze and crack in the air
and I trample them as I move on by.

I drive alone. Gritty snow piles up along the edges of county
roads. My body registers every shudder and bump of ice and
pothole, the bones in my fingers rattling on the controls as I
watch for mailboxes, watch for impatient drivers teetering on
the far shoulders swishing past, watch for oblivious dogs, for
stalled cars, and for signs.

My breasts swell under my heavy jacket and ache for Cole's
hands, even as I flip switches to lower the wing, broaden the
spray, shift the plow. I have to call Aunt June. She has to know.
Someone has to know that Dylan is the one who fills the holes
that loss digs. Otherwise, there'll be more Amaras, more like

me. But how will I tell my aunt that her son is a bad man? What
if she calls me a liar? Or worse. Perhaps she already knows
and, like priests who turn their heads away, or coworkers who
assume it's all in good fun, or a mother who loves her son, she
has chosen not to know.

At home in the bathroom, I sit on the cold toilet rim bent over
my knees, my hair falling around me. I have to phone my aunt
to tell her that her son is a pedophile. The last time I used
the phone in the hallway was the call from Donovan. When
he found his daughter in bed with his brother. When he didn't
know what to do and I didn't know what to tell him. The phone
hasn't rung since. I am going to pick up that gray and black
rectangle with the buttons that light up and I will wait until she
answers with her cheery redheaded voice and I will open my
mouth and this time I will tell her.

But first I'm going to click on Beckett's leash and step out
into the carpeted hall and push open the stairwell door to run
down three flights of stairs and out into the cold dark morning.
We will run as strong and as far I'm able, given that my hips
ache like crazy. Then I will turn to look at the fishing huts on
the snow-covered bay and wonder again how the fishermen
manage to stay warm without melting the ice under them. I
will think about augers for ice and augers for sand and salt,
and how the word augury means divination, especially by the
flight of birds, and how august means respected, and how my
baby could be born in that month. I will tug my dog's leash to
bring him back from whatever he's sniffing so we can cross
the road with its too-bright headlights to unlock the apartment
building's door, take the stairs two steps at a time to stretch out
the muscles until we arrive at our floor. After I unhook Beckett,
give him a treat, hang up my coat, and have a glass of water, I
will call my aunt.

But my dog and I don't run along the waterfront. We walk,
our breaths smoky in the air. How would my life be with a
daughter or a son of my own? Would I be able to cease my

grieving? Maybe we could buy a house a little farther north or west—Angus or Shanty Bay. Where I'd be landlocked, rocking a howling baby I can't calm, Cole working overtime and gigging on weekends? Could we be a happy little family? Do such things exist?

For now, I walk beside my dog, modulate my gait to accommodate the slide of my hipbones, and smell the winter air coming off the lake.

Snow is falling again. Somewhere a car skids into a ditch. Tom and Bob and the others are out there flinging sand around and double-scraping the shoulders. My cold but dry feet grip the inside of my boots like monkey feet, let go and clench up again.

Sweat pools under my arms and drip in two single lines down my sides. The phone cradle is empty. I consider using my cell phone to call Aunt June, but the landline seems more substantial, as if the cell phone's signal would float into an alternate reality whereas the "real" phone will carry my message with certainty. When I press the "find" button I hear muffled beeping from the living room. It won't stop until I either push the button again or find that thing and make the goddamn call. Beckett skitters across the parquet to stand at attention, his little black nose pointing at the couch. When I push the "find" button again the beeping stops. Beckett's body un-tenses. I go to the bathroom and pee two tablespoons. And then I go to the living room to dig the phone out of the cushions and call my aunt.

"Brett," she says, when she answers on the third ring. "You have news, don't you? I saw it in your cards, you know." Like hydrogen peroxide her voice bubbles right through the receiver.

It's true. That look she gave me at the sink when I unrolled the bag of raspberry leaf tea, the look she gave me over The Sun tarot card, the brush of her hand over my belly just before we got out at the airport.

"Yes, Auntie. I do. I am." The weight of my exhale pushes

me to the floor where I rest my head on the edge of the couch. While I take in a breath and hold it, Aunt June asks when it's due, informs me that I'm having a girl, and half-pauses to take in her own breath.

"But that's not why I'm calling," I say, flicking together the rough nail edges of my middle finger and thumb.

"Oh?"

The duvet rustles as Cole rolls over in bed. Hard snow taps on the window. Out on the lake a fisherman pulls in his line, and the long silvery body of a fish struggles with its own sudden weight.

"I have to tell you something."

"Yes?" She is patient, my aunt June, despite her exuberance, despite her insistence that all that can be divined can also be rectified, and despite the possibility that she may already know what I am about to tell her.

"It's about when Mama and I stayed with you," I say. "After the fire."

"Uhmhmm," she intones after a slight hesitation, as if she has pulled from her deck a card with swords in a prone man's back.

"When you and Mama went to the coast." I'm up now, moving, as if through snow, back to the small table by the door where there is an anchor for the phone.

A soft smack in the background like a trump card being played. "I remember," she says quietly.

"Dylan took care of me…" I trail off, look to Beckett, but he's of no help.

A pause followed by a measured suck of breath. "He did," she says.

"We got very close."

"Okay?" she says.

"Maybe too close." The phone is slick and hot. I want to let my clothes drop to the floor, open a window, call for help.

Cole stands in the bedroom doorway, his innocent penis swaying a little, his eyes not quite open. I gesture for him to carry on to the bathroom, a swoop of my hand followed by an air kiss of reassurance. He goes. The bathroom door clicks behind him, followed by the metallic rattle of curtain hooks, the complaint of faucet and the rush of the water.

"What are you trying to tell me, Brett? Please be clear." My aunt's voice is something durable like a tree or a road; a thing you could climb or travel on.

"He—I, I—we—" It's all I can do not to slam down the phone and run out the door. "I— Oh, oh, Aunt June, I'm sorry. I'm so sorry." This is what I didn't want to happen. I drag my sleeve across my eyes. "He…he…helped me, in a way. He didn't hurt me. You have to know that."

The line is quiet except for that almost imperceptible landline hum. This call needed to be from the landline because of its fixedness, its solid place by the door from where it never moves. Even though I can move—I could pace, go all the way to the bedroom, but I stand right here as if the receiver is still tethered, like in the old days, by a cord.

"Auntie?" I say. "Are you still there?"

"I am," she says.

"I thought you should know."

"Why is that? Why is it that you thought I should know?"

I suck in my breath, a hot fist grabbing me at the apex of my ribs. "Because," I begin and stop, deliberating. "Because of Amara."

"Amara?" she asks quickly, her voice cutting through the wires like pincers. "What about Amara?"

I lock my knees because they shake from the effort of standing. I brace myself with one hand on the door.

"Dylan and Amara?" Aunt June says. "He's very fond of her, I know."

For many seconds, neither of us speaks.

"They don't get to see each other very often, you know," Aunt June says.

"It doesn't matter, Auntie. I didn't get to see him much either." I will not cry. I will keep standing here. I will keep speaking if I have to.

But in the following silence, my resolve begins to waver. I could back out now. Stop. Stop talking. Stop speaking the words that need to be spoken and go back to being who I was before I saw that eleven-year-old girl's pelvis tilt into a forty-eight-year-old man's hip. Before I saw that and knew. That he had broken more than my heart.

I close my eyes and there are the mother wolf's steady gold ones watching.

"What I'm trying to tell you is that Dylan was fond of me too. More fond than he should have been. He was kind, but it was wrong..." I have to stop because a plow blade is scraping the inside of my chest.

"All right. Brett?"

"Yes?" I sniff.

"You can have him charged."

"What? What are you saying?"

"It's not too late."

It could be my imagination or a gas bubble, but a sensation like the tip of a wing turns in my belly.

"I'm pregnant, Auntie," I say.

"I know that," she says. After a short pause she continues, "You can still do it."

"You *want* me to do it?"

"For your baby, Brett. Do it for her."

"Auntie," I say.

"Yes, Brett."

"I also have cancer." Both of these truths feel cowardly. She is opening the cell door for her own son and I am shoving her into my ditch.

A sound like a hand being rubbed across the receiver is followed by a long, forced breath. Cole's singing comes through the water, the shower curtain, all the way through the door. It's the new song, the one about being lonely together. It's quite good, its incongruously jaunty tune works well against the heavy lyrics. The receiver sweats in my palm, its heat against my ear.

"Where is it?" Aunt June asks.

I don't know what she means. I'm in a courtroom telling stone-faced strangers that I opened my legs for my cousin's tongue.

"What kind of cancer?" my aunt says.

"Invasive cervical cancer," I say as if I am reading from that big blue book.

She comes back fast with: "That's a good one. Easy to treat. Have you been doing a parasite cleanse? Because if you are, you have to stop."

"Auntie," I wail. "Why aren't you mad? Why aren't you yelling? Because you knew? Did you know? Did you know about him—about us?" I pull the receiver away from my mouth, aware how loud my voice is. I ask her, "Why are we talking like this? Like it's a normal day? As if we're normal or something. As if this is an ordinary conversation? As if it can all be fixed with WD40 and duct tape?"

Beckett lets out a soft whine and scuttles over to me. I crumple to the floor to bury my face in the fur at the back of his neck.

"I didn't know," she says. "But I'm not surprised."

Maybe no one will be surprised. "I need to call Amara," I say at last. "I'm the only one who can."

"You can still have him charged." She sounds old and very, very tired.

"Perhaps I will." But not now. "I'm sorry, Auntie," I say. "I love you."

When I hang up, Cole is right there, his hair damp, his skin warm as a promise.

"You're shaking," he says.

I lean into him.

Beckett skitters to a stop in front of us and cocks his head, his tongue pink in his open mouth.

"It's okay," says Cole. "It's going to be okay."

"Okay?" I say, gripping the cloth of his shirt. "How is it going to be okay?"

"Because you've decided, haven't you?"

"What?" I say, the pang of panic in my tone making Beckett's body go rigid.

"To keep it."

"What are you talking about?" I can't make my mouth say more.

Cole leans back, far enough to run a hand over his belly. His breath warms and cools, like peppermint tea.

I squeeze my eyes shut. "I don't know what to do, Cole."

He will say that it's not his. "You could include me," he says.

"I'm trying," I say, but Cole shakes his head. "I'm pregnant and they want me to...to..."

He says, "I know."

"You know?"

He gives me a look that makes me feel very young and foolish, which makes me wonder how long he's known and why didn't he tell *me*. His look also causes a window to open inside. Cole may have always looked at me this way but perhaps for the first time I receive the intimacy of it. Cole knows me.

"I need to lie down," he says, and then does just that. I watch him lie down on the bed, pull the duvet right up to his chin, and close his eyes.

I roll off my clothes and quietly slide in beside him. The sheet scrapes against the little semicircle burn scar open on my arm and I put my hand there. It's never bothered me that much because the scars you can't see are worse and much deeper. The thing about this scar, the one on my arm, is that it is hooked in with those other unseen scars. Dylan kissed it before it had fully healed. The first time I cried after the fire was when he put his lips on that raw place. I imagined it was in the shape of Goldie's little mouth or her belly button. If I had known about God, then I might have thought that He threw that piece of burning wood at me, or let that beam go just at the moment that Daddy was saving my life. Cole used to like to kiss that scar. Maybe he kissed it in hopes that I'd be nice to him instead of a perfect bitch. In any case, ever since we got back from the Kootenays it's been on fire, that little moon-shaped scar on my forearm. This morning I woke up to find that I'd picked a hole in it, and now it's bleeding. I watch the creases in Cole's forehead contract and release and his lips twitch with dream words.

He's still sleeping at five p.m. when I push off the duvet and slide into my slippers. I hush Beckett when he pops up like a jack-in-the-box, promise him a walk and a big bowl of breakfast. As I pass by my desk on the way to the kitchen, I tear down last year's calendar with its tropical blue-blues and green-greens, crumple it, and let it drop into the wastebasket. In its place I pin the one Mel gave me.

I have the urge to write letters to those who are gone. To tell Goldie that she is like a phantom limb, attached but unseen. To tell my daddy thank you for being so much fun. For riding me on your shoulders, for taking me up the mountain to shoot grouse and hunt for morels and puffballs. Thank him for being funny and kind and for saving my life. I won't thank him for dying. That part has to just lie down and forget about itself. He made me when he was a young hippy draft dodger and deeply in love with Mama. I'd thank him for that.

I will never write to Mark. I hung on to him because he seemed sure. I wanted to have what I saw as confidence, to be able to deliver a swift kick to nail a point. I wanted his righteousness, his bravado. I don't want any of that now. My attempts to stay safe like that have rendered me sorry for everything.

Instead of letters, I write: *These are the lies I have told myself: It was my fault. I killed my family. Dylan loved me. I can't bear children.*

I tuck my jewel-crusted pen into my notebook and set it aside. I've got to figure this out. I need to know how much danger I'm in. An internet search reveals there are alternate therapies for cervical cancer that won't hurt the baby. The details about receptors and hormones are a jumble of medical jargon, but I get the gist and will do more research, ask more questions, follow through. Aunt June called my cancer easy. A good cancer, she called it. I do a deeper search. The results reassure me that this cancer is easily treated and slow growing. How slow growing is anyone's guess.

I close my laptop and reopen my journal. I draw lines on the page because my hand itches and my brain can't form words.

Cole comes up behind me and says, "That shape looks like a bone."

I cover the lines I've drawn with my whole hand, but he is saying, "A wish bone, Brett. It looks like a wish bone."

So I lift my hand and draw around it—more lines and swirls and little tiny dots.

"Mom used to do illustrations for her children's books," he says. "It reminds me of those."

I turn in my chair to look up at him, but he is staring at the new calendar.

"What happened to the Bali calendar?" he says.

"It's January," I say.

"Did you buy this?" he asks, tracing a finger along the picture of a snowy cliff where the shapes of dozens of wolves blend into the rock.

"Mel gave it to me."

"What about Bali?" he asks in a tone without undercurrent.

"I'm not going."

"Good," he says, dropping his hand to my shoulder to give it a light squeeze before leaving the bedroom. The room cools when he leaves, but a light fragrance like hope or cucumbers lingers in his wake.

18

Today the fog is so dense that we are inches from the car ahead when its taillights emerge. Last week's snow has been shocked by a sudden warmth and the entire county huddles in the gloom. Mel and I are on a maintenance run—straightening the signs the plows have bent, cold-patching the soggy potholes. When I found out we weren't on the plows this morning, I went straight to Mel, grateful to be able to sit beside him.

The blur ahead makes Mel sit forward as if those few extra inches might enable him to see farther. In this underwater-like landscape, it's impossible to discern what's ahead. We inch forward into nothing. I'm sweating. I can smell myself through my heavy jacket's open collar—whuffs of musk with every exhale. I want to tell Mel everything. Everything. My story ticks through my blood like an IED. I am an improvised explosive device. Mel grips the steering wheel and squints into the fog, his entire body contracted as I have never seen it. His fingers aren't draped and tapping out his internal rhythm. I want to invite him for a coffee at Tim Hortons. Not drive-thru, but to sit inside, across from each other at a table, where I will tell him things, such as how I caused my sister to burn, how my father died trying to save her, how my mother slipped out of her body, leaving its shell for us to clothe and feed, how I traveled as far as I could to get away and never succeeded, how I played at loving, how six years ago I made a choice that I regret, how I worry that my illness is payback for all my bad decisions, and how now, inside my damaged place, the son or daughter of a good man has already unfurled a spine, a heart, and tiny genitals of its own. And how I can't talk about it to the man who fathered it. I want to ask Mel what he thinks is the right choice.

We slide forward in the vibrating hum of the engine, the

clenched cords of concentration visible through the scraggle of Mel's beard. Brake lights ahead flash red. Mel's torso jerks as he, too, brakes. Through the dense white, I see a dark shape at the roadside.

"*Nimoosh*," I say, pointing.

Mel lets his foot off the accelerator, flips on the turn signal, and glides to a stop on the shoulder.

"No. No. No," I chant under my breath as I unhook the seatbelt and grab the door handle.

Before I can swing my legs out, Mel says, "*Ma'iingan*."

"Wolves don't get hit." I'm running, my boot heels striking broken rock through wet snow, and all time slows to jelly. I will never reach him. Dog. Wolf. Please don't be dead. Please.

At the creature's fine gold-brown head, I drop to the ground, snot freezing on my upper lip. No blood under its head or smear leading to its body. It must have been a corner blow to the skull. Along its underbelly is a row of long collapsed teats. I try to penetrate the fog for signs of her pups, a whimper or shift of tawny fur. She smells fresh and wild, like mushrooms and spring runoff. A fine layer of dew has settled on the tips of her fur. Ripples move through her coat as if by wind, but there is no wind. The air holds still.

Behind me, Mel casts no shadow.

I feel for a pulse. "She's alive," I breathe.

The animal stirs, a muted growl in her throat. I drop back on my haunches, glance up at Mel who is smiling as he digs in his jacket pocket. The wolf raises her head.

From Mel's hand flutters a gold-brown snow of tobacco. It drifts down through the fog and settles on the gravel by her tail.

The wolf's scrutiny of us is cursory. Her attention is on the hazy brush on the far side of the ditch. Her ears prick forward and she struggles to her feet, and then makes her unsteady way down the embankment and across the culvert. When she reaches the crest of the hill, she breaks into an easy jog, but then she pauses, one front paw lifted. She turns to regard us with her quiet eyes.

And then she is gone, not even a wrinkle in the fog where she slipped through.

Mel crouches, puts his ungloved hand on the bloodless spot where the wolf lay, drops his head, and begins to pray. *"Boozhoo Gzheminido, Mshkiki Nini Ndizhinikaaz, Rama ndoonjibaa, waawaashkeshi doodem."*

Mel's prayers are usually brief, but this time he continues. Our heads are so close I can make out the soft-syllabled words, and even though I don't know exactly what they mean, I do know that they are words of gratitude.

"I'iw nama'ewinan, maaba asemaa, miinwaa n'ode'winaanin gda-bagidinimaagom. Miigwech gda-igom n'mishomissinaanig miinwa n'ookomisinaanig jiinaago gaa-iyaajig, noongom e-iyaajig miinwaa waabang ge-iyaajig. Miigwech manidoog iyaajig noodinong, iyaajig nibiing, iyaajig shkodeng miinwa iyaajig akiing. Miigwech manidoog iyaajig giiwedinong, waabanong, zhaawanong miinwa epangishimok. Miigwech ma'iingankwe. Daga bi-wiidokawishinaang wii mino bimaadiziyaang. Aho."

He looks up at me and smiles. "No need to cry," he says.

After the metallic clunk of the truck door closing, I don't hear the truck's engine come to life. Mel is simply waiting, or perhaps not even doing something as active as waiting. Maybe he is just being. And I am still at the roadside watching the bank of fog where the wolf vanished sway toward me. I am waiting. Not for the wolf to return with her pups tumbling after, and I'm not waiting for the fog to lift. For the first time I am simply waiting in trust. Trust that if I wait, I will understand what has just been given.

Then I do understand. With a lift as though the pebbled ground under my boots is rising, I realize that I already know. She pierced the membrane between worlds to give me this.

When I get to the truck, Mel has already opened his window. He leans out a little to hear me.

"Could I have some *asemaa*?" I call up to him, but before the last syllable is out of my mouth, Mel stretches out a hand to place a pocketful of tobacco in my palm.

I will say my prayer the way *Mshkiki Nini* has taught me: to greet the Creator, say my name and where I'm from, and then to give thanks. Cars stop and go in the fog like wraiths with red blinking eyes. I move down into the culvert and up the embankment to the edge of the woods. I don't need skunks or tea leaves or the moon in Cancer. I have been given everything I need.

"Wait," Mel calls.

I stop.

"When you say your name, say, *Mshkiki Kwe.*"

"*Mshkiki Kwe?*"

He nods, unhooks the sweetgrass braid from the mirror, and hands it to me. "Go. Say your prayer now."

I light the sweetgrass and smudge the way Mel taught me. First the smoke cleanses my eyes so that I may see clearly, then my mouth so that I may speak true words, then my ears so I will hear well and my head for good thoughts, then my heart and organs. After wafting the smoke over the place where the wolf lay, I kneel in the snow-softened grasses and lay the tobacco. "*Boozhoo Gzheminido, Mshkiki Kwe Ndizhinikaaz,* Winlaw *ndoon-jibaa. Miigwech. Miigwech. Miigwech ma'iingan.*" It's all I know, but it's enough. I know that it is enough. "*Aho.*"

A foreign sensation has risen in me. I'll call it gratitude. I'm still alive and I can still choose. After all my stalling, all my foot-out-the-door of life, after all my saying no again and again, I'm still here. Here in the yard. Here in my body. Here, healing and gestating at the same time.

Mel opens the passenger door. When I haul my gear there, he stands there as if all he's ever wanted in life is to stand in a yard filled with yellow trucks—and white ones with blue county logos, plow blades, and brush cutters—and wait. I don't remember him holding a door for me. I've told Mel everything. He didn't know I had cancer and he didn't know I was pregnant. Maybe his Franny did, but he did not. Or so he claims.

I want to look right into his face to see what's really there—

not just what I think is there. And I want to thank him. Because
this a yard full of trucks and a job to do, because I am the
only woman among a dozen men, and because it's considered
confrontational by his people to look someone right in the face,
I can't stop and do these things. Word would get out that I'm
sleeping with Mel, which is what they all probably think anyway.
So I touch the front edge of my hard hat and walk beside him,
aware of how our footsteps sound like matching heartbeats.

"Mel," I say as we approach the office building.

His hand hesitates on its way to open the door. "Hm?"

"Thank you," I say. "*Chi Miigwech.*"

I am thinking about body parts—the good ones that leap to attention at the slightest provocation; the ones that respond even
when they shouldn't. The part in and of me that moistened and
opened like the peony petals. Petals open, not because they will
themselves to part, but because the sun touches them. Because
the bulb from which they spring is hugged by fertile earth and
because it is the flower's nature to open. It opens its mouth to
catch raindrops, unaware of its own scent. The crocus doesn't
stop blooming because the spring rains have come too early—
March, say—when frost is still a danger. No one tells the flower
it is too early, you are too young or too vulnerable. Even daffo-
dils push up through the crust of winter toward the promise of
quenching rains and the sun's warmth and light. No one blames
the flower.

I draw a shape on the empty white page.

It's time to stop this.

I've drawn an emerging slave breaking free from the marble.
It is a mother wolf who has been dazed by a blow.

I will pray for the babies and for the children. I will ask Mel
to help. I will ask to meet his wife. I will invite Norah to come.
I have learned to pray and I'm ready to set down this sack of
stones. I will lower them into a ceremonial hole, crumple a
pound of tobacco, smudge with sacred medicines, and ask my
feet to dance.

When Cole comes out of the shower, I'm at my little desk in the corner of the bedroom. It's seven o'clock in the evening and the apartment is dry and warm. Outside the snow has begun again, but the flakes are light and float through the haloes of streetlights. I'm trying to write something about what the wolf told me, trying to express what I understand about life, friendship, family, and love, but so far I have written only five words: *Time to unwrap the present.*

Cole is wearing only his faded Hot Stuff boxers and mismatched socks. The soft fuzz of his russet hair has been darkened by the shower. I turn to regard him and our eyes meet. He is so still I can feel a thumping inside my ribs. And lower, a flutter imagined or real, speaking to me in a new language I'm beginning to understand.

He will stay.

I will stay. I will do what the living do.

"If it's a girl," he says, "would you like to call her Goldie?"

"We," I say. My pen nib finds the page and I write, "Alex." "Her real name was Alex. Not Alexis or Alexandra."

"I remember," Cole says. "Brett and Alex. Strong names." He simply stands, hands loose at his sides. His body is at home with me. "Alex is a good name."

"Yes," I say and set down my pen.

ACKNOWLEDGMENTS

My bottomless gratitude goes to Sue Reynolds for her unflagging support and encouragement from start to finish. Almost every scene in this novel began in the safe space of one of her writers' sanctuaries. The scenes not written in Sue Reynolds' sanctuaries sprang to life in Barbara Turner-Vesselago's Freefall Writing retreats where I received her invaluable feedback and insight.

So many others who helped along the way deserve my gratitude—for their supportive feedback and encouragement. They are, in no particular order: Brian Foot, Cheryl McLean, James Dewar, Phil Dwyer, Trish Boyco, Beth Girard, Marie Lauzier, Terry van Luyk, Anna van Straubenzee, Christine Barbetta, Stephanie Curry, Kate Marshall Flaherty, Kari Jones, and Evelyn Lotfy.

I'd like to thank Paul McKerroll for introducing me to the bells and whistles of big snowplows and letting me sit up in the driver's seat. Big thanks go to Halli Villegas and Dawn Kresan for hosting a ten-day writing retreat on Pelee Island where I was able to put the finishing touches (or so I believed) on the manuscript. Chi miigwetch, Candice Sawyer-King, and Janissa King, for the Ojibwe language guidance, especially with Mel's prayer.

I am indebted to the cheerleading by beta reader and friend of my heart, Barbara Bergen.

Without Pat Schneider and the Amherst Writers & Artists Method she created, this book may never have been written. Focus on the writing's strengths offers assurance to the writer that perhaps not everything they write is garbage. For me, that assurance is priceless.

And of, course, a big thank you to Pam Van Dyk and Jaynie Royal, the fearless founders and editors at Regal House Publishing for taking a chance on this debut author.